PRAISE FOR TESSA BAILEY

"No one writes hot, dirty-talking alpha heroes like Tessa Bailey!"
—Laura Kaye, *NYT* bestselling author of *Hard to Come By*

"There are not many authors whose books completely, utterly, and totally wreck me. Tessa is at the top of that list, and I thank the stars for the day she started writing. As soon as I get a book from her, *nothing* else gets done until I finish it. My world is a better place because Tessa's books are in it."
—*NYT* bestselling author Sophie Jordan

"Sexy, witty, and completely irresistible, Tessa Bailey's writing is addictive. I can't get enough! Her dirty-talking heroes keep me up all night and always bring me back for more."
—Kelsie Leverich, *NYT* bestselling author of *Lovers Restored*

"Nobody writes hot guys, feisty girls, and fan-yourself sex like Tessa Bailey. Her books are addicting, and you'll continue to root for her characters long after you turn the last page!"
—Megan Erickson, author of *Make it Last*

"Tessa Bailey just keeps getting better and better. *Risking It All* is sexy, sultry, and sinfully delicious. Fair warning: clear your calendar, because you won't be able to put this book down."
—Robin Covington, author of *Temptation*

"There's alphas, there's Tessa Bailey's alphas, and then there's Bowen—the ultimate seductive playboy with a heart of gold. *Risking It All* is not only my favorite book by Tessa, but Bowen is easily my favorite hero she's ever written. Period."
—Lana, *Dirty Girl Romance*

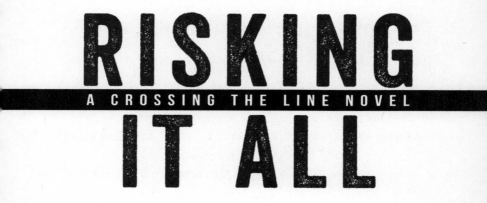

RISKING

A CROSSING THE LINE NOVEL

IT ALL

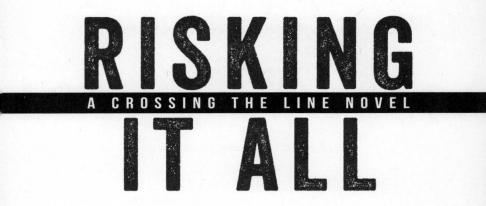

RISKING
A CROSSING THE LINE NOVEL

IT ALL

TESSA BAILEY

Entangled Publishing, LLC
2614 South Timberline Road
Suite 109
Fort Collins, CO 80525

Visit our website at www.entangledpublishing.com.

Edited by Heather Howland
Cover design by Heather Howland and Amber Shah
Photography from Shutterstock

Paperback ISBN 978-1-62266-564-8
Ebook ISBN 978-1-62266-565-5

Manufactured in the United States of America

First Edition January 2015

10 9 8 7 6 5 4 3 2 1

For Mackenzie.
Everything *for Mackenzie.*

CHAPTER ONE

Here's your meatloaf. Choke on it.

Seraphina Newsom crossed herself discreetly as she walked away from the customer's table, muttering a quick Hail Mary for good measure. No sense in letting her immortal soul go to the devil because the man had treated her ass like it was on the specials menu. Still able to feel the sting of his pinching fingers, she vowed, then and there, to overtip her waitresses for the rest of her life. Thirty percent or bust.

Sera took a deep breath and pushed through the double doors leading to the kitchen of Dooly's. Loud, tinny Greek music emanating from a portable radio greeted her, as did scraping silverware and dishes being submerged in hot, soapy water. Right on cue, the cook tossed two more plates of greasy meat loaf onto the dented metal shelf and *ding*ed the bell, even though she already stood there waiting. Squaring her shoulders, she reminded herself why a girl with a nursing degree and a budding career in law enforcement would be donning an apron in the Bushwick section of Brooklyn.

She was there to get up close and personal with her brother's murderer.

"Why you never try my meat loaf, waitress?" the cook asked her in heavily accented English.

"Er...gluten allergy?"

"What is this gluten everyone talks about?"

She started to answer, but stopped. "It's probably just a myth. Like Santa Claus and comfortable thongs." Satisfied with his frown and the fact that she'd avoided telling him his meat loaf resembled roadkill, Sera took both plates and backed through the doors.

Into the deathly silent dining room.

Discreetly as possible, she glanced toward the center of the silence. Two stools away sat Trevor Hogan. The man who'd gunned her brother down.

Hogan was a lifelong local who had started small-time. Stealing cars, robbing delis, brawling. His ambition had placed him in the right place at the right time, and with the help of a metal baseball bat, Hogan earned the trust of the boss and took over the protection racket. Loan-sharking, extorting local businesses, you name it — Hogan had both greedy hands in it.

Her brother, Colin, had been a rookie with the NYPD when Hogan began branching out, running an illegal gambling operation so large it had financed two successful nightclubs, ballooning his criminal influence even more. As inexperienced as Colin had been, he shouldn't have been anywhere near Hogan's case. He'd been too young, too cocky, wanting to land a major arrest his first year in the field.

But when your uncle was the police commissioner, exceptions were made, no matter how deadly.

She'd been working as an emergency room nurse at Massachusetts General in Boston when her brother died. Ironic, that. After taking a vow to save people's lives, she'd been unable to save the life that mattered most.

Sera smoothed a thumb over the Saint Michael charm that hung around her neck. She wouldn't go as far as to say the Newsoms were cursed, but…all right, they were pretty much cursed. The last three generations of Newsoms, including her father, had been killed in the line of duty. Her uncle was all that she had left, and he ran the city with an iron fist. As far as the people of this city were concerned, she didn't exist. To the little *family* she had left, she didn't exist, either. Seraphina Newsom was a ghost.

To her mind, that invisibility made her the perfect candidate to go undercover and find the key evidence to put away Hogan for life. Rumors of a ledger containing Hogan's unsavory business dealings had long swirled through the precinct hallways. The rumors were fueled by the fierce opposition he'd shown when his financial records had been subpoenaed during the tossed-out murder trial. Added to the fact that Hogan was cocky as hell, and low-level informants had reported seeing the ledger, she *knew* it existed. His secrets were written on those pages.

Not secrets that would take him off the street. Not the conventional way, at least. Information was valuable in this neighborhood, and she could use the names in that ledger to implode his operation from the inside out, bringing Hogan's operation down square on its head.

As soon as she'd felt confident enough that gaining possession of the ledger would be the key to outing Colin's murderer, she'd taken a personal week off of work, citing the upcoming three-year anniversary of her brother's death as the reason. And she'd gone undercover without a direct order from her uncle.

When this was over, she'd never again wear a badge. But she'd have bagged a murderer.

And then she would disappear.

Sera set down both plates of meat loaf in front of two burly male customers whose earlier loud conversation had devolved into subdued undertones with Hogan's appearance, never letting Hogan out of her peripheral vision. Ever since he'd arrived, Dooly's lively buzz had been switched off like a lightbulb, customers poking at their meals absently. Apparently unconcerned about the pall he'd cast over the crowd, Hogan sat with one arm draped over his chair, focusing on the UFC match raging on the ancient television.

Hogan's four-man crew stomped into the bar, making the sixth sense that ran in her family *ping*. Hogan leaned against the bar, gesturing animatedly as he spoke to the bartender. His friends laughed on cue and some of the customers began to relax. Hogan, his youthfulness beginning to fade along with his good looks, tossed back a shot of whiskey. He turned as he plunked the glass down on the bar, catching her eye across the dining room floor. Instead of cringing under his interest, Sera smiled back and sailed toward the kitchen, conscious of his hard gaze on her.

Everything happened quickly after that. There was a loud crack as Dooly's front door was kicked open. A man walked in, sweatshirt hood pulled low over his face, gun raised and pointed at Hogan. Every patron in the bar hit the floor as if it were a middle-school earthquake drill. Sera reached toward her hip for a weapon that wasn't there.

Hogan threw himself behind one of the four men who'd joined him, just in time for the man to take the bullet in his stead. The wounded man fell with a shocked curse, still shielding Hogan, who followed him to the wooden floor, scrambling for his gun. Hogan's other men wasted no time removing their own weapons, issuing threats at the already-retreating gunman, who managed to make it out the door before they could fire a single shot.

What had she just witnessed? An assassination attempt on Hogan? For a moment, she felt frozen to the spot, reeling at the fact that Hogan's life had almost been stolen from her. Justice for Colin did not include such an easy way out. No, it would have been unacceptable. Years of heartache, months of work… all for nothing. It had been so close. Too close.

The sight of blood broke Sera out of her stupor. It was everywhere. Splattered on the mirror behind the bar, the ground, the man who lay on his back clutching his upper chest. Before her conscious mind processed her actions, Sera moved toward the man, shoving aside the group of useless bystanders. She might have quit nursing to become a cop, but the oath she'd taken wouldn't allow her to stand by while someone died. Not when she could prevent it. "Get me the first aid kit from behind the bar." As she knelt down beside the bleeding man, she noticed no one had moved. "*Now*. And call an ambulance."

Feet shuffled around Sera, telling her someone had actually listened. Briefly, her eyes landed on the face of the wounded man. Young, dark, startlingly handsome despite the fact that his teeth were gritted from the obvious pain. She didn't recognize him from the case file, nor had she expected his type among this crew. Hardened, yes, but he didn't appear as if he'd slipped beyond redemption like the rest of them. With brisk efficiency, she pried his hand away from the wound, pushed open his leather jacket and ripped his white T-shirt open from collar to hem.

The first aid kit clattered down beside her on the floor. "At least buy him dinner first."

Hogan. She'd deal with him later. Relief moved through her when she saw that the wound had missed the man's heart by about two inches. Still, it could have hit his subclavian artery. She could keep him alive long enough for help to arrive, but it would need to be soon. As gently as possible, she eased her hand beneath his shoulder, relieved when she felt an exit wound. At least the bullet had gone clear through. She ripped off her apron, balled up the starchy material and pressed it against the wound. It had to hurt like hell, but the man barely winced.

She glanced up, meeting Hogan's eyes. "Did you call the ambulance?"

He leaned against the bar, chewing a cocktail straw. The utter lack of concern on his face reminded Sera she was in the presence of a monster. Her brother's murderer. Hogan shrugged, setting her teeth on edge. "You're doing a bang-up job all on your own. No need to involve uniforms."

Sera failed to hide her horror. "He could die without medical attention. Look at how much blood he's already lost." She wiped her bloody palm across her uniform shirt, unwittingly making her point.

Eyes narrow, he pointed at her with his cocktail straw. "Why don't you ask him what he wants?"

She looked back down at the injured man. "No ambulance," he managed through gritted teeth, face paling with the effort. "I'd rather bleed out."

Hogan's face lit up with amusement. "And there you go." He signaled the bartender for another drink. "You got a name, Florence Nightingale?"

He's colder than I could have imagined.

Sera took a deep breath and focused on his question. She'd planned her false identity down to the last detail. The name and cover story she would use if she ever got close enough to Hogan to actually employ it. She'd never expected to use it this soon, though, especially in this kind of situation.

"Sera."

He threw back the shot of whiskey. "Can you fix him up,

Sera? He's my cousin. If he dies, it'll piss off my mother."

Yes. She might be able to save him. No, she *would* save him. Despite the wounded man's vast difference from her brother, she wouldn't let another person die because of Hogan's presence in his life. Call it irrational, but in a way, saving this man might in small measure make up for her being two hundred miles away as her brother died on the cold sidewalk. None of this could be portrayed to Hogan, however. Or she risked her own neck. "Fix him?" She gave a disbelieving laugh. "He needs doctors...a hospital. I'm a waitress."

"Yeah? You don't talk like no waitress."

"You want to hear the specials or something?"

Hogan's laugh boomed through the bar, but he sobered just as quickly. He regarded her closely for a moment, then nodded to his cohorts. "Load Connor into the backseat. And for God's sake, put a fucking towel down first." Almost as an afterthought, he added, "She's coming with us."

CHAPTER TWO

Bowen Driscol kept the lit cigarette clamped between his lips as two police officers jerked his hands behind his back and shoved him forward onto the hood of their squad car. A group of neighborhood girls passing on the sidewalk stopped to gawk, giggling when he threw them a wink. The officer's hand between his shoulder blades kept him in place, cold metal clinking when the other uniform removed the piece he'd had tucked into his waistband and cuffed him. When the hand on his back pushed a little too hard, Bowen gave in with a sigh and spat the cigarette onto the curb.

"Look, I like it rough as much as the next guy, but we hardly know each other."

"Shut it, Driscol."

"You going to explain why I'm being arrested?" He swallowed a growl as the cuffs bit into his skin. "Or is this just how you get all your dates?"

"Your mother didn't seem to mind." The officer heaved him off the hood and stuffed him into the backseat, oblivious to the sore spot he'd just poked with his casual insult. "As for why I'm taking you in?" With a shrug, he slammed the door. "Pick something," he called through the glass.

Bowen kept his unconcerned expression firmly in place as the officers drove through the streets of Bensonhurst where he'd been raised. Where he'd likely die. He knew every corner, every alleyway, and the name of every shop owner. This was his home. He hated it as much as he loved it. Loved it for the familiarity, hated it for the prison it had become since he reluctantly accepted his legacy.

Even though it was torture being trapped in the back of a police car without the use of his hands, he couldn't deny a sense of relief. Had they finally caught him? Finally gathered enough information to put him away? God, a big part of him hoped they had, even if he would die before admitting it to these smug assholes. He was tired of looking over his goddamn shoulder when he walked down the street, wondering if today would be the day someone tried to end his reign as boss. He'd never wanted the job, but with his father awaiting trial at Rikers Island, it had landed on his shoulders like a ton of bricks. Yeah, he'd never been a saint to begin with, but now people feared him for reasons that had nothing to do with his penchant for street fights. Now they worried about their legs being broken over unpaid debts. Turned tail and ran when they saw him as if he were Death himself.

He racked his brain trying to figure out what had gotten him pinched. Sure they were required to tell him, but the NYPD never played by the rules. Not with him. They knew he ran South Brooklyn, they just hadn't been able to trace any crime back to him—a fact that pissed them off in a big way. It warmed his heart exactly how much. Would that all change today? Their silence was unusual, to say the least. Any other day, they wouldn't waste a chance to rib him.

Bowen frowned when they bypassed the turn for the local

precinct and proceeded toward Manhattan. "Where we headed, boys?"

"Don't worry about it," said the one driving.

"Never said I was worried." He wished for a cigarette. "I'm just wondering if I need to make arrangements for someone to water my houseplants."

The cops exchanged a glance. "*You* have plants."

"What? I don't strike you as the nurturing type?"

Bowen caught sight of himself in the rearview mirror and had to laugh. With a purple-black eye and a cut bottom lip, he looked like the opposite of nurturing. In fact, he looked like shit run over twice. Nothing new. He couldn't remember seeing himself reflected back without some sort of injury on his face. The utter exhaustion in his eyes, though…that was new. Quickly, he looked out the window to find them traveling over the Brooklyn Bridge. What the hell did they want with him in Manhattan?

"You know, I love this new air of mystery you boys have going. It's sexy."

Instead of responding, they turned up the chattering dispatch radio to drown him out. It took every ounce of willpower not to question the officers further when they pulled into NYPD headquarters a few minutes later. His heart pounded in his chest as they pulled him out of the backseat, but he did his best to look bored.

This is it. I'm done.

No more instilling fear, no more resorting to violence to collect money owed to him. No more issuing orders to soulless men who didn't know how to feel remorse. All done.

The officers led him through the entrance and every head turned; animosity and disgust targeted him from all directions. Bowen ignored the twinge of pain from his cut lip as he grinned at his rapt audience. "Afternoon, gentlemen." He wished he were wearing a hat so he could tip it. "Weather today is beautiful. Not a goddamn cloud in the sky."

He didn't have the pleasure of hearing any angry responses because the officers pulled him down a hallway, shoving him into the first interrogation room. Irritation clawed at his throat over being pushed around, but he didn't give them the satisfaction of showing it. If he weren't wearing handcuffs, he would have already swung on them and they knew it. They also knew he could easily take them both on and win. Fighting was in his blood. He did it often and he did it well. So he couldn't contain his surprise when they removed the handcuffs. It even managed to distract him from his anger.

"All right. I give up. What the fuck is going on?"

"Have a seat." The officer who'd driven them there kicked out the metal chair before leaning against the wall with his arms crossed. "You'll find out soon enough."

He remained standing, turning slightly when the interrogation room door opened again and an older man walked in, looking grave. Bowen's eyebrows shot up when he recognized the man. Police Commissioner Newsom.

He'd seen the man on television doing press conferences more times than he could count. That's what he did. Sound bites to reassure the masses. Public relations. He sure as hell didn't interrogate street toughs from Brooklyn. Newsom tossed a file on the metal table and nodded at him. "Why the black eye, Driscol? Don't you have men to do the dirty work for you now that you're in charge?"

No way would he tell him the truth about his perpetual black eyes. He wouldn't tell him that when he went to collect debts and the money wasn't ready, he always let the other man take a swing at him before leaving his men to deliver the rest of the message. He welcomed the pain that came with that single blow, craved it even. Lately, it was the only thing reminding him he was alive. Sometimes he even hoped the money *wouldn't* be available, as it hadn't been last night. Bitterness flooded his mouth at the memory of the man's desperate eyes when Bowen had shown up at his door.

No money for me, huh? Go ahead, take a shot at me. Do it. You'll be glad you did it in an hour when you wake up hating me.

"Why am I here?" Bowen fell into the chair without answering Newsom's question. "Not that I don't appreciate the stellar hospitality."

"Already you're living up to your reputation as a smart-ass." Newsom sat, scrubbing a weary hand over his whiskered face. "Look, I'm not here to play any bullshit games with you, so I'd appreciate the same courtesy."

"Fair enough." Bowen lit a cigarette. "Shoot."

Newsom's jaw hardened. Behind him, the two officers shifted, but stilled when Newsom held up a hand. "We have a situation and I've been informed you're in a position to help us."

Bowen paused in the middle of his second drag of nicotine. "Help *you*?" When the commissioner just looked at him, he laughed out loud. "Any minute now I'm going to wake up, right?"

"No, I'm afraid not." Newsom flipped open the file and scanned the contents. "And in case you're wondering, asking for help from some punk who we've been trying to take down for over a year wasn't exactly my number one choice."

"Flattery will get you nowhere." He took a deep drag of his cigarette and blew the smoke toward one of the scowling officers. "Okay. What do you need my help with? I'd at least like to know the particulars before I turn you down."

"You sound pretty certain."

"Good. That's what I was aiming for."

Newsom muttered something under his breath, but all Bowen could make out was the word "mistake." "How about I lay it out for you in black and white, then you decide?"

Bowen stayed silent, watching Newsom through a cloud of smoke.

The commissioner sighed wearily. "We've lost contact with an undercover officer. At the risk of sounding cliché, they've gone rogue. Went in without permission." He considered his hands a moment. "We'd like you to make contact with the officer, first and foremost to confirm they're alive and well. We need them extracted from the situation unharmed."

"Undercover." Bowen felt a tingle at the back of his neck. "Investigating who?"

"You think I'd reveal a name without your signed agreement to cooperate?"

Bowen didn't answer, the word "cooperate" hanging in the air like rank garbage.

"The officer is looking for evidence," the commissioner continued. "Frankly, it's evidence I—*we*—need. This isn't how I wanted to go about obtaining it, but they're *in* now."

"Evidence of what?"

"Corruption. Something you should be familiar with." He formed a steeple with his fingers. "Which leads me to your secondary task. If the officer is indeed alive and well, allow them a small window of time to continue the mission. If it proves fruitful and they uncover what we're looking for, you bring that evidence to me *before* they have a chance to lose it or get killed." He shook his head. "A damn rookie cop. No business whatsoever this deep in the game."

"This idea gets more appealing by the minute." Bowen sent a pointed glance toward the two flunkies. "Cops aren't exactly my jam on a good day. Some inexperienced rookie with a death wish? Why would I agree to that?"

"Because, Mr. Driscol, we can make life very difficult for you otherwise. We know about the circumstances surrounding your father's incarceration." Newsom paused, as if to let that statement sink in. Bowen kept his features carefully schooled so he wouldn't betray the shock pounding through his blood. He hadn't seen this coming. Couldn't have anticipated it in a million years. "We know you were aware of your father's impending arrest and didn't warn him because it would have put someone very close to you in danger. I think some of your associates would find it interesting that your sister was working as an unofficial informant, don't you?"

Grinding out his cigarette on the bottom of his shoe, Bowen felt sick. With guilt, with dread. "You can't prove that."

Newsom smiled without humor. "We wouldn't need to. The mere suggestion would put a target on your back. *Her* back." The commissioner paused as that horrifying statement sank in. "Until now, we haven't fully committed resources to ending your little run as king. That could very easily change. I suggest playing ball, Driscol. Unless you want to end up behind bars, just like dear old dad."

The impact of that statement sent Bowen back in his chair, but he made it look casual at the last minute. Just like his dad. He couldn't think about that right now. Not with these cops staring at him like a science project. He'd had Ruby's back since childhood and vice versa. She never would have given the police leverage to use against him. It would be a cold day in hell before she told another living soul. Unless...

"Let me guess." Bowen swiped a hand through his hair. "Troy Bennett is on the other side of that glass. He's the one who so graciously offered my services."

Newsom's lips twitched. "You catch on quick. Ever think of joining the force?"

The officers behind him laughed as if the mere idea of him being anything but a criminal was hysterical. For once, he didn't really blame them. Bowen turned toward the two-way glass and showed it his middle finger. Ruby's boyfriend, the man who'd managed to put the pool hustler on the straight and narrow, had been a fucking thorn in his side since day one. He should have known when Ruby hooked up with a cop that this was inevitable.

Seconds later, the door opened and Troy strolled in holding a cup of coffee. "Bowen."

He didn't return the greeting, jerking his chin at Newsom instead. "Before, my answer was no. Now, it's *hell* no."

Troy's mouth tightened. "Can I have a moment with him, Commissioner?"

Newsom gave a brusque nod and left the room, followed by his two flunkies. Bowen lit another cigarette and tossed his lighter onto the table. "You're wasting your time."

"Why haven't you been returning your sister's phone calls?"

The question threw him, before it circled back around and pissed him off. "What the hell is this? A family therapy session?" He pushed to his feet and paced. "There was a time when you didn't want me within a hundred yards of her."

"She misses you." Troy shrugged. "When she's unhappy, I'm unhappy."

Bowen ignored the stabbing feeling in his chest. "Yeah? She has a funny way of missing me. Telling her cop boyfriend the one thing that could fuck me over."

"It won't fuck you over, because you're going to help us."

"Not. Happening."

Troy walked to the metal table and flipped open the file.

Bowen watched as he sifted through some papers and pulled out a picture. "I'm not supposed to show you this until you agree to help, but I'm going to anyway. You know why?"

"I couldn't care less."

"Because I trust you," Troy enunciated. "Enough to convince Newsom that you're redeemable and could make a difference in this case. This is my ass on the line, too."

I trust you. Bowen didn't want to hear those words. Didn't like the way they made him feel. He shouldn't be trusted. Not after the things he'd been compelled to do. Not after he'd let his own father get put behind bars. Let his sister nearly get murdered. "Sorry to let you down, but I'll take my chances with a bull's-eye on my back."

"We don't have any other options here, man. You're a part of that world, and if the alternative is Newsom dropping a dime on Ruby—and finding a reason to put you in a cell— you have to do it." Troy shook his head. "You know I'll protect your sister. Even if it means we have to leave the city and never come back. Leave behind everything she's worked for. But I don't think that's what you want." With a curse, Troy threw the photograph down onto the table. Resolutely, Bowen kept his eyes up, refusing to look. Troy pointed down at the picture. "This is your chance to make up for the shit you've done. A chance to do something good. Ruby sees the good in you. Are you going to prove her wrong?"

"*Fuck you,*" Bowen said through his teeth, hating Troy with every cell in his body for using his weakness against him. He didn't care about many things in this world, but he cared about his sister. Which is why he'd completely cut her out of his life. "And while we're on the subject, keep her the hell away from me. I don't want to see her in the neighborhood."

"Still protecting her?" Troy asked quietly. "We both know

that's my job now."

"Then do it. Keep her out of Brooklyn."

Troy nodded thoughtfully, still watching him closely. Wanting to escape that observation, Bowen glanced away, his gaze accidentally landing on the photograph.

Everything inside him went still. He'd scooped up the picture to get a closer look before his brain registered the action. "Who is this?"

"That's the officer we've lost contact with. Going on a week now." Troy lowered his voice, putting his back toward the two-way glass. "She's investigating Trevor Hogan."

Bowen couldn't hide his astonishment. "This girl? This girl with the freckles and the rosary beads around her neck? She's undercover with Hogan's crew?" When Troy simply nodded, Bowen cursed under his breath. He didn't understand the reaction he was having to the photograph, but he couldn't deny the unwelcome surge of protectiveness. A pretty brunette smiled up at him, squinting into the sunshine, hand closed around the cross at her chest. She didn't belong anywhere near the ruthless Hogan, the man who had recently taken over North Brooklyn. If he suspected her for one second, she would be killed without hesitation.

Bowen knew something Troy didn't, though. He and Hogan had an upcoming deal, set to take place on May ninth. Little over a week away. A shipment of stolen computer hardware would land in neutral territory, thanks to a Brooklyn defector who had taken his theft operation overseas. At their contact's request, he and Hogan were going to split the hardware down the middle as a gesture of goodwill between North and South Brooklyn, since warring over the goods would up his chances of being caught. If Bowen wanted to cooperate with the police, he had a perfect opening to do it.

If he cooperated? Jesus, was he actually considering this? Absently, his finger smoothed over the picture. "What's her name?"

"Seraphina." Troy cleared his throat. "Hogan killed her brother and walked. Seems to me you can relate to wanting what's best for a sibling. Only she didn't get that chance."

A wave of sympathy moved through him. Could he do this? Turn...informant? By going in and protecting this girl—Seraphina—he kept himself out of prison and let his sister keep her shiny new life. And dammit, *someone* needed to bring this impulsive rookie cop home, right? This might be an old photo, but if she'd retained an ounce of that innocence, Hogan would have her for breakfast.

Who the hell was he kidding? There was no choice.

"How long do I have to get her out?"

"The sooner the better. No more than one week."

Perfect timing. "You have to tell me what she's looking for. I'm not going into this blind."

Troy lowered his voice. "Financial records. A ledger." He crossed his arms over his chest. "Men have gone undercover with Hogan before. They...didn't last long, but were in communication long enough to confirm he keeps track of business by hand."

Bowen decided it wouldn't be wise to mention he'd seen the damn thing himself. He reached into his jeans again for his packet of cigarettes. "Let's get this over with. I hate paperwork."

CHAPTER THREE

Sera hated the man on sight.

But since hating another person was a sin, she decided to *strongly* dislike him instead. He'd walked into Rush, Hogan's nightclub, five minutes ago and hadn't taken his eyes off her once. Nursing a glass of whiskey at the bar, he somehow fit in and stood out at the same time. He was in possession of a wicked black eye, yet he'd walked through the door with the confidence of a man who doled them out, not received them. Tall and broad-shouldered with the cut muscles of a working man, he caught the attention of women and men alike, drawing looks of appreciation as well as apprehension. The way he moved said *do not fuck with me*, louder than if he'd shouted the statement. His dark blond hair had been tousled in a way that looked purposeful, like a woman had just been holding on to it for dear life.

Sera shook herself, realizing she'd been openly scowling at him. These were not the type of thoughts she normally had. She shouldn't be picturing a woman in the throes of ecstasy with her fingers clutching some stranger's hair.

With a muttered admonishment directed at herself, she

picked up her tray and turned, resolving to ignore the stranger. She'd been waitressing at Hogan's nightclub for two weeks and she'd gotten no closer to incriminating him. He'd given her a room upstairs and ordered her to heal his cousin, whose condition began to decline, much to her alarm. She'd wondered if the man even wanted to survive. She'd begged Hogan to take him to a hospital, knowing the action would ruin her chances of bringing him down. No matter how hard she'd pleaded, Hogan had refused to pursue medical attention and against all odds, she'd managed to stabilize the patient after several days.

Once she'd made him reasonably comfortable and he appeared to be out of the woods, she'd thought Hogan would send her packing. He'd thrown her an apron instead. Whether he'd decided her healing skills might come in useful in the future or he simply didn't know what to do with her, she couldn't decide. Not having answers had begun to wear thin, making her jumpy. She'd even requested to be allowed to leave and return home several times so she wouldn't appear eager to stick around, but he continued to put her off, using his injured cousin as an excuse to keep her there. Sera had caught him watching her on a few occasions, a thoughtful expression on his face, as if he were deciding her fate. That cold calculation unnerved her, and his wariness hadn't exactly been conducive to her investigation, but she'd gotten a glimpse of the ledger book early yesterday morning. She refused to give up her chance at him.

Hopefully, all of her time-biding would come to an end tomorrow. She'd overheard Hogan on the phone yesterday as he sat at one of the tables in her section. He was going out of town for a week to check on operations at another nightclub he owned at the Jersey shore. If he let her remain behind to care for his cousin, she would finally have her chance to access the office downstairs he always kept locked.

Against her will, her gaze landed on the man at the bar again. Something about him was familiar, but she couldn't place the reason for such a feeling. Before he'd been appraising as he watched her; now he simply looked angry. Talk about confusing.

"Sweetheart, I'm dying of thirst over here."

Sera turned with a pasted-on smile and cleared away the three men's empty pint glasses. "Same round again?"

Grunts served as her answer. With a nod, Sera slipped through the rows of tables to retrieve their order from the bar.

At early evening on a Friday, Rush had started to fill up, and she knew from even limited experience the regulars were demanding. Rush lacked any similarity to the nightclubs she'd been to, which was admittedly very few. No frilly, overpriced drinks or coolly sophisticated customers. Here, they were rough and suspicious of newcomers, herself included. After a few shifts, they seemed to accept her only because she was with Hogan.

Sera propped her elbows on the wooden bar hatch until the bartender scanned her through bloodshot eyes. "Two bottles of Bud, one Carlsberg."

"You got it, honey." As he shuffled toward the other end of the bar to drag her beers out of the ice, Sera felt the staring man move closer. It annoyed her, the way her skin prickled as he sauntered toward her, taking his sweet time. She didn't want to talk to him and silently urged the weary bartender to hurry up with her order. No such luck, though. She'd be willing to bet he'd never hurried to do a single thing in his life.

"You know, if I were working for tips, I might smile more."

The words were spoken so close to her neck, the small hairs at her nape shifted, sending a wicked shiver down her back. An unusual stirring took place in her belly before exploding through her veins, hot and liquid-like. Her lips parted on a small gasp. At his audacity? At her reaction to this stranger? She didn't know.

Pull it together. Play your part. Allowing her lips to curve up at the ends, she turned to give him a playful retort, but the words died on her lips. She'd just looked up into the most strikingly handsome male face she'd ever seen. His gray eyes were noticeably tired, but intensely focused on her, mouth tilted in a smirk. From a distance, he'd been attractive, even with the painful-looking black eye. Up close…he affected her. A lot. Something she definitely couldn't afford while needing to keep her game face intact.

Sera took a step away from him. "I have a hard time smiling when I'm being stared at."

"Then you must not smile much, because you're a fucking stunner."

Whoa. Huh? The long pull of sexual attraction in her stomach came as a shock. That line had actually worked on her? She'd never had a thing for Brooklyn accents before, but the way he pronounced stunner like *stunna* did funny things to her insides. Or maybe the sincerity in his voice had done it. He'd said it like he *meant* it. Coupled with the steady manner in which he watched her now, the effect was potent. It figured that the first man she'd felt a physical pull toward would show up while she was undercover.

Can't do anything about it here. Put him off.

She wanted to kiss the bartender when he set her beers down on the bar. "Excuse me. I'm trying to work here. I have customers who need drinks."

"Yeah?" He took a slug of whiskey, throat muscles working. "Now I need one, too."

"You're not in my section."

Too late, Sera realized she'd said the wrong thing. Setting his empty glass on the bar, he swaggered past her toward the back of the club where tables were arranged. He dropped into the first available chair, close enough to the table of men that she couldn't deny it was her section, before looking back at her expectantly. She turned to ask the bartender for a refill on the rude man's whiskey, but he'd already set it down on the hatch. Apparently he *could* move quickly when he wanted to.

Teeth gritted with the effort to appear casual, Sera placed all four drinks on her tray, ignoring her smile coach's snort when she served the three men first.

"Took long enough," one of them commented. "Someone should talk to Hogan. Get him to light a fire under your perky ass."

Behind her, a chair scraped back with such force, she jumped several inches in the air. All three men at the table froze, eyes going wide when her admirer leaned over their table, supported by his clenched fists. "Apologize to her now."

One of them stood, hand out in a conciliatory gesture. "Shit, I didn't know she was with you. I-I didn't...she—"

A fist hit the table, knocking over one of the fresh beers. "I asked for an apology. If there's one thing I can't stand, it's asking for something twice."

A chorus of sorrys immediately went up, but all she could do was nod her acceptance. Who *was* this guy? The three men looked utterly horrified at having offended him, like their very lives were at stake. Slowly, he straightened and went back to his table, settling back in his chair. Everyone in the club had gone deathly still, but he didn't seem to notice or give a damn. Not knowing what else to do, Sera placed the full glass of whiskey in front of him. When she tried to walk away, his hand snaked out and grabbed her wrist.

"Can I get that smile now?"

"If I don't give it to you, what happens?" she asked, with a little more steel in her voice than intended. "Are you going to shout the smile out of me?"

His thumb massaged a circle into her palm, watching her closely. "Careful, Ladybug, you're showing your spots."

What is that supposed to mean? She snatched her hand back. "Maybe I keep the smile for my boyfriend only."

He leaned back slowly and sipped his whiskey, all traces of amusement gone. "If you do have a boyfriend, he's about to be sorely disappointed."

"Why is that?"

"I've never been much good at sharing."

Sera stared at him in shock. Instinctively she knew not to challenge him in front of the men sitting behind her, no doubt hanging on every single word. For some reason, they seemed to fear him, and until she knew the lay of the land, making a scene wouldn't help her cause. She set her tray down and lowered her voice to a whisper. Still, she couldn't let him get away with that comment. Share her? As if she were a can of Coke? "Who do you think you are?"

His gaze dropped to her lips. "I'm the guy who's going to kiss you tonight."

"Like hell you will," she sputtered, crossing herself before she could resist the urge. "I don't even know your name."

A single eyebrow rose. "Did you just cross yourself?"

She shifted on the balls of her feet. "I'd tell you to try it, but it appears to be too late for religion where you're concerned."

"No arguments here." He leaned forward, clasping his hands between his knees. The way his head tilted to the side probably sent most girls into a squealing fit. It hadn't escaped her notice he still hadn't revealed his name. "I'll make you a deal—"

"Oh no." She shook her head. "This is how every episode of

Dateline NBC starts."

"Ah, sweetheart," he murmured so low she could barely hear it. "How did you end up here?"

Sera didn't know what to make of his confusing question, so she picked up her tray and started back toward the bar, but his voice brought her up short.

"If I can make you smile, I get that kiss." He rose and gently pried the tray from her hands. "That's the deal. Harmless enough for you?"

"Nothing about you is harmless." The statement slipped out on a whisper. "Aren't there other girls you could be kissing?"

"Sure there are." Without looking, he tossed her tray on the table. "But none of them bless themselves after saying 'hell' or make me crazy to see them smile."

"You appear to be crazy regardless."

His lips twitched. "How about it, then? If I'm so crazy, there's no harm in the deal. No smile, no kiss."

A slight hesitation was her mistake. Before she could protest, he grabbed her hand and tugged her toward the back of the bar. "Wait. *Wait.* I have customers."

"They'll live." His calloused fingers twined with hers as he led her down the back hallway, past the bathrooms, and into the kitchen. The short-order cook and his assistant glanced up, looking completely unconcerned to see her being dragged through the kitchen by the insane customer. She opened her mouth to ask for their assistance when her kidnapper greeted them both by name. *Fabulous.*

"Where are you taking me?" Sera might know how to defend herself, but it wouldn't be wise to go somewhere alone with this man she knew nothing about. She threw a desperate look at the cook. "Stop him!"

Laughter sounded behind her as she was pulled into the alleyway behind the club, the kitchen door slamming shut behind them. Never having been back there before, she took a moment to take in her surroundings. A loud extractor fan above the door hummed, and street sounds greeted her ears in the distance. It had rained earlier, leaving damp asphalt in its wake and water dripping from the drainpipes of the apartment building across the alley. A cool breeze whipped down the passage and Sera wrapped her arms around herself to protect her exposed skin.

Her kidnapper still held her hand tightly, but had stooped down to scoop up a pebble off the ground. As she watched in stunned silence, he lobbed the pebble up at the closest window of the building on the other side of the alley.

"What are you doing?"

He held up a finger, smiling when a light illuminated the window. "Wait for it," he drew out.

When the window flew open on a barked curse, his hand squeezed hers, pulling her closer to his side. Sera stumbled into the crook of his arm, the smell of whiskey and smoke wrapping itself around her like fog. Above them, a white-haired woman in a housecoat appeared at the window, squinting into the darkness and looking less than thrilled by the disturbance.

"Mrs. Petricelli, you're looking extra beautiful this evening," her kidnapper shouted. "Sing for us, would ya?"

"*You*, huh?" She propped a fist on her hip. "This ain't a free show."

He slapped his free hand to his chest. "My undying love isn't enough payment?"

Sera blinked in surprise when the woman began to primp, patting the back of her hair. Her former irritation over the kidnapping turned to intrigue. She couldn't stop herself from looking up at him, wondering how this playful man had put the fear of God into three men twice his age only moments ago.

When she'd gotten her first look at him at the bar, she'd judged him to be older, thanks to the weariness in his eyes. Now, with a roguish grin playing around his mouth, a twinkle replacing the fatigue in his eyes, she changed her earlier assumption. He couldn't be older than thirty.

Her assessment was interrupted when the most beautiful sound she'd ever heard floated through the alley and arrested her on the spot. Mrs. Petricelli leaned partially out the window, singing an opera song that Sera recognized as Puccini. She wasn't shy with it, either. With wobbly arms outstretched toward the night sky, her voice rose and fell in such haunting perfection that Sera temporarily stopped breathing. One by one, windows in the building began to slide open, neighbors popping out to listen, joy written on their faces. Having lived in the area for even a short while, she knew that quiet respect was rare among the residents, making their utter silence almost as poignant as Mrs. Petricelli's song.

She didn't want the moment to end. *Never* in her life had she experienced something so spontaneous and wonderful. In all the hours she'd spent in church, listening to choirs sing, nothing she'd ever heard could compare to this. How ironic that it was taking place in a Brooklyn alley that smelled like stale garbage, with a man who had managed to infuriate and attract her within minutes of their acquaintance.

Sera glanced up at him. Instead of watching Mrs. Petricelli, he watched her, as if she were the main attraction. "You're smiling."

Her fingers flew up to trace her mouth. She *was* smiling. "Uh-oh."

"Yeah. Uh-oh." His thumb brushed her cheek. "I get that a lot."

She couldn't move as he angled his body toward hers, pulling her into the circle of his arms. In that moment, she forgot about her job. About being undercover or the fact that this man was an enigma that needed solving. With opera gilding the cool air around them, the masculine lips descending toward hers became her whole universe. She wanted him to kiss her. Badly. Even suspected it might be the kind of kiss she'd always dreamed of but no one had ever delivered.

The song ended on an abrupt note, breaking the spell. Sera jerked away from him. *What is wrong with me?* Letting him kiss her would be a mistake. Of that she was positive.

"Thank you," she called up to Mrs. Petricelli, before racing back toward the kitchen as quickly as her legs could carry her. The door didn't slam behind her as fast as it should have, telling her she'd been followed. Breath raced in and out of her lungs as she entered the hallway. Just a little farther and she'd be away from him.

A hand curled around her elbow just as she reached the dining room. "Welching on deals in this neighborhood can get you into trouble, Ladybug." He turned her around, bringing her up hard against his muscular chest. "You'd do well to remember that."

She couldn't help it. Her gaze fell to his mouth. "Kissing you seems like worse trouble."

"Yeah, but it's the fun kind." He glided his hand up the back of her neck, gathering her hair into his fingers. Such a proprietary gesture, it gave her pause, feeling a flood of tantalizing heat rush though her system. His eyes flared at whatever he saw taking place on her face and he didn't waste time taking advantage. Cursing once under his breath, he yanked her up against him and fused their mouths together.

Ohhh. Oh, wow. Sera's body melted along with her reservations, curves conforming to his hard planes in an effort to get closer. Because of their height difference, her head had fallen back to receive the aggressive kiss, but as his tongue skated across her lips, parting them, she pushed up on her toes and engaged him enthusiastically. A guttural groan met her action, the hand in her hair tightening as he backed her against the hallway wall.

She needed to breathe, but he seemed unwilling to let her do so. Worked for her. Breathing would give her time to think, and even a tiny flash of clarity could talk her out of this and it felt so *good*. His tongue worked deep inside her mouth, claiming her, leaving no room for protest. Then, oh *then*, his hips fit to hers and began mimicking the rhythm of his tongue. Slow, measured grinds that were somehow a little frantic at the same time. A thrum built between her legs, becoming unbearable. When she whimpered, he bent his knees and came up more firmly between her thighs, plastering every inch of them together.

Finally, as dizziness set in, his lips left hers. "Jesus," he grated at her lips. "I said a kiss. You're begging to be *fucked*."

His words barely penetrated the desire still blanketing her mind. Quick rushes of breath seemed to be amplified in her ears as she drew them. "I…I am?"

He searched her eyes for a moment, his regard so intense she nearly missed the hardness pressed against her belly. But once she felt…it…nothing could prevent her face from heating, reddening.

Bowen's gaze fell to her flushed skin and he released a tortured laugh. "Ah, sweetheart, I don't fuck around with virgins." His head dipped, teeth closing around her ear and tugging. "But I'll get down on my knees and eat that untouched pussy like a motherfucker."

"Well, shit, Driscol. Looks like you've met my new waitress."

Hogan's voice brought Sera's surroundings back to her in a blinding flash. She shoved out from underneath the hard body pinning her to the wall, needing to escape into the dining room before her mortification swallowed her whole. But Hogan's words halted her in her tracks.

Driscol. She'd heard that name before. Countless times.

When it hit Sera whom exactly she'd just let kiss her within an inch of her life, it took all her willpower not to buckle on the spot.

She'd just made out with Bowen Driscol, recent heir to South Brooklyn's most ruthless criminal enterprise.

CHAPTER FOUR

*H**ear that? It's the sound of your plan backfiring. Twice.*

Doing his best to appear unconcerned at Hogan's sudden arrival, Bowen watched Sera's face as she processed her boss's words. His last name and everything that came along with it. Why did he feel a surge of pride when she didn't even flinch? He could pile it right on top of every other insane reaction he'd had to her since walking into Rush, because he sure as hell didn't have a fucking clue. While he might not understand the fierce urge to protect a virtual stranger, one thing had become instantly clear. He wasn't leaving her there to fend for herself. Not a chance.

When they'd briefed him at police headquarters, he'd told them he would do this his own way or not at all. It would be a cold day in hell before he took orders from the police, so they would have to trust him to handle it. When Newsom had balked at this condition, he'd managed to convince him that the closer the cops came to Sera, the more danger she would be in. He'd meant it, too. Everyone in this neighborhood knew one another. They craved the familiar.

It was one of the reasons he knew Sera's time was limited.

Already, the idea of her being harmed had him by the

throat. *She'd* had him by the damn throat since the moment he'd arrived. After seeing the photograph of her, he'd expected to walk in and find a wide-eyed Girl Scout seconds from her death. Only half of that expectation had come true. There was innocence, so much innocence, but she'd done a bang-up job hiding it underneath skintight jeans and a crop top. Rich brown hair, drizzled with a honey color, brushed where he knew her nipples would be if he lifted her shirt. Just enough makeup to fit in without looking unnatural, like most of the girls who frequented Rush. No spray tan, no glittery eye goop, just a rosy glow that made his hands itch to touch her skin. On sight, she'd affected him so much it hurt to look at her, while at the same time it hurt worse to look away. Then her lips parted and that husky voice had come out, stroking over every inch of his body.

At that moment, his game plan had changed from simply making her casual acquaintance to daring anyone to come within ten feet of her. And the quickest way to ensure her safety, in his mind, had been to put a stamp of ownership on her. Right there in the middle of Rush.

Which is about when his plan had gone to shit. Anyone who knew him was aware that Bowen's relationships ended as quickly as they started. Usually within the same night. It only took a few whispered words and a nod toward the door to convince a girl to leave with him. He sure as hell didn't dry-hump them in plain view of the dining room, keeping his mouth locked to theirs until his brain forced him to breathe. Like he'd done with Sera, right in front of several neighborhood lifers who were no doubt more curious about her than before his ass had ever walked through the door. So, yeah. Now instead of *Bowen's latest hookup*, she'd become a possible target.

But *Christ*. She'd tasted so damn good. With her perfection pressed up against him, her eager tongue tangling with his, he'd lost his cool. That kiss had complicated the shit out of everything. A virgin. She hadn't needed to say it out loud; he'd seen the answer in her eyes, the surprised noise she made when he'd shoved up between her legs.

No time to think about that now, though. He was the only thing standing between her and possible death. Time for damage control. He adopted his best shit-eating grin and faced Hogan. As he'd anticipated, the man looked suspicious. "Someone's got to keep the waitresses in line when you're not around, right?" Bowen put his hand out and after a slight hesitation, Hogan shook it. "I came by to talk. Guess I got a little distracted."

Hogan still appeared dubious, but he nodded once. "Can't say I blame you. She's quite the little distraction."

It took every ounce of Bowen's control not to grab Hogan by the throat when he gave Sera a lustful once-over. "Why don't we let her get back to work?" Hogan's features tightened at Bowen's not-so-subtle command, warning him to reel back his obvious interest in Sera. "I'll buy you a drink."

Hogan very deliberately rubbed his jaw. "All right, Driscol." He turned his hard gaze on Sera. "Enough standing around. You're downstairs to serve drinks."

Fists clenched so hard he thought the bones might shatter, Bowen followed Hogan to the bar. He somehow resisted the impulse to turn around and gauge Sera's expression. Pass on some sort of reassurance that he'd handle Hogan. But not only would she reject such reassurance from him, she didn't know he was on her side.

And she couldn't know. He'd agreed to keep his involvement in the investigation from her. Newsom had explained that his niece's stubborn nature might cause her to make rash decisions if she knew the police were monitoring her, possibly getting ready to swoop in and put an end to her impulsive mission. *She's got nothing to lose*, he'd said. *No care for her own well-being.* Bowen damn well wished he hadn't agreed to that condition now so he could talk some sense into her.

When he reached the seat he'd left vacant what felt like hours ago, he slid onto the stool and signaled for a whiskey. God only knew how much he needed it.

Hogan took the seat beside him, looking thoughtful. "You know, I hadn't quite decided not to have her for myself." One by one, he popped his knuckles. "How was she?"

Stay calm. Stay calm. "I wouldn't know. You interrupted us before we got to the good part, man."

The other man smiled tightly. "Are you expecting an apology?" He picked up the shot of top-shelf tequila the bartender had placed in front of him. "I don't know if I like you coming into my club, handling my waitress. We might be making peace, but that doesn't mean I have an open-door policy."

Since he would rather chew nails than apologize, Bowen stayed silent. Eventually, Hogan laughed and slapped him on the back, making him stiffen.

"So let's talk." Hogan leaned close. "Everything still in order for next week's shipment?"

He nodded, the familiar pit opening in his stomach that always came when discussing business. "All set. I need to know what kind of manpower you're bringing, so I can match it. With that much cargo, we'll need a decent number, but they've all got to be trustworthy. No last-minute additions."

Hogan rubbed his palms together, turned on by the promise of the upcoming score. "Not a problem. I've handpicked every one of them. They know what happens if they talk." Rapping the bar with one hand, he looked back toward the dining room. "I'm not taking any chances with this one. It's too big. Which is why I hope you got the waitress out of your system."

Bowen's blood ran cold. "Meaning?"

Hogan's voice dipped low. "I kept her around because one of my guys got his ass shot a couple weeks back. She seemed to know what the fuck she was doing, and I sure as hell didn't have time to play nurse to anyone. So I brought her here." He shrugged. "He's up and around now. And she's not exactly waitress of the year. In fact, there's something about her…"

"Besides those legs?" Bowen interjected, wanting to distract Hogan from that suspicious line of thinking.

He acknowledged Bowen's comment with a cold smirk. "She's been around too long. I can't be sure what she's heard or seen." A touch of concern laced his tone. "Anyway, in the spirit of taking no chances leading up to this next shipment, I'm not keeping an outsider around longer than necessary."

The clawing in Bowen's throat was back. "Seems a little hasty, doesn't it?"

His comment earned him a jab in the shoulder. Hogan actually had the nerve to look amused after so casually mentioning his decision to get rid of Sera. "Should I take that to mean she's not out of your system yet?"

Hating the words he was about to say, Bowen made an indifferent gesture. "I wouldn't mind finishing what we started first." His stomach turned over. "After that, it's none of my business."

Hogan leaned back on his stool, eyes focused sharply on Bowen. "Tell you what. I'm heading to my Jersey club for a week to knock some heads together. Until I get back, she's your responsibility." One of his shoulders lifted. "Why not let you have your fun?"

Bowen felt like breaking something. "I got no problem with that."

"I bet you don't." Hogan turned, gesturing Sera closer with

a crooked finger. "But just to be safe, I'm going to have my cousin Connor keep an eye on things."

"You mean keep an eye on me." Bowen couldn't soften the harshness of his statement. "I don't need a babysitter."

"Think of it more like insurance. Nothing is going to stand in the way of this job, Driscol, especially your cute piece of ass. You've got one week."

Jesus, how many times would he have that same warning issued in his direction? One week. The world would apparently end in one damn week.

Sera arrived then, splitting a glance between him and Hogan. If she'd shown up a second later, Bowen strongly believed he would have given in to the urge to bury his fist in Hogan's smug face and blow the whole operation.

"Yes?"

Hogan tossed back his shot of tequila. "Sera, you've met Bowen, haven't you?" He laughed at his own joke. "He's going to be your host while I'm gone. I have a feeling you're going to be playing a different kind of nurse."

"In his dreams, you mean?" She felt, rather than saw, Bowen stiffen. It made little difference. He was about to throw a serious wrench into her engine. "I'm not going anywhere, unless I decide to. Not with him or anyone."

"Are you sure about that?" A hard glint entered Hogan's eye. "Right about now, he might just be the lesser of two evils."

Several things occurred to Sera at the same time.

First and most disturbing, she'd been marked as dispensable. Connor now required minimal medical attention for his wound, apart from the occasional changing of his bandages. If she'd outlived her usefulness in that department and Hogan didn't feel comfortable letting her remain behind in his absence without a watchdog, then he didn't trust her. Trust was paramount in his underworld, and she hadn't been given enough time to earn it. Lack of trust could be tolerated only if he had leverage of some sort on her, and she'd given him none.

Had Bowen somehow convinced Hogan to keep her around as his…plaything? She tried not to have a visceral reaction to that thought, difficult as it was. Just imagining what the sisters at Holy Angels Academy would have to say about her being bartered as a bed partner made her cringe. *Moving on.*

This new development put a major puzzle piece within her reach. In all the research she'd done, there had always been a giant question mark beside Bowen's name when it came to the major crime player's location the night her brother was murdered. Had Bowen been there? Did he have the answers she needed?

In a matter of days, Colin would have been twenty-nine. She owed him answers.

God, she'd just let a hardened criminal turn her into a shivering pile of lady hormones, without even finding out his name. How could she let her guard down like that? This was everything she'd been working toward for months, years if you started the clock when Hogan killed her brother in cold blood.

Her mind traveled back to the alley, when he'd only been a stranger, instead of the man who'd inherited a huge portion of the city and its illegal activities. Nestled against his warmth while the bright, brilliant strains of opera split the cool air. The way he'd looked at her. As if her smile were the most amazing part of the moment, not the woman belting Puccini from the second-floor window. It had felt like magic, but now she saw it was only an illusion. Bowen's notorious way with women had even made it into his thick police file, and she'd just let herself become another victim.

Unless...

She could use this to her advantage. Her week of personal leave had officially expired, meaning her uncle would start to look for her soon—if he wasn't already. She needed to take this turn of events and make it work for the investigation. Whether she wanted to accept it or not, Bowen's interest in her might have bought her the precious time she needed to continue investigating Hogan, while playing another angle at the same time. Namely, Bowen. It would mean using her body to achieve an end. Was she ready for that? Was it worth setting aside her principles and giving away an important part of herself?

Her brother's face flashed through her mind. *Yes*, it was worth it. How could she even question that when Colin had given up everything for this job?

When a sliver of excitement breached her resolve, Sera shoved it away.

She had to play this exactly right to ensure she didn't get made. Keeping her bravado would be key.

"Where are you going?" she asked Hogan, since she wasn't supposed to know about his trip to New Jersey. She also knew from experience that his employees didn't usually question him. Unfortunately, thanks to her loss of composure the night they met, he knew she had a backbone. While she might tread carefully, she also couldn't suddenly start playing meek.

His lips curled. "Aw, what's wrong? You going to miss me?"

To Sera's surprise, Hogan reached out as though he were going to touch her face. In the two weeks she'd been there, he hadn't made a pass at her or even flirted. Why now? Her question was answered when Bowen's hand shot out and grabbed his wrist, just before it reached her face.

Hogan threw back his head, laughing as he jerked his hand back. "Someone has a crush on you, cutie. Better get him upstairs before someone makes the mistake of breathing the same air as you."

Sera glanced at Bowen, who'd managed to keep his temper off his face, but his anger was broadcast through bunched-up fists. "He doesn't look like he needs a nurse. But if he thinks I'm going home with him, maybe a shrink would be a better idea."

That set Hogan howling again, but her focus remained on Bowen. For some reason, her insult seemed to calm him down. What sense did that make? "There isn't a shrink in the world that could figure me out, sweetheart."

"You won't know until you try, *sweetheart.*"

Her boss pushed back his stool and stood. "Good luck, Driscol. You're going to need it." As he skirted past them toward the exit, he raised an eyebrow at Bowen and lowered his voice. "Told you...*something* about her. Use the head on your shoulders."

Sera pretended not to hear, smoothing a hand down her apron to free it of wrinkles. "I'm going to get back to work," she said to Bowen. "I'd rather you weren't here when my shift ends."

"That's a shame. I just got comfortable."

She narrowed her eyes. "Listen, I don't care what arrangement you made with Hogan. I'm the only one who decides how I spend my time."

He sipped his whiskey, rolling it around on his tongue before swallowing. "You didn't mind my company when I had you up against the hallway wall."

Sera knew her face flushed when he chuckled. "Momentary insanity," she mumbled.

"You saying I drove you insane, Ladybug?" He winked. "I'll

take that as a compliment."

"Don't."

"I'll be right here when you finish."

The double entendre in his voice was so glaringly obvious, she almost laughed. Almost. She worked with cops, after all. She'd quickly grown used to sexual innuendo. Not that she ever participated.

Throughout the remaining three hours of her shift, she had to take several bathroom breaks to cool off, patting her face down with wet paper towels. On the occasions she gave in and looked over at Bowen, he was staring in a way that made her pulse skitter and race. She felt sweaty and hot in an unfamiliar way. The distraction wasn't appreciated, and yet after a while she began posing under his watchful eye. Angling herself toward him, arching her back when it wasn't necessary. Flipping her hair over her shoulder like an idiot.

Yes, her goal had changed with Bowen's unexpected arrival. She'd decided to use this attraction between them to her advantage, but it made her nervous exactly how much the prospect of his hands on her again excited her. The only way to survive was to immerse herself in the role. Stop thinking like Seraphina the cop and simply be Sera, the waitress. Bowen wanted her and she could admit to wanting him back, much as it annoyed her. After all, she had no guarantee he hadn't had a role in her brother's murder. That in itself should be enough to eliminate any inconvenient attractions. Why didn't it?

When ten o'clock rolled around, she untied her apron and tossed it into the waitress station cabinet. With a fortifying breath, she turned, intending to leave through the fire escape exit leading upstairs. She stopped short when she saw Bowen propped against the wall, waiting for her.

This is it, Sera. Too late to turn back now.

He pulled open the door. "After you."

Choosing to ignore him until he made the first move, Sera ascended the dim staircase, so physically aware of Bowen behind her, her neck prickled with shiver-inducing heat. The exposed skin at her back singed under the gaze she felt resting there. The sound of his work boots landing on each step echoed through the enclosed space, matching her thudding heartbeat. Would he follow her into her room? Probably. Why else would he be tracing a path behind her up the stairs? In a matter of minutes, she could be naked with one of Brooklyn's most sought-after criminals.

When they reached her door, she tugged the key out of her pocket and turned it in the lock. She pushed the door open to reveal her small, windowless room, half of which was taken up by a twin bed. The clothes that had been lent to her by one of Rush's waitresses sat in a neat pile on a single chair propped in the corner.

Bowen looked horrified. "Not exactly the lap of luxury, is it?"

"It's a good thing they didn't ask me to fill out a comment card," she muttered, walking inside. "But it's only temporary, until Connor gets back on his feet."

He made a thoughtful noise in his throat and reached down to test the doorknob. "You keep this locked at night?"

She frowned. "Yes."

"Good." He shoved his hands into his pockets and looked at her hard. "Lock it behind me when I go and don't open it for anyone."

He was leaving? Downstairs, he'd given the impression he wanted to sleep with her. Hadn't he?

"Don't do that, sweetheart."

Her eyes snapped to his. "Do what?"

"Look disappointed that I'm taking off. It's killing me."

She scoffed at that, holding the door wide for him to pass. "Now who's temporarily insane?"

"Nothing temporary about my insanity." He stepped closer, *too* close, but she held her ground. "I'll be back in the morning. Have your things ready to go."

"Why would I do that?"

His laughter held only the barest hint of amusement. "You have no fear, do you?"

"Of you?" She gulped when he closed the distance between them. "Should I fear you?"

His mouth came down on hers, kissing her long and hard. Lips meshed, teeth scraped, tongues tangled. When he pulled back, his breath came in harsh pants. "Why do you think I asked you to lock the door?"

Before she could formulate a response, he'd left, disappearing at the end of the hallway.

CHAPTER FIVE

Bowen pulled himself up from the top stair, where he'd spent the night propped against the wall. Not wanting to leave Sera for a second on the chance Hogan changed his mind and decided to take care of her sooner, he'd spent the night in the stairwell, watching her door. He still hadn't trusted himself enough to bring her home last night. Not when he'd been starving for her. It had taken every measure of willpower to walk out of her room. If he'd taken her back to his place, no doubt she would have ended up on her back. Watching her move around the dining room for hours on end last night, her firm ass swishing in those jeans, the air-conditioning causing her nipples to bead, he'd been strung so tight by the time her shift ended, his vision had started blurring. Dangerous territory. Especially when despite her protests, she'd clearly wanted him to stay.

He hadn't exactly gotten the most restful night of sleep on the metal staircase, so he'd had a lot of time to think. Sure, he made a living out of being underhanded, but the kind of deceit it would take to sleep with Sera without her knowing his role in her investigation? Even he didn't lack enough conscience for that.

Worse, after she'd given him so little protest over entering her room, he had the sneaking suspicion she planned on seducing information out of him. Or distracting him with sex while she continued to pursue Hogan. The physical connection he felt with her couldn't be faked, but the idea of her using it against him made him undeniably angry.

A hot-to-trot virgin. Wasn't that just his fucking luck?

He wouldn't know the first thing about being with someone inexperienced. He'd never been anything but hard and fast with a woman. As soon as they'd been pleasured, he took his own, having already mentally moved on.

Scrubbing a hand over his morning beard, he made his way toward her room. Or more accurately, her prison cell. When they got back to his place, he planned on putting her in a room she could breathe in. A room with a window. Granted, it would be clear on the opposite end of the apartment with plenty of distance between them. Bowen had to laugh at himself. As if it would matter. He would know she was there, sleeping in his sheets, showering in his bathroom. Naked.

This was going to be a long week.

Bowen reached her door, testing the handle to make sure it was still locked. When it opened with little urging, panic rushed in and overwhelmed him. He shoved the door open, his heart stopping when he found her bed empty. Her clothes were still stacked in the same spot as last night; her bed looked slept in. Where the hell was she?

Oh, God. He rubbed the heel of his hand against his chest, cursing himself for not taking her out of this place last night. What had he been thinking?

"Sera!"

He pivoted on a heel and strode out of the room, only to be brought up short at the sound of a musical laugh. Even though he'd never heard the amused notes before, he immediately knew it was Sera. Relief swamped him at the sign she was okay. The rest of him wanted to know who had managed to get a laugh out of her. Following the sound toward an open door, he banished the panic. No more. It would be a cold day in hell before he let her out of his sight again.

Panic morphed to swift, consuming jealousy. It whooshed through his system like a hot wind, obliterating rational thought. Sera sat cross-legged on the bed with a shirtless man, folding a bandage in her lap. The ends of her mouth were tilted in an absent smile, the smile he'd had to work double time to get a glimpse of last night. She hadn't noticed him yet, but the man leveled a steady gaze at him from his position against the pillows. The only thing saving the guy's life was the fact that Sera had all her clothes on. The life-threatening injury he sported didn't hurt his cause either.

"Sera," shirtless man rumbled, nodding toward Bowen.

"Huh?" Her eyes met his. "Oh."

Oh?

"Get off the bed."

Wisdom won out and she didn't argue with him, coming to her feet almost immediately. But irritation at following orders replaced self-preservation. "Don't order me around."

"You're mine for the week. Or did you forget?"

Angry color flooded her cheekbones. It was the wrong thing to say, but he couldn't see reason. A foreign possessiveness had taken up residence in his chest, and until she moved away from the shirtless man, nothing could breach it.

He jerked his chin toward the patient. "You got a shirt or something, man? Not that I'm not fucking dazzled."

Shirtless ignored him. "I'd ask Sera to introduce us, but based on your temper, I think I can guess who you are."

"Impressive." He crossed his arms. "Shirt."

With a heavy sigh, Sera moved toward a chest of drawers and pulled out a shirt. It didn't help ease his irritation she knew which drawer they were in. She walked over to the bed and handed over a red shirt, nodding once when the guy thanked her.

"Bowen, this is Connor Bannon. Mr. Hogan's cousin." She glanced between the two of them. "Call me crazy, but I smell a budding friendship."

Both of them snorted.

Connor finished pulling the shirt over his head. "Wasn't expecting you so early." One dark eyebrow lifted. "You must have slept here or something."

Bowen made a mental note not to underestimate Connor Bannon. "Or something." He turned his attention back to Sera. "Get your things. I'm taking you to my place."

"Doubtful," Connor said.

"Excuse me?"

"I *said*, doubtful." With a wince, Connor swung his legs over the side of the bed. "I know Hogan spoke to you about our arrangement."

"Hogan can talk to me if he has a problem with her leaving." He moved closer to Sera, letting his hand drift across her lower back. A gesture of possession he shouldn't be making, but couldn't seem to stop. "Or doesn't it bother you the girl taking care of you has been sleeping in a broom closet?"

A muscle jumped in Connor's cheek. "I don't make the decisions."

"Yeah? That's *all* I do." He felt Sera studying him and looked down at her, reeling a little over seeing her face in the light of day for the first time. Those gorgeous big brown eyes hit him like an uppercut, the scattering of freckles making her so fresh. So beautiful. So out of place in this world. He needed to stop staring, but not absorbing every nuance of her face seemed like the worst crime. "Hey, Ladybug."

"Don't 'hey Ladybug' me."

He couldn't contain his grin. Shit, he was in trouble. Still not taking his gaze off her, he spoke to Connor. "She's coming with me. You want to check in on us, that's up to you."

A drawn-out pause. "Oh, count on it."

"Great." Bowen laced his fingers with Sera's and led her toward the door. "Try and show up wearing clothes when you do."

Sera followed Bowen up the three flights of stairs leading to his apartment, wishing he hadn't been so silent on the ride over. He'd waited in the hallway and she stuffed her things into two grocery bags and fifteen minutes later, they were in his working-class neighborhood of Bensonhurst. Soon, she would be inside the home of Bowen Driscol, known felon. If she hadn't been in deep before, she'd just sunk to the bottom of the ocean with no oxygen tank.

He lived above an Italian restaurant called Buon Gusto. As they'd walked past to the adjacent entrance, two porters having a cigarette break greeted him as if he were a god returning to Olympus after winning a battle. They'd watched her with open curiosity until Bowen put a hand on her shoulder, his features darkening. Both cigarettes had been crushed underfoot, the restaurant door slamming as they ducked back inside in their haste. She'd wanted to question him about his behavior, but his rigid posture hadn't exactly invited conversation.

It frustrated her she didn't know where they stood. One

minute, he was snarling at anyone who came near her, the next he seemed to be restraining himself from touching her. Last night, she'd sworn she had him pegged. A self-entitled ladies' man who thought he had the right to "keep her" until Hogan returned. As far as she'd been concerned, Hogan and Driscol were one and the same. Then he'd left her alone last night, even warning her to lock the door behind him when he left. Perhaps his seduction style was to confuse his prey until they grew too dizzy to put up a fight?

Obviously Bowen had been tasked with keeping an eye on her until Hogan's return, but knowing what she did about Hogan, if he was suspicious of someone, they wouldn't live to see the next morning. Bowen had intervened on her behalf. But why? If he didn't plan on pursuing a fling with her, what did he want her for?

The sound of Bowen's key sliding into the lock dispelled her musings. One hand knocked against his thigh, in a gesture that seemed almost nervous. "I don't bring girls here during the day. And at night, the lights always stay off."

She didn't bother hiding her confusion. "Was that meant to reassure me?"

His breath escaped in a rush. "I have no idea. Did it?"

"No."

"Yeah, well." He pushed open the door. "That's probably a good thing."

Sera hefted her plastic grocery bags higher in her arms and followed him inside. The second she crossed the threshold, she came to a dead stop.

Murals. Everywhere. On every available inch of the apartment wall, loud, swirling, chaotic colors jumped out at her. So many shades, she could never count them all, careering through the space like a kaleidoscopic dream. Slowly, she turned in a circle, trying to find a pattern in the chaos. Too many scenes, too much to look at.

Some were abstract shapes painted in dynamic shades, wedged between almost frantic depictions of city landmarks, such as the Brooklyn Bridge. Yankee Stadium. A subway train. In each vignette, half of the perfectly rendered landmark remained intact, while the other half disappeared in flames. The more scenes she took in, the more the theme became obvious. Two conflicting outcomes: the murals had split personalities. She didn't need him to confirm he'd been the one to paint them. It was obvious.

"Is this why you keep the lights off?" She searched his face for answers.

Her breath caught in her throat at the intensity he radiated.

"Among other reasons."

Tamping down the urge to pry more, she walked into the central living room between an open kitchen and a hallway she assumed led to the bedrooms. She dropped the plastic bags to the ground, her hand stretching out of its own accord to trace the outline of a woman's face. With a frown, she cast a look around the room and realized the same outline appeared every few feet. No features, just the shape of a head with long brown hair. Running through the strands was a streak of hot pink.

"Who—"

"Your room is behind the kitchen." He pinched her waist. "Come on, stop gawking."

She rubbed the tingling spot. "I'm not gawking."

"You're one of those drivers that slows down to watch someone get a speeding ticket, aren't you?" His disappeared into a door she hadn't seen before, just off the kitchen. "A rubbernecker."

"You're just trying to change the subject."

He sighed as she entered the room. "Waitresses aren't usually so astute, Ladybug."

"Guys like you aren't usually mural artists."

Before she could blink, he lunged toward her, sending her back against the wall. "Guys like me?" He rested his palms above her, leaning down until his breath feathered her lips. "And what exactly do you know about me?"

Sera realized her massive error. His playful side had allowed her to get comfortable, but she needed to remember whom she was dealing with. She'd already gotten a glimpse of his notorious temper. "I don't know anything," she whispered, letting real fear show. "I was just surprised."

"Surprised," he repeated slowly. "While you're here, you need to be more careful what you say and who you say it to. Comments like that can get you hurt. And then *I'll* have to hurt that somebody back. It'll be very ugly, Sera. Do you understand?"

She nodded, then gasped when he ground his hips against hers. The steel of his arousal pressed against the softness of her belly. He bit his bottom lip and closed his eyes, an expression that struck her as pained. *Move*, she silently commanded him. *Touch me.* When he didn't grant her the friction she wanted, she lifted her hands and dug them into his thick, haphazard mane of burnished gold hair. With a snarl, he grabbed her wrists and pinned them to the wall above her. The loss of control sent exhilaration snapping along her skin. She shouldn't like it. As a cop, the ability to defend herself should be paramount, but something about being put on display made her feel exceedingly hot. Tempting.

His gaze raked down her body, lingering on the rise and fall of her breasts. The thin material of her T-shirt hid nothing, telling him without words that she was turned on. For him. By him.

"Stop begging me for it." His voice shook. "I'm hanging on

by a goddamn thread here."

She didn't understand his plea. He obviously wanted her, and her willingness couldn't be clearer. Why was he holding back? "Can I ask you a question?"

"If I say no..." Appearing to give in a little, he ran his tongue along her lower lip and groaned, "Would it stop you?"

"Probably not."

"Maybe I'll kiss you to shut you up. You'd love that. Wouldn't you?"

It wasn't a question, but a statement. Going on instinct, she gave a long, slow roll of her hips. "Do it."

He gave a sharp curse. "Ask the question," he rasped at her ear.

"Why did you bring me here, if not for this?" She tilted her head, hoping he would take the hint and kiss her there. When he didn't disappoint, she moaned in her throat. His damp lips were smooth where the rest of him was hard, rough. They traced the skin beneath her ear with unerring accuracy, homing in on the sensitive spot she hadn't even been aware of. "You locked me in my room last night...and n-now I'm in a separate bedroom. It seems counterproductive." His teeth closed around her ear and she whimpered. "Did Hogan tell you *not* to touch me or something? Becaus—"

"*What?*" His head whipped up, the hands holding hers against the wall flexing hard. "Listen to me, if I wanted to fuck you, I'd end anyone or anything who got in my way. Nothing would stop me. Not a locked door. Not some lowlife. Nothing."

"If?" she repeated, embarrassment cooling her desire. "You don't want to?"

His laughter was harsh. "Want to? *Want* to?" One of his hands loosened its grip to drop down and grasp the bulge in his pants. "I didn't even know it was possible to ache this bad. It hurts to breathe, baby."

The heat came rushing back in full force. "Then I don't understand."

"I can't. We can't." He pressed his forehead to hers. "See, I'm wondering if keeping my hands off you will buy my way out of hell. God knows I'll have experienced the worst hell has to offer already. You think he'll make me go through it twice?"

The suffering in his voice lacerated her. There was so much more going on here than sexual frustration, although there was definitely a healthy dose of that. He seemed to think there would be consequences for getting physical with her. But that didn't make any sense. Since when does a man who rules streets with fear care about consequences for anything? This man took what he wanted and damn the outcome. Right?

Without thinking, she took the hand he'd dropped and brushed a stray piece of hair off his forehead. His body went liquid, melting against her for long moments while she held her breath. "Aren't there other ways to buy yourself out of hell?"

"Not for me."

No sooner were the words out of his mouth than someone pounded on the door.

CHAPTER SIX

Safe. Keep her safe.

Bowen jerked away from Sera, his body going on full alert. No one just walked up and pounded on his apartment door without advance warning. No one, except for one man. A man who absolutely could not be allowed anywhere near Sera. His jaw clenched against the urge to bury her in the closet underneath a pile of clothes. It might give him peace of mind, but it would make her suspicious. He couldn't afford that, nor did he want it. For some reason, her being comfortable around him mattered. A lot.

Sensing how closely she watched him, he ran a casual hand through his hair. "I need to discuss some business. Make yourself comfortable."

She nodded carefully and sat down at the edge of the bed. Oh, God, what would it be like if he nudged her onto her back, settled himself between her thighs and worked them both into a sweat? His need for her hadn't calmed in the least. In fact, it only raged higher now that a threat was nearby. He couldn't allow anything to touch her. Not even himself.

She looked so out of place in this bedroom, fire and destruction raging on the walls behind her. When he'd painted that particular mural, he never imagined a cop sitting in the room with him. He would have laughed out loud at the very idea. Yet there she sat, looking like a lamb on her way to slaughter. Instead of flames outlining her head, she looked more suited to wearing a halo. When she looked up at the ceiling, he followed her line of vision and nearly laughed out loud. He'd painted the scales of justice one night after a particularly bad run-in with a gang that had been dealing drugs in Bensonhurst, the one thing he would never abide. Now the undercover cop would be sleeping beneath them. If that wasn't irony, he didn't know what was.

To her credit, she showed no reaction except for an arched eyebrow. "Shouldn't you get the door?"

Christ, he'd been so wrapped up in her, he'd completely forgotten about the man waiting outside. "Right," he said gruffly. "I'll be right back."

"Bowen?"

"Yeah," he said, looking back over his shoulder.

"They're kind of great." She pushed her hair behind her ear. "The murals."

Something heavy inside him shifted so dramatically, it surprised him she didn't react to it. Very few people had ever seen what he did in his spare time. Judged the tool he used to occupy his mind in order to think about anything other than what he did for a living. He'd never thought to show it to anyone, let alone have the work appreciated. Even more, she seemed to mean what she said.

If he stood here looking at her a second longer, he wasn't sure what the odd mixture of pride and gratefulness would make him do, so he took a deep breath to compose himself and walked into the living room, looking at the murals with fresh eyes. Wondering what Sera saw when she looked at them. What they made her think about him. Pushing those thoughts to the side, he opened the door.

His father's oldest business partner, Wayne Gibbs, stood in the hallway, the day's racing form sticking out of his front pocket.

"Wayne."

"You mind letting me in? I'm catching a cold out here."

When he made a move to pass him, Bowen blocked his path. "Let's talk downstairs."

"You can't invite your godfather inside?" He clucked his tongue. "I know Lenny taught you more respect than that."

His tone was teasing, but Bowen heard the underlying steel. Jesus, these old-school guys didn't take disrespect lightly. Neglect to invite them in for coffee and you signed your own death warrant. Furthermore, Wayne never failed to bring up his father every time they met. Bowen knew he was suspicious about the events leading to his business partner's arrest, but since he didn't have concrete evidence of Bowen's role, he settled on needling him every chance he got.

He didn't want to invite Wayne inside, but not doing so would be suspicious. The last thing he needed was added scrutiny while he had Sera under his protection. He'd just have to hope Sera knew enough to stay out of sight in the back bedroom.

With a tight smile, he stepped back. "Coffee?"

"Nah, I'm good. I only got a minute before I have to split."

He shoved his hands into his pockets, doing his best to ignore Wayne's usual amusement over the paint-covered walls. "What's up?"

"That crew from Central Brooklyn we took care of a few weeks ago is back." The older man picked up a paintbrush and let it drop. "One of our guys said they were selling again down on Kings Highway. Either they've got balls of steel or they can't read a map. We told them to keep it in their territory, but they ain't listening."

Bowen inwardly cringed, knowing Sera could hear everything from the back room. It wouldn't matter to her he had immunity with the police as long as he cooperated. But immunity didn't mean he hadn't committed crimes. It only meant he wouldn't pay for them. As soon as she was clear of this personal crusade, he and the NYPD would be back to playing cops and robbers, just like before.

It was for the best his criminal status stayed fresh in her mind. As often as possible, she needed to be reminded to keep her distance. This is who he was. Not a painter or someone she should be letting kiss her neck.

Bowen leaned back against the kitchen counter. "We'll pay them a visit tonight and remind them. Although after the last time, I'm not sure what'll get through to them." He hated the look of anticipation that entered Wayne's eyes. "Anything else?"

"Yeah." Wayne chuckled. "Our boy Tony still hasn't paid for the big hit he took on the Jets' loss last week. He's been ducking me."

Bowen massaged his eyes with the heel of his hand. "God, this guy doesn't learn."

"Let's hope not. That's how we make money."

A sour taste flooded Bowen's mouth. "If I wanted a punching bag, I'd go to the gym. He's *never* good for it on time. Why do we keep taking his bets?"

Wayne spread his hands. "We get the dough eventually, don't we?"

Exhaustion washed over Bowen. "Give him another couple days to make good before we go see him."

"You can't go easy," Wayne warned. "You go easy, word spreads that you're soft."

"I'm not soft." His voice quieted. "I don't see you throwing the punches."

Distracted, Wayne bent down and fished a lacy pair of underwear from the plastic grocery bags Sera had left in the living room. "What's this?" Bowen tried not to react. "You wearing ladies' underpants now?"

"Are you really asking me that question?"

Looking uncomfortable, Wayne shifted on his feet. "You got a girl here?"

Again, Bowen repressed the need to hide her in the closet, before guarding it with his life. "I don't see how that's any of your business."

"Not my business?" His lowered voice vibrated. "We're out here talking shop while your latest piece of ass can hear everything we say? That sure sounds like my business."

Rage filtered through his body at hearing Sera referred to as a piece of ass, but he managed to keep himself in check. "She's asleep," he said through clenched teeth, hoping she would overhear and follow suit. "I spent the morning wearing her out. Been a while since you did that to a woman?"

"Touchy, aren't we?"

Bowen ignored the question. "Are we done here?"

"Not until I'm satisfied she didn't hear anything. You know what happens when people have the misfortune of hearing too much."

He took a step closer. The older man arched an eyebrow at the action. Very rarely did he challenge Wayne, even though he technically held rank over him. He'd known the man since childhood, had once even viewed him as a father figure. With Sera's safety in question, he didn't hesitate to pull rank now.

"Are you questioning my judgment? I wouldn't suggest it."

The older man's chin went up. "That's the first time you've ever reminded me of your father. It's almost enough to bring a tear to my eye."

Nausea roiled in Bowen's gut. Even though the comment had been insincere, it still made him feel ill. "Then you know how Lenny would deal with someone who questioned him."

Wayne gave an exaggerated nod. "Very well, kid. If that's how you want to play it."

At the use of the old nickname, Bowen's hands bunched into fists. "Time to go, old man."

Wayne threw back his head and laughed on the way to the door, but it held a hint of menace. "Out of everything, I never thought pussy would be your downfall, Bowen. Can I at least count on seeing you tonight, or are you taking her to a Broadway show?"

He didn't wait for Bowen's response, but closed the door softly behind him. After flipping all three dead bolts back into place, Bowen released a pent-up breath and went to the guest bedroom. What he saw made his heart squeeze in his chest. Nestled under the covers, Sera had obviously overheard him and pretended to be asleep, even going so far as to make the bed look mussed from sex. Now she sat up, watching him with a wariness so different from the pleasure she'd shown when talking about his murals, it increased the queasiness he was experiencing.

Bowen cleared his throat into the silence. "What time do you work tonight?"

"Five."

He nodded. "Be ready to go at four thirty."

"Okay, sure."

Frustration gripped him. He wanted to shout at her, tell her she was in over her head. He wanted to beg her to go home and let him deal with the fallout. He wanted to climb into the bed with her and see if she still planned on using her body to keep him happy while she went behind his back to bring down Hogan. So many things he wanted and couldn't ever have. In the end, all he could do was walk away and leave her there, looking like his personal version of temptation.

Sera set down a plate of hot wings in the middle of the table, smiling softly at the chorus of masculine thank-yous that went up. Since Bowen's intervention the night before, she'd apparently been upgraded from low-level peon to respected member of staff. While it definitely made waitressing more pleasant, it galled her it had taken threats from Bowen to earn her basic human decency. Not just threats, she amended, casting a glance at him where he sat sipping whiskey at the bar, daring anyone with his eyes to mess with her. Constant observation.

People obviously thought they were an item, and it made them curious about her. She didn't need that, nor did she want his protection. Her goal had been to keep her head down and gather information. His oversight left very little opportunity for recon. And her time was running out. Even more so than before.

He'd let her overhear everything being said in his living room. *Everything.* Hadn't even made a basic attempt to keep his voice down while talking about collecting illegally earned gambling money, following through on threats to drug dealers. That could mean only one thing. He didn't plan on keeping her around long enough to let her tell anyone what she'd heard. She had to work fast.

Lying in bed that afternoon, she'd thought it was already

over. The realization had been unlike anything she'd experienced before, and she wouldn't go there again. She'd actually been surprised at the way Bowen spoke about her, at his obvious indifference to her hearing an incriminating conversation. *Stupid.* She had been stupid. And naive, just as her uncle had always accused her of being. Whatever good she thought she'd glimpsed inside Bowen was a facade, and remembering that might just save her life.

Furthermore, she'd allowed the tentative friendship she'd developed with Connor to make her complacent. Make her feel safe in this world. Their brief discussions about his ailing mother, his life before coming to Brooklyn, didn't mean he would save her if presented with a crucial choice. It was unlike her to let down her guard like that. Had she developed some weird case of Stockholm syndrome? She might have nursed Connor back to health, but in this world, the bottom line was all that counted. Making money, staying alive. Protecting your interests. She'd learned early not to depend on anyone but herself, and a lapse in judgment could mean her life.

She didn't understand why Bowen had moved her into his apartment, but thinking about it had become a distraction. Based on the conversation he'd had with Wayne, he would have to leave at some point to go pay his visit to the outsiders who'd had the audacity to invade his territory. That would be her chance to gain entrance to Hogan's office, and she had to take it. She could feel the walls closing in around her. Until today, she'd felt relatively safe in her assumed identity. Now it had all begun to crumble around her ears.

Her uncle had never had any faith in her, choosing to place it all in her brother. When her father died in the line of duty so long ago, she'd been a child. She'd desperately needed approval, encouragement. Her mother's subsequent death when her grief drove her to drink and drive one horrible night had left Sera precious little resources for that. Instead of giving her a solid foundation to rebuild on, her uncle's response had been to send her away. As an adult, she could understand why a busy man opted out of raising two children, but that rejection had also instilled a need to prove herself to him. To everyone.

Focus now. Stop dwelling on what you can't change. Your plan is to find the evidence, expose Hogan, and become invisible again. Just like you have been forever.

Having finished serving the table, she straightened, intending to return to the bar. When she ran straight into Bowen's solid figure, she couldn't contain a yelp of alarm. He steadied her with both hands on her elbows, gaze narrowed suspiciously. "You all right?"

"I'm fine, I just didn't expect you to be standing there."

"Okay." He drew the word out. "I have to leave for a little while, but I'll be right back."

She tugged away and pasted on a casual smile. "Who's going to glare at me from the bar while you're gone?"

"Nobody better. If anyone does, you tell me." After what seemed to be an internal debate, he slid a hand around her waist and pulled her close again, as if offended to have her so far away. "Think you can manage to kiss me without turning into a wildcat?"

A mere breath separated their lips. "You didn't seem to mind before."

"Baby, you're making me hard right when I need to walk out the door. It's goddamn inconvenient." He sampled her mouth with a wet tug of his lips. "Don't stop."

As though it were the most natural thing in the world, her hand slid up his chest and disappeared into his hair. He snaked his arm around her body so it rested against the small of her back and drew her close. So close. Their mouths came together on a groan. The sensual devastation reached to her toes, then slithered back up to settle between her legs. How could he do this to her? One minute he was the enemy; the next he drew reactions from her body, scrambling her brain. Made her question everything she knew about herself.

Bowen released her mouth on a curse. "Watching you work fucks me up. You have any idea what it does to me when you bend over a table and smile? It makes me want to pull up your skirt and turn that smile into a scream."

His words shivered down her back. "Do you talk to every girl like this?"

"I don't even turn on the lights for other girls."

Why did that kick up a spark of pleasure? It was just another line. She *knew* it and yet, combined with the way he looked at her, she felt like the only person in the room. "That's just bad manners."

Gray eyes twinkled. "They're the only kind I have."

"You're confusing me, Bowen." She took a deep breath. "I need to get back to work."

When she tried to extricate herself, he didn't budge. "That's the first time you've said my name." He rubbed their lips together. "Whisper it again in my ear, then I'll go."

"You're a lunatic." He simply raised an eyebrow and she sighed, annoyed at the traitorous smile playing around her mouth. Holding his shoulders for support, she pressed up on her toes and laid her mouth against his ear. After taking a moment to inhale his smoky leather scent, she let his name fall from her lips. "*Bowen*."

He actually shook. The arm banding her waist tightened, and the breath whooshed from her lungs. Then just as quickly, he let her go. "I'll be *right* back."

All she could do was nod.

CHAPTER SEVEN

Bowen bit the inside of his cheek to silence the screaming in his head, the churning sickness in his stomach. His knuckles ached and he needed to wash them off before he saw Sera. It helped to think about her, so he hung on to the image of her lying in the middle of his guest bed. Any minute, he would get out of this car full of jackasses bragging about the beatdowns they'd just delivered and see her again. And maybe she'd let him pretend like earlier. Maybe she'd let him kiss her and call her Ladybug and fantasize they weren't so different. Maybe, maybe, maybe.

Not one fucking certainty in his life, except for pain. The giving of it and the receiving of it. Not a day went by anymore where he didn't condone the use of violence. As a teenager and even through his early twenties, he'd loved fighting. Lived for it. He'd loved the fact no one ever got the drop on him; he could use his fists to get out of any situation. That time had long passed, and now it was work. The kind of work that breaks you down until nothing registers. For a while now, he'd experienced slips into numbness. It got a little easier every time, to issue the order. A little easier to think of people as dollar signs instead of living, breathing human beings with souls.

Had *he* been born with a soul? He'd often wondered if it were possible to walk upright, communicating and living life with just the idea of where his soul should be. Worse, did people see that lack in him? Is that why everyone left in the end?

An image of the woman, hair streaked full of pink, replaced Sera in his mind, but he grabbed on to her and held tight, the way he wished he could do in real life. He didn't want to think about the woman or why she'd left or if it had been something he could have prevented. Something he could have done differently. Right now, at least he had a purpose. Protect Sera. Keep Ruby's involvement in his father's arrest confidential. If he could do those two things, maybe he could look back one day and say he'd done something that mattered. Keeping his own ass out of jail didn't quite rate in comparison, but it drove him, too. No way would he pass his father in the Rikers Island cafeteria and see smug satisfaction on his face.

Finally, after an eternity, the car pulled over to drop him at the curb outside of Rush. The other passengers were still in their element, mimicking the cries of pain they'd induced tonight, already talking about the next time.

Irritation snapping behind his eyes, he stooped down and leaned into the passenger side window. Everyone shut up, attention zeroing in on him. "Listen up. You assholes want to go out and get your dicks wet, get drunk? Have at it. But keep your fucking mouths shut. You're about as inconspicuous as a couple of Macy's parade floats. This isn't your first fight and it won't be your last, so quit acting like it. You're embarrassing yourselves and me in the process."

The driver held up his hands. "You got it, boss."

God, he hated being called that. Boss of what? A car full of shitheads. He straightened and patted the car's roof once.

"Take it easy on them girls."

Spirits somewhat restored, the car full of men pulled away as Bowen walked into Rush, nodding in greeting at the bouncer. As he wove through the crowd at the bar, he heard his name spoken several times. Some of the voices female, some male. He ignored them all. The moment his eyes landed on Sera, the screaming in his head died down to a whisper. Face flushed, hair falling out of its ponytail, she looked more than a little flustered. Since he'd left, the place had grown busy, the typical Saturday night crowd looking to get rowdy. The tray full of drinks in her hand looked seconds from gracing the floor.

Good Lord, the girl was a horrible waitress. Why did that make him want her even more?

He didn't even realize he was walking toward her until Connor stepped into his path, bringing him up short. "Driscol."

Bowen gave a quick nod, angling himself so he could keep an eye on Sera. "Look at you, fully clothed. Is there a special occasion?"

"Nah." Connor shrugged. "I just don't have a beautiful girl in my bed at the moment."

His vision swam with red. "I'd be more careful about what comes out of your mouth. I don't care if this club belongs to your cousin. Don't talk about her."

Connor considered him in a way that made Bowen almost uncomfortable. This wasn't a typical neighborhood guy. Too much went on behind his eyes. A quick glance at the man's forearm and the navy tattoo told him Connor hadn't spent his entire life in Brooklyn, like the rest of them. "I just wanted to confirm my suspicion."

"The suspicion that I'd like to kick your ass?"

"Nope." He tipped back his bottle of Heineken. "The suspicion that the ladies' man I'd heard so much about is gone over one chick."

Bowen accepted a glass of whiskey from the bartender, not bothering to deny it. He'd already screwed himself with his possessive behavior. "So what? You want to go paint our nails and talk about it or something?"

"Funny. You know why I brought it up." His voice trailed off when the music quieted between songs. When another one kicked in, he spoke again. "She overheard something. Something she shouldn't have."

"Excuse me?" Bowen swore he could feel the blood turning to solid ice in his veins. "We're talking about Sera?"

"No, the other girl you almost ripped my throat out over."

"Talk," he gritted out.

Connor finished his beer and set it on the bar. "Last week. Hogan had a phone conversation in the hallway outside my room. He didn't realize she was inside changing my bandage." He glanced over his shoulder at Sera where she took a drink order. When he turned back, his eyebrows were drawn low. "It was the date of the shipment. She heard it. No location, but it was enough to worry my cousin. That's why she's marked, man."

Even having already known Hogan wanted Sera gone didn't ease the blow of hearing it spoken aloud. Over his dead body would those words ever come true. "The question is, why are you telling me this?"

"I'd be dead if it wasn't for her. I repay my debts."

Difficult as it was to admit, Bowen believed him. He'd had a lot of experience dealing with liars, and this guy wasn't one. Second, he knew all too well the way Sera could work her way under your skin, make you question your own loyalties. Watching her call an order to the bartender, his throat squeezed. He needed to distract himself or he would carry her out of there over his shoulder. "How'd you end up here?"

Connor raised an eyebrow.

"Going from the navy to running small-time game in Brooklyn?" Bowen shrugged. "That's pretty far to fall."

"Thanks, man." He pulled his wallet out of his pocket. "You want to go paint our nails and talk about it or something?"

"Fair enough." Bowen watched as Connor laid a twenty-dollar tip on the bar. "Listen," he said, uncomfortable expressing gratitude. "I owe you one. I repay my debts, too."

Connor turned to leave, then stopped. "You might want to clean the blood off your knuckles before you go see her."

Bowen showed no reaction, continuing to sip his whiskey. His gaze sought Sera over the rim of his glass, Connor's parting words echoing in his head. What kind of man had to clean blood off his hands before going to see his girl? A man too tainted to touch her. The glass froze at his lips when he didn't immediately see her in the dining room. Quickly, he scanned the bar, panic like a hot poker in his stomach. *Relax, she's probably just in the bathroom.* But when several minutes passed and she didn't emerge, fear replaced panic. No way could she have passed him and left the bar. He would have sensed her walking by, would have seen her. She had to be somewhere inside the bar.

His attention snagged on the kitchen, his feet beginning to move before any type of decision registered. When they'd gone out to the alley on Friday night, he'd noticed a door inside the kitchen, one he presumed led to the basement. If she'd gone down there, he prayed she was alone. That she hadn't been taken down there against her will. Jesus, why had he let Connor distract him? Had it been intentional?

The cook called his name as he entered the kitchen, but Bowen ignored him, taking the stairs leading to the basement two at a time. Her name burned his throat, dying to be shouted, but he didn't want to alert anyone to his presence until he knew what he was up against. When he reached the bottom, he saw light coming from another door. An office? He went closer, stopping short when he saw Sera, rummaging through a drawer, flashlight wedged between her teeth.

Hogan's office. She's looking for the ledger.

The ledger I'll have to take away. One my name is definitely in. Probably multiple times.

His first instinct was to drag her from the office, tell her to forget everything she'd seen. The more she knew, the more imminent the danger to her life would become. What if someone else, not him, had come down and seen her? Hundreds of customers were upstairs. People loyal to Hogan who would jump at the chance to score points with him by turning in Sera. How could she take such a stupid risk?

Then logic resumed. This was her job. This was why she was there in the first place. It hit him then, how much danger Sera had put herself in. God, if something happened to her...

No. He wouldn't allow it. She might be on a mission to bring down Hogan and get justice for her brother, but that undertaking conflicted with his own. Keep her alive and safe. He'd justified his role in guarding Sera as a way to protect his sister, but it had become more than that the second he met her. So much more.

It had become everything.

With a heavy swallow, he walked back up to the top of the stairs and slammed the door, before descending once more, slower than before. As he entered the basement, she walked out with a smile, holding up an object. A cell phone.

"Found it," she said. "Hogan took away my cell phone. Figured there was no harm in getting it back while he's not here to bully me."

It was a weak cover story. She knew it. So did he. Bowen grew sick as he registered the look on her face. Fear. Of him. She might be trying to brazen it out, but she thought she'd been caught. Thought it was over and he'd be the one to mete out her punishment. He could see it in her wide brown gaze, the bracing of her shoulders. In his life, he'd never been more ashamed of his reputation, the life he'd led.

With one hand outstretched, he went toward her. "Ladybug—"

"Have to get back upstairs." She came through the office door and skirted him, heading toward the staircase. If he let her go, she'd run and never come back. That much was obvious. A part of him wanted to let her. The rest of him rebelled at the idea of never seeing her again, letting her leave fearing him. It was selfish and yet he couldn't let it happen.

Adrenaline blasted through Sera as she hastened toward the stairs, dodging Bowen's attempt to grab her. She'd been too desperate, too impulsive, and now she would pay for it. Unless she could somehow make it up the stairs and escape through the kitchen into the alley. Knowing Bowen and how he made his living, her chances were slim. No matter what connection she'd imagined between them or kisses they'd shared, it would all go out the window now. For some reason, the realization hurt badly. Why did it have to be him who caught her?

Dammit, she'd seen him occupied in a conversation with Connor and thought she'd have at least five minutes. Had she been longer than five minutes? After what she'd discovered, time had blurred, then stood still. For all she knew, an hour had passed as she stood there, staring disbelievingly at Hogan's black book of debts.

She hadn't wanted it to be true. Didn't see how it was possible. But there it had been in black and white.

Her brother, Colin, had been taking payouts from Hogan.

Later. She would think about it later. Right now, she had to get away from Bowen. She might have taken her chances fighting him off as she'd been trained, but she was unarmed and didn't know if Bowen carried his gun. As her foot came down on the bottom step, she cringed over the anticipation of a bullet entering her back. *Please don't shoot.* She chanted it over and over, calling on Saint Michael for protection, even knowing it would do her no good. He wouldn't let her leave alive after catching her snooping.

An arm snagged her around the waist and yanked her backward. One second she was free-falling, the next she came up hard against Bowen's chest. Without hesitation, she began to fight like hell, attempting to bring her foot down on his instep, but he anticipated the move and shifted his foot. Her elbow managed to connect with his gut, although besides a grunt, he didn't react.

"Stop *struggling*." His voice sounded pained, confusing her. "Please, just stop."

Sera gathered her strength to renew her struggles, but went still when his mouth nuzzled her ear. "Let me go."

"I wish I could."

Tears gathered in her throat. This was it. Her uncle had been right. She wasn't cut out to be a cop, and it all ended now. And after what she'd just discovered, it had all been for nothing. *Colin, how could you?*

As quickly as the thoughts came, she grew angry with herself. How could she lose faith in her brother so easily? Not to mention herself. There had to be an explanation for Colin's deception. She simply wouldn't believe otherwise. With a burst of renewed energy, she twisted from Bowen's grip, throwing her elbow as hard as she could into his sternum. To her relief, his grip loosened momentarily and she scrambled up the stairs. She'd almost reached the top when a hand circled her ankle, halting her progress.

"Goddammit, Sera." His hand gripped the waistband of her skirt to gain leverage, his bigger body covering hers in seconds, keeping her pinned on her side. Her breath sounded like a windstorm in her ears as one calloused hand slipped around the back of her neck. "I'm not going to hurt you," he grated. "How could you think I would?"

His words partially broke through the fogbank of fear. It didn't seem possible that he could have accepted her cell phone explanation. He was too smart for that, wasn't he? "I know... I'm not supposed to be down here. I thought you might tell Hogan."

"No." He shifted their position, so that her bottom rested on a stair, his hips wedged between her thighs. His forearm supported her back, cushioning her against the hardness of the stairs. Her worries dimmed when his closeness registered. Bowen became aware of it at the same time, because the pace of his breathing increased. "Look at me. You have nothing to fear from me. Ever. Do you understand?"

The moment was so honest, his voice so full of passion, she couldn't stop her own truth from escaping. "I don't know who you are."

He shook his head slowly. "Baby, I don't know either."

She shifted beneath him and he groaned. The raw sound sent blazing heat spiraling through her. After what she'd just learned, how it had ripped her beliefs to shreds, followed by the possibility of being caught, maybe killed, the emotions crashing around inside her needed an outlet. *Now*. His hard body between her thighs, his mouth so close, promised a distraction. A distraction she'd been wanting since they'd met, if she was honest with herself. Even in the dim light of the basement, his base, hungry sex appeal radiated from him, dragging her under. Of their own accord, her knees rose on either side of his hips, ankles locking at the small of his back.

"*Oh, God*, don't do that." His hand slid down from her neck to hitch her leg higher around his waist, contradicting his words. Rough fingers stroked down the outside of her thigh, his hips rolling once on a choked curse. "You just ran from me. Forced me to catch you. I don't know if I can say no after being challenged like that."

"Don't say no."

He stamped his mouth over hers, as if to chastise her for what she'd said, but almost immediately his lips softened and he granted her a deep, hot kiss. The hand resting on the outside of her thigh continued its path and cupped her bottom, kneading, squeezing. They broke away, panting at the intimate contact, frustration coating his expression. "I can't let your first time be on the stairs of a nightclub."

"You're not the one who decides what I do with my body," she argued, with a lot more confidence than she felt. Yes, this might be new to her, but she didn't want to stop feeling this way. She didn't want his weight, his touch, to leave her. It would give her time to think.

Something primal, possessive flared behind his eyes. "I've got my cock pressed between your legs. For the sake of my sanity, let's say I *am* the one who decides."

His gravelly request sent liquid warmth pooling in her lower belly. Worried he would feel the wetness, she tried to scoot back and close her thighs, but he wouldn't let her. Almost like a warning, he gave a quick thrust of his hips, sending the rigid fly of his jeans dragging up the center of her damp silk panties.

"Oh my God." Desire flashed like lightning, fast and jagged inside her. The tug low in her belly was becoming unmanageable. She wanted to squirm to relieve the growing ache, but the friction would drive her higher and she needed to stay grounded. Right? It didn't help that Bowen had buried his face in her neck, his breath rasping along her skin. When his teeth sank into the side of her neck, accompanied by another deliberate drag of his erection against her core, Sera decided embracing the overwhelming sensations was better than letting him stop. *No, please don't let him stop.* She closed her eyes and allowed her thighs to fall open, praying, begging him to do it again.

Her gesture of permission seemed to break something free inside him and he began rocking against her, his tongue licking up the side of her neck. "What sound would you make the first time I sink in, Sera? Would you scream for me or your God?"

Feeling a sense of desperation, needing an anchor, she turned her head to ask for his mouth, but he anticipated her. Their mouths fused together in a wet slide of lips, throaty sounds of satisfaction. She felt a pang of surprise when he released her backside to work his belt buckle. He'd just said he wouldn't take her on the steps. Had he changed his mind? She opened her eyes to watch his progress, her heartbeat pounding out of control when he unzipped his jeans and removed his thick, lengthy arousal.

"I'm not going to put it in you, baby, I just need to…" He dragged the head of his fisted erection along the seam of her panties. "Fuck. Fucking *Christ.*"

White light blossomed behind her eyes at the contact with her clitoris. "D-do that again. *Please*, Bowen," she implored, hips rising to encourage him.

Teeth gritted, he used the head of his length to circle her, over and over, silk clinging to damp flesh. She moaned and begged, the sound mingling with Bowen's dark curses. "Once I broke you in, you'd be a sweet little fuck, wouldn't you, Sera? You've got innocent eyes, but a hot, greedy body. God help me, I would never stop banging you."

He punctuated his final word by pushing his hardness against the silk at her opening, using his thumb to apply pressure to her clit at the same time. The material prevented him from entering, but his round tip nudging her there, his gorgeous face awash with agony as he gave her pleasure...all of it sent her rocketing over the edge. Broken sobs ripped from her throat as her sex trembled and clenched, every muscle in her body seeming to spasm simultaneously.

"*Bowen.*"

"That's right, sweetheart." He cupped her jaw and tilted it, so she was looking up at him. "You say *my* name when you come now, don't you? Every time from now on. *Again.*"

"Bowen," she panted. Before she'd fully formed the word, he'd reversed their positions, settling himself on the step with her straddling his thighs. With her legs spread, she knew the dampness he'd created was visible on her underwear. Maybe after what had just happened, modesty was a little ridiculous, but she attempted to pull her skirt down anyway.

"Don't even think about it. It makes me hot as fuck to see what I did to you." He smoothed his palms over her breasts, then yanked her tank top and bra down in one swift, almost angry motion, exposing her to his eyes. She'd never shown a man her naked breasts before, but had always wondered what it would be like. Her fantasies didn't compare to the lust on Bowen's face. His eyelids dipped as though he couldn't hold them up, tongue snaking out to wet his lips. "I can't have your pussy, but I'm going to make these mine. Right now." He gripped his arousal and began to stroke. "Play with your nipples, Sera. Tease me."

Seeing how she affected him made her feel so desirable in that moment. Their surroundings had faded into nothingness, leaving only Bowen and his deep, hypnotic voice. She traced her fingers up her rib cage slowly, excitement blooming once more as she watched his mouth fall open, letting out a groan. As she'd only ever done by herself, she pinched her nipples, tugging them a little between her thumb and forefinger. Between their bodies, the pace of his stroking accelerated along with his harsh breaths.

"Tell me you wish I'd fuck you," he demanded. "Tell me you want it bad."

"I…"

"Say it, baby." He sucked in a breath, eyes beginning to look glassy. "We both know it's true."

He was right. She *did* want him. In a way that startled her. But once she said it out loud she wouldn't be able to take it back. Still, the words climbed her throat, wanting to escape. She desperately wanted to see him climax. To be the reason he lost control. *Let go, Sera. Just once.*

Keeping her gaze locked on him, she squeezed her breasts tight, then let them fall out of her hands and bounce. "I wish you'd fuck me." She leaned down, bringing their mouths close. "I want it so bad, Bowen."

"*Oh, God.*" His body reared up, hips pumping, a growl erupting from his throat. He worked his length up and down so fast his hand became a blur, then she felt warmth between them, coating her throat and breasts. It shouldn't have turned her on or filled her with feminine pride, but it did. Seeing the physical result of her touch, her voice, it made her feel powerful. Sexy.

Two feelings she'd never experienced until now. With Bowen.

When his body stopped shuddering, he looked at her through hooded eyes that coasted down her body with appreciation. Then stopped. As if a switch had been flipped inside him, he jerked upright and began wiping her off with his T-shirt.

"Dammit. You make me crazy, Sera. You know that?" Color still high on his cheekbones, he shot her a look, half disbelief, half amusement. "By the way, I didn't think you'd actually say it."

Heat crept up her neck. "It worked, didn't it?"

His lips tipped into a smile. "Yeah, Ladybug. It worked." He dropped his T-shirt, then leaned forward to press a kiss to her mouth. "What the hell am I going to do with you?"

"I could ask you the same question."

Just then, the door at the top of the stairs began creaking open. In a split second's time, Bowen wrapped his arms around her and jerked her into a protective hold. With her face pressed against his throat, she felt his neck turn to see who'd interrupted them. When she heard Connor's familiar voice, she sagged into Bowen.

"Jesus, Driscol. Control yourself, huh?"

He only drew her closer. "What do you want?"

"A couple of Hogan's guys just walked in. I don't think it would be wise if they saw you two coming out of here together." Bowen tensed at Connor's warning. After a moment, Connor added, "They're not going to care that you just came down here to mess around."

Keeping her blocked from Connor's view, he tried to fix her clothing, but she slapped his hand away and did it herself. After giving her a look, he relented and pulled his own T-shirt back on, seemingly unconcerned about the dampness at the hem. "Do you have a suggestion or did you just come down here hoping to get an eyeful?"

Connor snorted. "There's another staircase leading to the hatch we use for deliveries. Down the hallway, past the office. Use it."

They were already on their feet, moving down the stairs.

"Thank you, Connor," she said, pausing at the bottom, watching a silent communication pass between him and Bowen.

Connor nodded. "Listen, Driscol?"

"Yeah."

"This is my last favor."

CHAPTER EIGHT

Sera woke up staring at the scales of justice painted on the guest room ceiling. In another time or place, the irony of it might even be funny. Right now, mere hours after allowing one of New York City's most notable criminals access to her body, *ehh*, not so much. To make matters worse, she'd actually been disappointed last night when they came home and he didn't try to touch her again. He'd told her to make herself something to eat, then closed himself in his room without another word. She'd stood at the kitchen counter and eaten a bowl of Cheerios before reciting her nightly ritual of Our Fathers before heading to bed.

She should have been grateful for time to think and regroup. Instead, she'd found herself staring at the door, willing it to open. This attraction she felt for Bowen didn't seem possible to control. It was getting in the way of her investigation, clouding her judgment, distracting her. Last night, after finding her brother's name in Hogan's ledger book, she'd welcomed that distraction, but in the light of day, hiding wasn't an option. Colin had to have had a solid reason for taking payouts, and now her job would include finding it. Otherwise, bringing down Hogan could mean incriminating her brother in the process.

Last night, she'd gone down to Hogan's office seeking answers, but today she only had more questions. Bowen's easy acceptance of her cover story still made no sense. Unless, of course, her first theory still proved true. Knowing they would dispose of her once Hogan returned meant it didn't matter what she knew. It would follow her to the bottom of the East River or wherever they planned to dump her. But she couldn't reconcile that outcome with the Bowen she'd spent even a short amount of time with. He wasn't a callous man, at least when it came to her. On the contrary. She thought back to the tender kiss he'd given her after their encounter on the steps. The penetrating way he'd looked at her. Could he spend a week with her, then hand her over to Hogan? Just the idea of it hurt.

Not good, Sera.

Even more baffling than Bowen's behavior? Connor had assisted them last night. Yes, they'd formed a fledgling friendship while she'd been attending his injury, but he was related to Hogan. Why would he *help* them?

She pushed her hair out of her face and sat up in bed. When she swung her legs over the side, something caught her eye. Just above her pillow, a white oval had been painted. No, not an oval. A halo. She couldn't remember if it had been there yesterday and she just hadn't noticed. How could she have missed it? After a final curious glance, she left the room and went to shower.

Twenty minutes later, she'd showered and changed into leggings, an oversize button-down shirt, and ballet flats. She sat on the windowsill staring out toward Manhattan, piling her hair into a bun, when Bowen walked out of his bedroom, wearing nothing but a pair of partially unbuttoned jeans. Immediately, she noticed his body had been marked in several places. Fresh bruises, faded scars, all layered over rough-cut muscle. *Powerful*. After she managed to drag her gaze away from his distracting physique, she registered immediately how exhausted he looked. Stubble darker than his hair covered his jaw; dark circles formed half moons under his eyes, telling her he hadn't slept well. Even after the pep talk she'd just given herself about holding herself back from him, lest she forget why she came, Sera wanted to go to him. Run her fingers through his hair…and see if her touch could get him to sleep.

Whoa, don't get too racy with the fantasies, Saint Sera.

She ignored the sarcastic voice in her head and waved. "Morning."

He walked toward her as if compelled, not stopping until he stood so close, she couldn't inhale without taking in the masculine scent emanating from his skin. The way he looked at her would have been unnerving if she hadn't already witnessed his intense nature. He scanned her from head to toe, as if to reassure himself she was in one piece. It made her want to laugh and cry at the same time, but she had no idea why.

"Hey," he said softly. "How'd you sleep?"

She answered honestly. "I dreamed I was scuba diving."

His quick laugh seemed to surprise him. "Oh yeah? How'd that go?"

"Not good. They dropped me into the water and tossed instructions at me. Only, the instructions dissolved the minute they touched the water. I tried to tell them I didn't know how to scuba dive, but my words came out sounding like Charlie Brown's teacher."

He shook his head at her. "What did you eat before bed?"

"Cheerios."

"That explains it." He crossed his arms over his broad chest. "Cheerios made you think of life preservers. Life preservers made you think of the ocean."

"You're good at this." She tilted her head. "How do you explain the Charlie Brown voice?"

"Oh, that just means you're weird." They shared a laugh, the sound intimate in the stillness of the morning. "What were you thinking about when I walked out here?"

The gruff quality of his voice made her shiver. Knowing she couldn't tell him the whole truth, she went with an adjusted version. "I was thinking I haven't been anywhere in the last two weeks. Apart from here and the club." She glanced back out the window. "I'm officially an indoor kid."

He ran a hand through his sleep-mussed hair. "Well then, we need to get you out of here, baby."

Oh, God, until he'd agreed, she hadn't realized how badly she needed to get some air. Bowen's apartment was a million miles from her tiny room above Rush, but the possibility of getting outside and stretching her legs sounded like heaven. She stood, smiling so big it hurt. "Really?"

For a moment, he just stared at her, before visibly shaking himself. Stepping away from her, he reached into his back pocket and took out a pack of cigarettes, lighting one. "Let me grab a shower. I'll take you anywhere you want to go, Ladybug."

She lifted an eyebrow. "Anywhere?"

Cigarette clamped between his teeth, he nodded, but his eyes grew suspicious. "Why? Where are you thinking?"

Sera breezed past him and took a jug of milk out of the fridge. "Church."

Later. She'd get back on track with how to proceed later.

This isn't happening.

As Bowen walked down the sidewalk of his familiar neighborhood, Sera's hand warm inside his, he tried to remember the last time he'd been to church. Had he *ever* been to church? Once in middle school, he might have sneaked into the rectory and stolen wine. Did that count? He tried to picture what the inside of Saint Anthony's looked like, but could only remember the abandoned lot behind it, where he'd once watched his father end another man's life for shorting him by fifty bucks on payback of a loan.

Learning from his father had been his sick version of church. Sure, he'd listened to sermons, but they'd been about instilling fear and brooking no disrespect. Running numbers, inflicting pain, evading the police. His bible had been a notebook filled with debts, passed down when his father got pinched.

How could he walk into a church, holding this girl's hand? He'd be an imposter, a hypocrite. And hell, that was if he didn't burst into flames first. Why had he agreed to take her?

He knew the answer to that. She'd looked like a bright, beautiful mirage sitting on his windowsill when he'd woken up this morning after a mere hour of sleep. An antidote to the grisly images tattooed on the back of his eyelids. Images he added to every day, with situations like last night. Situations that left blood on his knuckles and another piece of him lying discarded in the gutter. One look at her, though, and he forgot everything, at least momentarily. She'd opened her mouth and said *church.* *Yes* had been his only possible answer, because she *wanted* it.

Make her happy. Keep her safe. The mantra had played on a loop in his head last night, keeping him awake as he painted every free inch of space in his room, until he'd run out of wall space. Before he knew it, he'd been standing at the foot of her bed. He'd fed himself the excuse that he just wanted to make sure she hadn't tried to sneak out, maybe head back to Rush for another shot at stealing the ledger. But minutes had passed and he'd still stood there, heart thudding in his chest as he stared down at her peaceful form. What would goodness and purity feel like wrapped around him nightly? He'd had to put a stranglehold on the need to crawl into the bed with her and try to absorb it. The fear it might have the reverse effect had stopped him.

What if he dirtied her instead?

God, he'd come close on that stairwell. So damn close. Tackling her on the stairs, his head had been fucked up. She'd just looked at him and seen her death. He'd *known* it. That certainty had been the equivalent of a shotgun blast to his chest. Minutes later, the reassurance in her eyes had been like a balm over the blast wound. He'd gotten lost in her, his need for her... He didn't know how long he could go without touching her again.

Church was certainly a good start.

Thankfully, when they reached the steps leading to Saint Anthony's, everyone had already gone inside. Everyone in Bensonhurst knew him, or at least knew *of* him, and would wonder what the hell he was doing there. He didn't care about the scrutiny on himself. He'd grown used to it. But he didn't want anyone making Sera uncomfortable. Not today, when it felt so goddamn perfect walking down the street, holding her hand. Since he didn't know if he'd ever get the chance again, he needed to savor it.

When they walked into the church, Bowen swore he could hear a record scratching. The priest actually paused in his opening welcome. One by one, every head in the church turned to face him, a few mouths even dropping open at the sight of him. Obviously sensing his discomfort, Sera pulled him into the very last row, a resolute smile on her face. After a beat, the priest resumed his welcome, before opening the Bible on the altar and beginning a reading.

"I guess you don't get to church much," she whispered. "They seem surprised to see you."

So, that's how she was going to play it. As if she wasn't aware of the real reason they looked horrified to have him in their sacred midst. "It's not my fault. They keep turning down my application to be an altar boy."

Her lips pressed together, laughter in her eyes. "You're not missing anything. The robes are itchy and all that kneeling is murder on your knees."

His dropped his head forward. "Don't tell me you were an altar—"

"Person. We prefer altar *person*."

"Unbelievable." He couldn't stop himself from pulling her more securely against his side. For the first time since he could remember, he felt comfortable. At ease. Even knowing she was only staying with him long enough to get the goods on Hogan didn't matter. He let himself trust the gut feeling that she felt something, too. He chuckled when he noticed a woman in the second row craning her neck to get a look at him. "You see that lady in the green jacket...the one with white hair?"

Sera nodded. "The gawker?"

"Like recognizes like." He just barely blocked her elbow from connecting with his stomach. "That's Mrs. Cormac, my fifth-grade teacher."

"No way."

"Oh, *way*." He began massaging her palm with his thumb. "There's a reason she doesn't look happy to see me. I once put a live chicken in her desk."

She slapped a hand over her mouth, but not quickly enough. Her clear, tinkling laugh sailed past her lips, drawing everyone's attention. None of them looked remotely happy about the interruption. While Sera hid behind the yellow program they'd picked up on the way in, all Bowen could do was shrug and give them all his most apologetic smile, teeth and everything. Apparently his apologetic smile was a little rusty, though, because it only seemed to piss them off more.

"She's just so happy to be here," he called, making Sera bend at the waist to hide her face between her knees. "Please, continue."

They managed to make it through the rest of the Mass without any more outbursts. Bowen found himself enjoying the hour-long service. Not that he listened to a word the priest said, but sitting there in the daylight, his arm draped across a smiling Sera's shoulders, he let himself imagine doing it every Sunday. Having that certainty, that routine. Knowing she would be there to sit with him, letting him hold her. Going home with him afterward without question, because it was *her* home, too. Not just a guest anymore. In his apartment or his life. Permanent.

Could he bring her into his world—to stay? If a miracle happened and she stuck around after the dust settled, could he rest a single second? Sera would be his vulnerability. A way to get to him. Not safe. Never safe. No, he'd have to change for her. Change into what, though? He didn't know how to be anyone else. Sera rested her head on his shoulder and his throat went tight. He could learn. He could learn to be someone else, do something else, if it meant keeping her. He'd do anything.

After it ended, they walked back to his apartment, only stopping to pick up bagels and coffee. He had business to deal with, but it could wait until tomorrow. Sera didn't have to work tonight and although spending the remainder of the day with her alone in his apartment would be an incredible test of his will, not spending time with her sounded much worse.

As they climbed the stairs leading to his apartment, she squeezed his hand, drawing his attention. "Bowen?"

"Yeah."

"Did you paint a halo over my head last night?"

He sighed. "Yeah."

When he tried to keep walking, she pulled him to a stop just before they reached his door. She started to say something, but surprised him by going up on her tiptoes and kissing him instead. It started as a peck. But when he curled a hand around her wrist and felt her pulse racing out of control, his good intentions deserted him. Fisting her shirt, he tugged her close and let his tongue explore her perfect texture, slow and deep. A little whimper jumped from her mouth into his, making him hungry to hear it again. Louder. God, her tempting body was rubbing against his, lighting him up like a pinball machine.

He needed to let her breathe, but wasn't willing to let her go, so he released her mouth in favor of sucking at her neck. Her skin smelled like his soap and *fuck*, he loved that. It made his cock swell in his pants, the realization the same object had touched both of their bodies. He wanted her walking around smelling like him all the time. Not just his soap. *Him*. All of him.

Sera's fingers tugged at his hair, the hard points of her nipples visible against the material of her shirt. "Why did you take me to church just to turn me right back into a sinner?" He bent her back over his arm so he could rake his teeth over her covered nipple. "You could take me to Mass every day for the rest of my life and I'd still be the kind of guy who would finger you in the back row."

"Bowen, take me inside. I want…"

He drew her upright and pressed their foreheads together,

unable to resist the urge to bite and drag her plump bottom lip forward. "What do you want, Sera? I told you, no fucking."

"What we did last night." She closed her eyes and he immediately missed them. "Can we do that again?"

Just like earlier when she asked him to take her to church, he only had the ability to say yes. He suspected that would be the case no matter what she asked. Bowen, scale the Empire State Building. Bowen, take me to Mars. Bowen, make me come. *Yes, yes, yes.*

"Come here, sweetheart." He trailed his hands down her back to grasp the taut cheeks of her ass. With no more encouragement than that, she twined her legs around his waist, trailing kisses on his face as he walked them to the apartment door. Before he could open it, however, the door swung wide.

Terror unlike he'd ever known whipped through him. Fast as he could, he whirled, putting himself between Sera and the unknown intruder. He expected to feel the sting of a bullet any moment, but he didn't care about the pain. Once he was incapacitated, he couldn't help Sera. She'd be alone. In one swift motion, he set Sera on her feet, drew the gun from his jeans waistband, and pointed it...at Ruby?

His sister.

CHAPTER NINE

Like any smart girl who'd grown up in this section of Brooklyn, Ruby's knees hit the floor and she raised her arms over her head. "Jesus, Bowen. Put the gun down."

It took him a moment to process that there wasn't a threat to Sera. The gun shook slightly as he lowered it to his side. When a sense of calm and relief pervaded him, he realized it was because Sera stood behind him, rubbing circles into his back. Her fingers slipped into his hair, bringing his heart rate back down to normal, forcing breath into his lungs.

"How did you get in?" Ruby raised an eyebrow at him and he shook his head. "Never mind." A stupid question, when he'd been the one to teach her how to pick a lock. His half sister had been raised from a young age to make money illegally, just like him. But her weapon of choice had been a pool stick. For years, they'd been sent by his father to bilk unsuspecting marks out of money. When they inevitably wanted their pound of flesh, not to mention their money back, Bowen had stepped in and made them regret it.

"Here's a better question." She gained her feet, gaze still focused on his weapon. "When did you start carrying a gun?"

"You think we could have this discussion inside?" he snapped. "Or has dating a cop taken away your common sense?"

"Don't be like that." She jerked her chin toward Sera. "Are you going to introduce me?"

Apparently his possessiveness of Sera included his sister, because he didn't want to share her with *anyone*. "This is Sera. We met at church."

"Bullshit."

"Look, I'll be right in," he said impatiently. After casting a final curious glance in his direction, Ruby sauntered back into the apartment. He took a deep breath and turned to face Sera. The touch of hurt in her brown eyes brought him up short, until he remembered what he'd just said. *Or has dating a cop taken away your common sense.* Beautiful. And he couldn't even apologize for the comment because he wasn't supposed to know she *was* a cop. God, in that moment, he wished he could scoop her up into his arms and get the hell away from this place. Take her somewhere where it didn't matter who they were and no threats to her safety existed. Instead, he smoothed a thumb over her lips still swollen from kissing him. "You okay?"

"I'm fine." She stooped down and picked the white paper bag full of bagels off the floor. "Who is she?"

Was that jealousy he heard in her voice? She'd hid it well, but hadn't been able to completely cover it up. One thing he knew for certain. He craved that jealousy. It didn't come close to matching his own where she was concerned, but it meant something to him. It gave him hope that her goal with him stemmed from more than bringing down Hogan. "She's my half sister, Ruby. Different fathers."

"Oh."

"Oh?"

"Hmm."

"Hmm?" He tugged her chin up. "Listen to me. This conversation between me and her…it isn't going to be pretty. The only thing that's going to get me through it is knowing I get to have bagels with you on the other side."

"Why won't it be pretty?"

"Things with me rarely are."

She scrutinized him for a moment before heading through his door. Bowen walked in to find Ruby and Sera sizing each other up from opposite ends of the kitchen. If he were a different man, maybe one who worked a nine-to-five desk job, it might have even been funny. As it was, he had an undercover cop sharing oxygen with the pissed-off ex-pool-hustler sibling he'd been avoiding for months.

Ever since she found out they were blood relatives. A fact he'd kept from her since childhood.

He honestly didn't know where he stood with either one of them, which made him angry, since they were both important to him. Most importantly, he didn't know if Troy had clued Ruby in to his involvement in the investigation. Probably best to figure that out right off the bat, and he definitely couldn't begin that line of questioning in front of Sera. Thankfully, Sera seemed to sense their reluctance to talk in front of her and started toward the bedroom. On impulse, he grabbed her wrist as she passed and planted a kiss on her forehead, and watched her until she disappeared inside the bedroom.

Bowen ignored Ruby's shocked expression, studying the cuts on his knuckles. He knew she was dying to ask about Sera, so he spoke before she could. "What are you doing here? I told Troy to keep you out of Brooklyn."

Ruby flinched. "When did you see Troy?"

She doesn't know. "We meet for lattes and girl chat once a week."

"Fuck that. Answer me."

Bowen shrugged off her question. "You've been in Manhattan too long, Ruby Tuesday. Lighten up."

She obviously didn't like his evasion, but let it go. "How are you?"

He laughed without humor. "Please tell me you didn't break into my apartment to make small talk."

"So what if I did? We used to talk all the time."

Bowen stayed silent. What did she want from him? She'd made a better life, and being associated with him would only screw it up. Why wouldn't she just move the hell on?

"Last time I was in the neighborhood, you said things were bad." She took a hesitant step toward him. "Have they gotten any better?"

He pointed toward the window. "This doesn't *get* better. Don't you understand that?"

"Troy and I can help. Let us."

Troy's intervention wouldn't save him. It was too late. Hell, the day he was born, it had already been too late. He had only one option and it was why he'd agreed to aid the police in the first place. Save the people he loved from being dragged down with him. And he fucking loved his sister beyond words. Which is why saying what came next caused him physical pain. "I don't want your help. I want you to get lost."

"No." Tears brimmed in her eyes. "It's not fair, Bowen. All those nights spent hiding in alleys and parking lots, freezing cold, hungry. Scared. You knew I was your sister. I just want to spend time with you knowing you're my brother."

"The knowing doesn't change anything."

She slapped the countertop. "Yes, it does. It changes everything. You don't get to shut me out. We're your family."

He went still. "We?"

Red stained her cheeks, but she raised her chin. "She just wants to make things right, Bowen. It won't kill you to hear her out."

Their mother. She meant their mother. Everything inside him rebelled at the thought of seeing her. "Is that why you came here? To set up some tearful mother-son reunion? You're wasting your time."

"Hey, she left me, too. Okay?" She closed the distance between them and grabbed his arm, but he yanked it away. "I'm not exactly over it, either. But aren't you even a little curious? Don't you at least want an explanation?

"I couldn't give less of a fuck."

"Oh, yeah?" She spun around, gesturing toward the living room wall. "Is that why you've painted her all over the apartment?"

Her barb stuck in his chest. "Go back to Manhattan, Ruby."

"She's downstairs."

At once, he felt like he'd just run a marathon. He couldn't seem to get enough air, but the need to escape the situation overrode everything else. Trapped. He felt trapped. Ruby was still talking to him, but nothing could break through the rush of white noise in his ears. Trying to regain some semblance of control, he strode toward the front door. "You crossed the line this time. I don't want to see her. Or you. Get the hell out and don't come back."

"Bowen, don't do this." She looked desperate now, shifting on her feet, mind racing behind her eyes. "You're hurting me. You're the one person I never thought would hurt me."

Dammit, she knew him too well. Knew saying that would kill him. But right now, when she'd forced him into his own personal nightmare, he couldn't, *wouldn't*, comfort her. "Yeah, that's too bad. Hurting people is what I do. Live with it."

Needing to get away from the pain on her face, he turned and yanked open the door.

And came face to face with his mother, Pamela Hicks.

She stumbled back a step, as if she hadn't expected him to open the door so fast. He didn't want to look at her, but he couldn't look away either. He hadn't seen her since he was a child, but somehow she looked exactly as he expected. She still had the streak of pink in her hair, still looked like a roadie for the Grateful Dead. With ripped jeans and a bullet belt, she looked like the furthest thing from a mother you could get. Which was totally accurate. She wasn't a mother.

When he realized he'd been standing there, numb and dumbstruck, he swallowed hard and turned back to Ruby. "*Go.*"

"Don't blame her," Pamela said, recapturing his attention. "I was supposed to stay in the car. I guess doing what the hell you want runs in the family, huh?"

The joke fell flat, as she seemed to expect it would. "I don't have a family."

"You could."

His laughter was even painful to his own ears. "What happened? Did you run out of money or something?" He reached into his back pocket for his wallet. "If I lend you a couple grand will you go back to wherever you came from?"

Behind him, Ruby spoke up. "Knock it off, Bowen."

"I don't need your money," Pamela said.

"Then that concludes our business." He held the door wide and looked at Ruby. "I don't want to see you here again. If you come back, I'll be more than happy to fill your boyfriend in on your occasional trips to Brooklyn. Still hustling for old time's sake, Ruby?"

Her face went white. "How...did you know?"

"I know *everything* that happens here. Why do you think

it's so hard for you to get a game?" He pointed to the hallway. "Go on, beat it."

Still looking shell-shocked, Ruby walked out the door. She didn't even meet his eyes as she passed, or kiss his cheek like she normally did. He knew then he'd damaged their bond. Possibly beyond repair.

He looked up to find Pamela staring past him into the apartment, her gaze zeroed in on the painting he'd done of her face, her hair. A tear tracked down her cheek. "I'm sorry."

"Yeah." He hit her with a disgusted look. "You sure are."

Bowen shut the door and locked all three dead bolts. Now that the moment had passed, now that he didn't need to put on an act, hundreds of emotions he'd kept at bay for so long rushed in all at once. Helplessness, rage, sadness, pain, regret. They stormed through him, overturning everything in their wake. The grip he'd had on them finally slipped. He needed an outlet. He needed somewhere to put it all.

Sera appeared in the guest room doorway.

Before he'd made a conscious decision, he'd started toward her.

I should probably run now.

Sera knew it would be the smartest move, and yet her feet were glued to the floor. *Deer in the headlights* would be the correct term for what she probably looked like. Except *this* Bowen, the one who stalked toward her with an air of menace surrounding him, had to be scarier than a vehicle heading toward you at full speed.

She'd only heard the tail end of the argument with his sister, thanks to their voices rising. Curiosity getting the better of her, she'd opened the door a crack and seen him standing in the doorway with another woman. The pink-haired woman on his wall, who she'd pieced together had to be his mother. Even without knowing the history there, she knew with absolute certainty the visit had been hard for him. Very hard. And now the Bowen who'd taken her to church this morning and made her laugh was long gone. Replaced by a man she didn't totally recognize.

If his threatening demeanor weren't layered with an almost tangible vulnerability, she would have turned on her heel and barricaded herself in the bedroom. But she did see it. She saw his need to release frustration, maybe even pain. Pain she could heal. Healing was in her blood, thanks to her years as a nurse. Bowen brought that quality out of her like a bullet being fired. *Heal. Fix. Repair.*

Those acknowledged desires were her final thoughts before he reached her. His mouth slammed down on top of hers, stealing her breath. Rough hands dug into the skin at her hips as he walked her backward. It only took a second for his desperation to grow contagious. Her instincts were crying for her to ease his torment, to be the one who cured him. She plastered her body to his, circling her arms around his neck and digging her fingers into his hair.

Her legs met the edge of the bed and they toppled onto it, Bowen catching himself on his elbows so he wouldn't crush her, but his mouth never stopped moving over hers. The kiss didn't carry even a hint of sweetness. It was sex. Pure and simple. A hot, mind-blowing *using* of her mouth. His lower body found the notch between her thighs and bore down. She broke away from his mouth to moan, but he jerked her face back and bit her bottom lip.

Briefly, their eyes met and Sera felt the beginnings of alarm.

She didn't see Bowen in there anywhere. More than anything, she wanted him. Wanted this. But she wouldn't be experiencing it with Bowen. She would regret it and so would he.

He growled as he pinned her arms over her head. "I bet you thought your first time would be with someone *nice*. Someone who would sprinkle rose petals on the bed and ease you in." He bent down and ripped her shirt open with his teeth, buttons popping off onto the bed, exposing her lacy black bra. His hot gaze raked over her breasts as he worked his hips in a grinding circle. "Not me, Sera. I don't do easy."

"*Bowen*." She just managed to bite back a moan. "Look at me."

"All I *do* is look at you," he practically shouted.

A knot formed in her throat at the sincerity in his statement. "You can be that nice guy. You *are* that nice guy."

When his gaze darkened, she knew it had been the wrong thing to say. "You think I'm *nice*?" He leaned down and spoke against her ear, his tone reminding her of cut glass. "I don't even know what that word means. I would ram my cock so deep into that virgin pussy, I'd hit your back wall on my first thrust. Do not fucking doubt me."

Even knowing his words hadn't been intended to arouse, they set a sharp ache pulsing between her thighs. "No, you wouldn't. You wouldn't cause me pain."

"*Yes, I would.*"

"No." She wriggled one of her hands free to stroke the side of his face, relieved when he squeezed his eyes shut and turned his face into her hand. "Not like this, Bowen."

When his eyes opened again, the glazed-over quality had mostly gone. He seemed to become aware of his surroundings again, really *seeing* her for the first time. As if a string had been cut, his body dropped heavily onto hers. He pushed his face up against her neck on a shuddering breath. "I'm sorry. I'm so fucking sorry."

She wrapped her arms around him. "I know."

"Please don't be scared of me, Ladybug," he said hoarsely. "I won't be able to stand it."

"I'm not."

He turned onto his side and gently pulled her against his chest. As if she'd done it hundreds of times before, she tucked her head under his chin. Her eyelids started to feel heavy almost immediately, the fingers stroking the bare skin of her back not helping matters. Every few minutes, he would tug her closer, each time feeling like another apology. Still able to feel the tension in his body, she searched for a way to distract him.

"How did you get the live chicken?"

The fingers stroking her back paused, preempting his rumbling laugh. "Off the back of a truck in Crown Heights." His fingers traced her earlobe, making her shiver. "He came with me so easily, I think he knew I was saving him from slaughter."

"Chickens are intuitive like that."

"Yeah?" His voice held a smile. "What about you? Are you intuitive?"

Her head bumped his chin when she nodded.

"Then what am I thinking about right now?"

Since she could feel his hard, jean-encased length against her thigh, she had a pretty solid idea. But something about the moment didn't feel right for that. He still seemed distracted by what had happened with his sister and mother. "You're thinking about bagels."

"Let's pretend you're right."

"Okay."

Neither one of them moved to get up. With every moment that passed, every stroke of his fingers, she grew more and more tired. After her difficulty sleeping last night, it was impossible to stop herself from nodding off. Just before she faded into unconsciousness, Bowen whispered into her ear.

"I'm sorry. I think I have to keep you, Sera."

CHAPTER TEN

Sera woke to darkness, shooting straight up in bed. She'd slept so deeply, it took her a moment to remember everything from the day. A quick glance at the clock radio on the side table told her it was eight o'clock. She flopped back onto the pillow to give herself a moment to let the grogginess dissipate. In the mornings, she never had a problem waking, but she felt as though she'd just woken from a coma.

When she shivered, Sera realized she still wore no shirt. The cold must have woken her, which meant Bowen had left only recently. It had felt so good, *too* good, to lie there with him and forget her responsibilities. She should be ashamed of how easily it had happened. Sleeping beside someone meant letting her guard down. Trusting the other person. She knew she needed to be more careful, but the voice of stern caution that usually spoke from within seemed to silence itself in his presence.

Was she naive to believe the Bowen Driscol she'd read about in police files wasn't the real man? There was no denying he'd done terrible things, but her instincts couldn't be this far off. He had *good* inside him.

She climbed out of bed in search of Bowen and found him

sitting on the couch, hands clasped between his knees. His head came up when he sensed her, a sad smile moving across his face. Almost like he'd read every thought she'd had in the bedroom.

He cleared his throat and gestured to the wall. "You want to paint?"

"Yes, please." In addition to being grateful for the distraction, she couldn't deny a spark of excitement. "But I should warn you, I only have two specialties."

"Which are?"

"Kitty cats and houses with smoke curling out of the chimney." She sat cross-legged on the floor, surveying the paintbrushes. "I'm not sure if those will fit in with your theme."

He frowned. "What theme?"

Sera ducked her head, feeling suddenly uncomfortable under his scrutiny. Was he actually unaware of the pattern his murals created, or did he just want to know what she thought? She picked up a paintbrush and gestured to the painting of the Brooklyn Bridge, half intact, half engulfed in flames. "Good and evil," she started quietly. "The battle between the two. Don't you see it?"

His gaze tracked around the room, as if seeing it for the first time. "I never saw it like that before." When he looked back at her, his eyes were serious. "What side do you think wins?"

Going into this investigation, she thought she knew the answer, but it didn't seem quite so clear anymore. "I think maybe they both win once in a while."

A beat of silence passed before Bowen broke eye contact, swiping an impatient hand through his hair. "Listen, I've been a shitty host. You need to eat something."

On cue, her stomach groaned. "I could go for a bagel. Or nine."

He stood. "Coming right up. Go ahead and get started."

"Where?" The word froze on her lips when she saw a fresh white space on the wall. Right where the painting of his mother's face had been.

"There."

"Bowen—"

"I want to replace a bad memory." He popped her bagel into the toaster and shot her a devilish grin. "Draw your cathouse."

Sera bit her lip to stop a laugh. "I don't think we're on the same page." She picked up a container of purple paint and squirted it onto an ancient-looking palette, stained with dozens of color blotches. Using a medium-sized paintbrush, she stirred the blob of paint. With a sigh, she stood and approached the wall.

"A purple cat?"

She jumped a little when he spoke from right behind her. He'd moved so quietly. "If you're already criticizing, this is going to be a long night."

"I'm not." He held the bagel to her lips, giving her no choice but to bite. His eyes darkened as she chewed. "Just wondering about your color choice."

Feeling self-conscious, she took the bagel from his hands. "Purple is the color of royalty. Maybe he's heir to the kitty throne."

"You're putting some thought into this."

She took another bite to save herself from having to answer. Truthfully, even though talking to him came naturally, she was feeling out of her element. Standing here with this dangerously beautiful man who brimmed with sexual confidence. This man, with swollen and lacerated hands, who held the paintbrush like an extension of his body, magnetized her like no other.

The glowing lamplight cast shadows around the apartment, and the soft sound of paintbrushes sliding along the wall was in direct contrast with the tension visible in Bowen's face and shoulders.

Unlike her, not all his tension seemed to be sexual. What took place earlier had obviously affected him greatly, even if he tried to put on a good show for her. She couldn't help wanting to ease the burden. As a nurse, she'd been known for her bedside manner. She'd never had the ability to remain emotionally detached when someone was in pain. She couldn't leave him suffering in silence, not with her commitment to heal.

"Is Ruby your only sibling?"

He paused mid-stroke. "I'd rather not talk about her."

"Okay," she agreed, before trying a different tack. "My brother and I were nothing alike, but we found little things in common. We both liked the old-school version of Tetris. Our tournament lasted five years." She painted a bow tie on her kitten, remembering the hours they'd spent in the boarding school recreation hall clutching those controls. "When our ancient Nintendo went belly-up, we pooled our allowance, bought one on eBay, and picked up right where we left off. I was winning when the tournament ended."

"Why did the tournament end?"

"It just did." She wasn't ready to say the rest out loud yet, and his nod told her he sensed it. "Playing Tetris…it was the only time we talked. I wished we'd played more, especially when we got older. When we got too cool."

Bowen was silent a moment. "With my sister…things are more complicated." He tossed the paintbrush down and lit a cigarette. "She's just too stubborn to see I'm doing what's best for her."

"What about what's best for you?" When confused eyes flashed to her, she shook her head. Hadn't anyone ever asked him that before? "I'm sorry, I'll leave it alone."

He blew a long, slow cloud of smoke toward the open window. "Tell me what happened to your brother, Ladybug."

His low, ominous tone dared her to give him anything less than the truth. "Someone killed him. They never found out who," she added quickly. Uncomfortable with his scrutiny, she got down on her knees and continued painting the bottom half of her cat. She tried to ignore him when he came up behind her, but his calloused hand slid into her hair, tilting her head back so she looked up at him from her kneeling position.

Cigarette still clamped between his teeth, he nonetheless spoke very precisely. "I don't like seeing you upset. It makes me want to go out and do something about it."

Surely he wasn't offering what she thought he was offering. After only knowing her for a few days? "You can't."

"Oh no?" He reached over to the side table on her left and stubbed out his cigarette in a ceramic ashtray. "You'd be surprised what you can do when you're numb."

"You're not numb," she whispered, rotating around to face him on her knees. Their provocative position became apparent to her. And she was fairly certain he'd just offered to *kill* for her. Unbelievably, her opinion of him hadn't changed with that fact, even if his expression told her he'd expected it to. He looked rubbed raw. Full of trepidation...*hunger*.

Her gaze dropped to the fly of his jeans and her breath caught when she saw the enormous swell pushing against his zipper, inches from her mouth. Her stomach fluttered and contracted at the sight, as if she'd just free-fallen from a great height. Between her legs, a telltale pulse jumped to life, warmth pooling instantly.

"Obviously I'm not numb with you, am I?" Features strained, Bowen pulled lightly on the strands of her hair still wrapped in his fist. "Get off your *knees*, Sera."

She made no move to stand. Pain. There was so much pain in his voice. She wanted to take it away and appease her own curiosity in the process.

"Look." He sounded a little desperate now. "Earlier in the hallway, you had your legs wrapped around my waist. Then I almost fucked you through the wall of the guest room." Another halfhearted tug at her hair. "The last seven hours, I watched you sleep in nothing but a bra and those ridiculous tights or whatever you call them. I'm just strung a little tight where you're concerned. Would you, *please*, just stand the hell up?"

Giving in to an impulse, she leaned forward and nuzzled her cheek against his erection, before planting hot, openmouthed kisses along the bulge.

"*Jesus Christ.*" He pressed closer with his hips. "You have to *stop.*"

Sera was beyond listening. Her fingers unsnapped his jeans and lowered the zipper before he made a more solid attempt to stop her. Seconds later, she'd freed his heavy arousal. The first time she gripped him in her hand, he hissed a vile curse. Paying close attention to his face, she stroked him up and down, running a thumb over the head with each upward stroke, the way she'd seen him do last night in the stairwell.

"You want to jerk me off, baby? Fine." Sweat had started appearing on his forehead. "But don't you dare put me in that innocent little mouth. I'm warning you, I won't be able to keep myself from fucking it until you know what I taste like."

The tingle between her legs graduated to a relentless ache. If he thought his warning would stop her, it had the opposite effect. Knowing he teetered on the edge of losing control because of her made her feel bold. Defiant.

Drunk on the feeling, she leaned forward and licked the

underside of Bowen's erection, root to tip. Then she lowered her mouth over the hard flesh as far as she could.

And sucked.

Holy, holy shit. I'm going to die.

Please, for the love of God, just let her finish me off first.

Thoughts, warnings, that conflicted with the indescribable pleasure he was getting from Sera's mouth tried to bombard him. He blocked them as best he could, but some of them made it through. He'd meant what he said to her. The day had been jam-packed full of sexual frustration, something he'd never dealt with, not *ever*, and now her *perfect fucking mouth* threatened to cut the strings holding his control in place.

With her head in his hands, the monstrous urge to thrust into the heat of her mouth battered his conscience. He could hear words falling from his lips that made no sense, belonged to no particular language. Or maybe he'd just been saving them for her, stored in some corner of his mind. A language solely reserved for Sera. That theory made him feel like slightly less of an asshole. It reminded him she was special. Not some girl he could prop against the wall and push too deep.

This could be her first time on her knees for a man, and he wouldn't fuck it up. No, it *was* her first time. He could see it in the gorgeous brown eyes that watched him, making sure she did it right. *Reassure her. I need to reassure her.*

"Anything, everything, all of it. It's perfect, sweetheart. You're so fucking perfect."

At least, that's what he *thought* he said. It might have come out sounding more like Swahili. Oh God, oh *God*, it didn't feel like her first time. She was sucking him so hard, he felt his soul dislodge and settle into a new spot. How could she look up at him so innocently, when her mouth worked him like the baddest girl he'd ever met? The contrast was blowing his mind, shooting him into a different realm. He wouldn't lie to himself anymore. His no-virgin rule obviously hadn't been created with Sera in mind. Not a single one of his rules had. Her lack of experience turned him on. It meant all those moments could, *would*, belong to him. No one else. Sure, that made him a greedy bastard, but he was beyond help.

She slowed down a little, letting him slide in deeper than he'd gone before. A strangled noise escaped him, abdomen tight, thighs quaking. His hands moved of their own accord, tangling in her hair. "Baby, baby, please. Can you take a little more? Just a lit—*ahhh fuck*."

He almost came then and there, without warning, but managed to reel himself back as much as possible. Not much longer and he'd lose it, though. She'd started making little humming noises in the back of her throat, shooting vibrating heat straight into his belly, his balls. Her hands joined the party then, *both* of them, riding his slick cock in time with her mouth.

The rush started, the dizzying buildup. He'd never gotten there so fast. How unfair was that when for the first time, he didn't want it to end? "I'm going to come, Sera. Take me out of your mouth." More painful words were never spoken. But the pain never came because she took him *deep*. Her hands slid around to his ass, fingernails digging into his flesh, tugging him close as her mouth pulled, licked, sucked.

His control evaporated with the oncoming release, consciousness narrowing down to her mouth. Acting on their own, his hands tightened in her hair. Hard. His hips rolled, meeting every stroke of her mouth. "You going to let me come in that virgin mouth? You going to make me a god?"

She scraped him with her teeth and his world exploded. He expected her to stop him once his climax struck, but *Jesus Christ*, she didn't. Her mouth pulled on him in greedy strokes, taking everything he had to give. A sound of enjoyment left her throat to ripple over his cock, shooting him into another dimension.

He didn't remember dropping to the floor or drawing her up against him, but he'd gotten there somehow. Deep breaths expanded his chest under her cheek. How could she feel so fragile against him when she'd just shaken him up so thoroughly? The frantic need to look into her eyes hit him hard. With a still-trembling hand, he tilted her chin up.

And felt like he'd been cold-cocked.

Lust. It expanded her pupils and blocked out all the beautiful chocolate brown. Her face flushed red, lips swollen and parted. Her nipples were sharp points pressing against her thin shirt; her thighs squeezed together on and off, on and off. The sight was so goddamn stunning, it sent his already-pounding heart into overdrive. It filled him with wild determination, purpose. *Give her pleasure. Give her relief.*

When he wedged his hips between her thighs, she moaned so loudly, so impatiently, he couldn't help but match it. Her pain equaled his pain. Her pleasure, his pleasure.

She was mine before. Mine *doesn't even begin to cover it now.*

He ran a hand down between their bodies and cupped her pussy, growling when he found the material of her tights damp. "Ah, sweetheart. Did you get wet while sucking me off?" Using the heel of his hand, he ground circles into her heat, his dick getting hard again from watching her hips writhe. "You have any idea how good you are with that mouth?" He leaned down and kissed her gently, knowing it would frustrate her into deepening it. She did. *Fuck yes*, she did. "Those lips are the best fuck I've ever had. But not for long. Isn't that right, Sera? We both know it's only a matter of time before I'm pounding the purity right out of you."

Without waiting for a response, he yanked the tights down her legs and threw them across the room. He said a prayer of thanks when she ripped her shirt over her head, revealing a black bra and tiny matching panties. *Jesus*. He could barely handle her fully clothed. Half naked? It hurt to look at her.

"Bowen, please. I need something to stop the hurt."

The fact she didn't even *know* what she needed set off an odd burn in his chest, but it also filled him with hot, pumping anticipation at the idea of showing her. "I know what you need, but that's not what I'm about to give you. I'll always give you *more* than you need, Sera. Every time."

He peeled the scrap of underwear down her legs, his vision fraying around the edges when he finally saw her uncovered pussy. *Mine. It's mine. She's mine. Mine.* His instincts were screaming at him to pin her down, spread her open, and fuck her. But he couldn't let the urges win. After what she'd given him, he owed her pleasure.

Still, this need to claim her in some way had him reaching for his thinnest paintbrush. He dipped it in purple paint and brought it to her lower belly. Knowing she couldn't wait much longer, he wrote his name quickly, but clearly. *Bowen*. It might be insignificant compared to how he wanted to mark her as his own, but it would have to do for now.

He tossed the paintbrush aside, blowing on the drying paint as he ran his hands up the insides of her smooth thighs. When they met at the sweetest part of her, he ran a knuckle down her seam to find her wet. His cock surged against his belly, his body begging to be inside her, to use the wetness to his advantage.

Instead, he pushed his middle finger into her tight heat, groaning at how little room he had to move it.

In the hopes that kissing her would remind him to go slow, he crawled up her body, sinking into a kiss as he fingered her. "Let me ask you a question, baby. What kind of dickless morons have you been around your whole life that not one of them made a play for you? For this?" He added a second finger, pushing a little deeper than before. "Not that I wouldn't want to end their miserable lives for them right now if they had."

Finally, he'd loosened her up enough that he could massage her G-spot with his middle finger. "All-girls' school," she gasped, her hips jerking off the floor. "Do that again."

Bowen obliged, keeping his fingers working between her legs as his open mouth skated across her cleavage. "You like that, don't you? I haven't even touched your clit yet."

"Maybe you sh-should?"

"Not yet." He moved back down her body, his tongue licking a path along her shuddering stomach, circling her belly button. "My tongue wants the first stroke."

As soon as the words left his mouth, he grew impatient to do exactly as he'd said. Losing his battle to be gentle, he shoved her thighs wide, taking a moment to look her over. Memorize the moment. Her back was arched off the floor, her eyes on him wide and trusting, hips shifting with the need he'd built with his fingers. What had he called her when they met? A stunner? How fucking inadequate. He didn't have words to describe her. She glowed. She'd somehow fallen out of the sky and landed in this unworthy place, with an unworthy man.

He threw her legs over his shoulders, lowered his head, and took the first delicious taste of her. Firming his tongue, he licked up her center and went right to work, worrying her sensitive bundle of nerves. Fast, slow, fast, slow. She liked it both ways, begging for one, then the other. Her fingers pulled frantically in his hair, making him even hotter to get her off.

"*Bowen*. Don't stop. *Please*, don't stop."

He worked two fingers into her, never pausing in the worshipping of her clit. Already she was beginning to tighten up, contracting around his fingers. One suck of her nub into his mouth, a pinch of her flesh between his lips, and she went flying, screaming his name in a way he knew he'd replay every damn day of his life. He'd never seen anything like her, the honesty that twisted her body, blanketed her beautiful face. She climaxed with every part of herself, wringing each drop free as if it might be the last time she experienced it.

Bowen had to laugh at that.

As soon as her thighs went slack on his shoulders, he pushed them up, bringing her knees even with her chest. "More, Sera. I'll always give you more."

His mouth didn't stop until her throat was too hoarse to scream his name anymore.

CHAPTER ELEVEN

Sera leaned against the kitchen counter, eating a green apple and trying not to stare at Bowen's closed bedroom door. Even after what they'd done together last night, he'd retreated to his own room after depositing her limp body in the guest room bed, underneath her halo where he claimed she belonged. His behavior grew more and more confusing, and while she should be focused on the case and not examining his actions, she couldn't help it. His huge presence had taken up permanent residence in her mind, and no way could she shake him.

He continued to be honorable, sticking to his guns and not sleeping with her. Even the nuns at Holy Angels would approve. She should be grateful. Really. Even without sleeping with him, she'd started feeling…an attachment to him. A dangerous realization if she'd ever had one.

She could hear her uncle now. *You see all the good in people. Never the bad. You're too soft to be a cop.* The familiar rhetoric was so ingrained in her mind, she could hear his voice like he stood in the room.

Originally, she'd justified coming to stay with Bowen as a way to further her investigation while finding out if he'd played a role in Colin's death. Yet here she stood days later without even one attempt under her belt. She'd become too comfortable and she needed to step back, view the situation objectively again. Already this morning, she'd done a quiet search of the apartment that yielded no results. Not that she'd expected much in the living area or guest room, Bowen being smart enough to keep any possible incriminating evidence somewhere safe. Away from prying eyes. Where, though?

Sera pushed off the counter. It would only take her five minutes to get to Bowen's car and back. She could clear her head and cross one more searchable location off her list. It had to be done. After tossing her apple core in the trash can, Sera pulled on a light jacket and went to the door. Unlocking the dead bolts sent three loud *clank*s echoing through the silent apartment, making her cringe. She held her breath and waited to hear movement in Bowen's room, but nothing came. With a relieved exhale, she gently pried the door open and slipped into the hallway.

Hands tucked in her pockets, she moved quickly down the sidewalk, grateful that residents in this neighborhood appeared to be late risers. Most of the shops hadn't rolled up their metal gates for the day. The fewer eyes on her the better.

Bowen's car sat parked just around the corner from his building. She only felt safe taking five minutes to search, knowing that Bowen could wake up any moment. It wouldn't be a pretty scene if he found her room empty. Five minutes wasn't very long, especially when you had no idea what you were looking for. Or in this case, hoping you didn't find. Her brother's case had been labeled cold—*officially*, anyway—and it had been years since his death, so she didn't necessarily expect to find evidence. However, she *could* search for a link between Bowen and Hogan. Weapons. The one that killed Colin had never been recovered.

Sera's hands clenched inside her pockets. What would she do if she found something incriminating? As soon as she asked herself the question, something became glaringly obvious. She was in *deep*. Into the investigation, yes, but even more so with Bowen. When evidence was found, it went to the department. There *were* no other options. In her case, it went to the department and she vamoosed as soon as she was sure Hogan was gone. And she'd go alone.

Why did that make her feel so empty now?

When she reached Bowen's car, she let the slim jim she'd found beneath Bowen's sink fall from her jacket sleeve into her palm. She slipped the tool between the car window and rubber seal, making quick work of the lock. Quickly, she popped the trunk and retreated to the back of the car, pushing the slim jim up her sleeve as she went. Inside, she saw nothing. A brand-new tire iron, a Brooklyn Nets sweatshirt. She lifted the lining and felt around, all the while praying her fingers didn't connect with anything except the spare tire.

After her search yielded nothing, she heaved a sigh of relief and skirted the bumper to the front passenger side, flipping open the glove compartment. Clean. Not even a crumpled-up parking ticket. No, wait…a folded-up piece of paper tucked inside beneath the plastic manual. The yellow edge jumped right out at her because it was the only thing out of place in the clean car, appearing as though it had been stored in a rush. She pinched the very corner and drew out a yellow pamphlet, laying it on the seat.

Her hand rose to her throat. The church program. Bowen had kept it. Along the bottom edge, he'd written yesterday's date in heavy script, circling it once. Guilt swarmed in the air, before swooping in to break right through her rib cage. Guilt and…something else. Maybe she hadn't gone out there looking for evidence against Bowen. Maybe she'd been looking for something to justify her desire to save him. God, she wanted to. It had taken this gesture to kick her in the ass. Make her realize exactly how vital that additional mission was to her.

Without searching the rest of the car, Sera replaced the church program exactly as she'd found it, locked the car, and returned to the apartment. To Bowen.

Bowen drew on his cigarette as he watched Sera from across the street. She removed the rolled-up newspaper she'd used to prop his building door open and slipped back inside with the grace of an adorable cat burglar. When the door closed behind her, some of the tension lifted from his shoulders. Although he'd suspected she would sneak out at some point, watching her knowingly deceive him bothered him more than it should. A *lot* more.

He'd walked into this with his eyes open, knowing Sera would be playing a part. It shouldn't be driving him out of his mind she hadn't confided in him yet. Why would she? They'd known each other for four days. Did he honestly think she would jeopardize all her hard work on the chance he turned out to be a decent man?

Hell, he wasn't a decent man. He'd been treading water before, but she finally managed to drag him below the surface last night. Her mouth, her taste, her voice. All things he couldn't be without anymore. Necessities. Even standing across the street from her felt like miles, instead of yards. If he had his way, if the world were perfect, she would have her arms twined around his neck every second of the day. Her mouth within kissing distance, curves fitted against his. It wouldn't feel so right, so *essential*, to touch her if she didn't feel anything on her end. Right?

Deciding enough time had passed since she walked into the building, Bowen crossed the street, but was brought up short when his cell phone vibrated in his pocket. He drew it out and stared at the screen. Manhattan number, but not one he recognized.

He answered anyway. "Yeah."

"What the fuck did you say to her?"

"Troy." Bowen took a final pull of his cigarette and ground it out under his boot. "I'm surprised it took you this long to call me."

Silence met him on the other end.

"Look, I told you to keep Ruby out of my neighborhood. If you can't keep tabs on your girl that's not my problem. She give you the slip again?"

"I knew she went," Troy responded tightly. "I know *every* time she goes."

He encountered a kick of surprise. "You don't care that it's dangerous for her here? The girl who managed to put my father behind bars?"

"She's never in danger. Don't question my ability to protect her." The pause that followed was full of frustration. "I do what I need to in order keep her. If that means letting her retain a piece of her old life, so be it."

"I'm not that piece."

"No, you're not. And don't worry. I think you finally managed to convince her. She's walking around like a ghost. I'd like to kick your ass for that."

"Been there, done that, got the bloodstained T-shirt." Bowen's own anger rose to match Troy's. Brought on by guilt, having his hands tied where Sera was concerned. It poured over his head like hot water. "Is this what cops do all day? Sit around and whine about your girlfriends and their mood swings? As a taxpayer, I, for one, am appalled."

"Fuck you, Driscol."

"No, fuck *you*. The longer Sera is out here, the more she's in danger. Try focusing on that." Bowen ran a rough hand through his hair. "They're suspicious. She's good at what she does, but it's not enough. Not here."

"You can't keep her safe?"

"No one. Is going. To touch her," Bowen whispered furiously. "As long as I'm breathing, *nothing* happens to her."

"So it's true. She's staying with you."

Bowen dropped his head forward on a disgusted laugh. He'd been played. The realization tasted bitter in his mouth. "You could have just asked. You didn't need to piss me off in order to find out what you needed to know."

"Even us whiny cops need entertainment." Troy sighed wearily. "You weren't going to tell us. Why is that?"

"You're the detective. Figure it out." As soon as the words left his mouth, a wave of self-loathing battered him, but it was too late to take them back. "Your only rule was she doesn't find out I'm working with you. I haven't broken it. You didn't say I couldn't enjoy myself while I sell out."

He could practically see Troy shaking his head. "Jesus, Bowen. I don't know why, but I expected better from you."

"Your mistake." He felt a fierce sudden need to have eyes on Sera. To hold her and apologize for what he'd just implied. For blackening her good name by connecting it to his own. "Listen, we agreed I would do this my way. The safest place she can be is with me. Are we done here?"

"For now."

"Fucking swell."

Bowen hung up on Troy's disappointment, refusing to examine why it actually bothered him. Since when did he give a shit what that asshole thought about him?

He started to reach for another cigarette, but changed his mind. Compelled by the craving to see Sera and reassure himself she was okay, he jogged toward the building. Before he jerked the door open, something caught his eye—or some*one*, rather. A block away, a man sat watching him from a parked car.

Dread settled in his gut. He started toward the car, but it pulled away from the curb. Very slowly, he reached behind his back and molded a hand around the butt of his gun. A moment later, the car passed and he got a glimpse of the driver inside. A driver who was looking right at him, expression inscrutable.

Connor.

CHAPTER TWELVE

When Bowen walked through the front door of the apartment, instead of exiting his bedroom as expected, Sera's heartbeat skidded to a halt. She sat in the windowsill, a bowl of Cheerios in one hand, spoon in the other. Oh, God, what if he'd seen her? She braced herself for questions, brain scrambling for a believable cover story that would explain why she'd broken into his car.

He tugged on the collar of his leather bomber jacket, restless energy radiating from every inch of him. "You want to get out of here, Ladybug?"

"What?"

"Come on." His fingers harassed his hair. "We've been stuck in here since last night."

She let him take the bowl of Cheerios from her hand. "Where were you?"

"Picking up smokes."

"Okay." The stores were still closed, though. She'd only been back ten minutes. They couldn't have opened that quickly. How could she have missed him leaving the apartment? "Let me get dressed." Something was wrong. She couldn't put a name to the look in his eyes. Anxiousness. Forced casualness.

"Where are you going?" she asked as he followed on her heels.

"With you." He smiled, but it was strained. "Let me pick something out?"

Sera watched dumbfounded as he rummaged through the neat stack of clothes on her side table, casting a look at her over his shoulder as if to make sure she was still there. Within seconds, he returned with a green short-sleeved sweaterdress. He shoved the garment into her hands and reached for the hem of her sleep shirt, tugging it up her bare thighs.

"Bowen." She grabbed his hands. "*Stop*." Their gazes connected, but she didn't think he saw her. "What's wrong with you? Did something happen?"

On a long exhale, he pressed their foreheads together. "Sometimes I feel a little trapped here, baby. In this place. Does that ever happen to you? Have you ever felt trapped?"

She thought of her years at boarding school, being kept at a safe distance while working in Boston, even living above Rush for two weeks in that tiny room. "Yes, I have."

His jaw tightened, gray eyes snapping. "Now I wish I hadn't asked."

"I don't feel trapped now," she said, realizing she meant it. Not here, not with him. She stepped back and pulled the T-shirt over her head, leaving her standing before him in a bra and panties. His nostrils flared, muscular chest shuddering once. When his hands flexed at his sides, she thought he would touch her. She mentally begged him to, begged him to seek comfort in her. Instead, he dragged the dress over her head and fixed it over her curves in a series of jerky moves.

"Shoes?" He snatched up the ankle boots at the foot of the bed. She was forced to grab his shoulders for support as he placed them on her feet, one at a time. Task complete, he straightened and jerked his chin at her. "Before you insist on doing some girlie nonsense to your hair, it looks great. Let's go."

Bowen took her hand and pulled her from the room, barely giving her enough time to collect her purse off the counter. Here she went again. "Not until you tell me where we're going."

He paused at the door, facing her slowly. "Do you trust me, Sera?"

His entire world seemed ready to crash and burn if she gave the wrong answer. That responsibility scared her. If he placed this much importance on trust, *her* trust, what would happen when he inevitably found out her full identity as a police officer? What would happen when they had to go their separate ways?

Her throat started to close up, but she managed a nod. "Yes."

Tension left his shoulders gradually. "Try not to think about it so hard next time."

"Try not to ask questions that require thought before I've had any coffee."

He draped an arm around her shoulders, holding her close as he locked the apartment. "Fair enough. You like the beach?"

"*Yes*. I love it." They walked side by side down the hall. "Is the beach kind of an escape for you, from being trapped?"

"Sometimes." Bowen shrugged, the edginess returning. "Today it's just a backdrop, though. You're the escape, sweetheart."

His words knocked the wind right out of her. The way he'd murmured it, almost as an afterthought, made it more meaningful. It proved it hadn't been a line or a joke. Just pure, honest Bowen. Not just the Bowen she wanted to save. The Bowen she…wanted. Period. Oh, God, she'd fallen for him. The word "fallen" didn't suit how she felt, though. "Fallen" implied that she'd already landed, when her entire being still soared, gravitating toward him. Solid ground wasn't even in her sight line. The practical part of her screamed bad news, but her heart only sped faster. After her investigation ended, could she walk away from him? Even thinking the words made her entire body rebel, hurting head to toe.

Bowen sent her a tentative smile as they reached the bottom of the staircase. He squeezed her to his side so tightly, she could barely breathe. His eyes scanned the street as he hustled her to his car parked at the curb and opened the passenger-side door. The second she settled into the seat, he slammed the door closed behind her.

Obviously something had happened between last night and this morning that had him worried. He said he'd left the apartment to buy cigarettes. Had he run into trouble instead?

They drove along the parkway with the windows down, crisp morning air tunneling through the car in a wash of white noise. It wasn't exactly beach weather, but she knew they weren't going for the usual reasons. Would he tell her if she asked?

Who is the man I'm free-falling for? The man who'd been so genuine with the offer to kill someone for her? Or the man who painted a halo over her head?

Bowen parked the car and they walked to a diner, ordering food to go. They took their wrapped breakfast sandwiches and ate them on the boardwalk, looking out over the Atlantic. Seagulls called to one another; people passed behind them speaking mostly in Russian as the ocean crashed in soothing intervals. It occurred to Sera she'd seen and experienced more with Bowen in the last four days than she had in years. She didn't know whether to be grateful or depressed by the thought.

"You're thinking too hard again."

Sera held up her paper cup of coffee in response.

He chuckled from his position on the railing. It didn't escape her he had a view of anyone coming up behind her. "When is the last time you were at the beach?"

She ate her last bite of sandwich as she dug through her memory. "When I was a senior in high school. Which is just sad, when you get right down to it."

"Hmm. Who were you with?"

"A pack of nuns."

He choked on a sip of coffee. "You make them sound like wolves."

"Oh, you've met them?"

His crack of laughter drew the attention of some passing joggers. "That bad, huh?"

She collected their garbage and tossed it in the nearby garbage can. "Let's just say, wearing a habit at the beach in ninety-degree weather doesn't put someone in a good mood to begin with. Throw in thirty teenage girls who are seeing boys with their shirts off for the first time…it's not pretty."

Bowen's eyes narrowed on her. "You were gawking again, weren't you?"

"Guilty."

His voice dropped. "We'll sort that out later, won't we?"

The air grew thick between them, heating her even in the cool morning breeze. It would be so easy to stand and wrap her arms around him, but she wanted to take this opportunity to know more. To understand him better as a person before their labels, their real lives, intruded and she'd never get the chance again. Her throat grew suddenly tight. "What about you? Last time at the beach."

He opened his mouth to answer, but frowned and shut it again. "I don't remember. I might have been here last week…" She could tell from his tone he meant it. If he wanted to, he could have easily made something up. Clearly, he couldn't call to mind the last time he'd been, and it bothered him tremendously.

"Just tell me about any time you were at the beach, Bowen," she offered quietly. "It doesn't have to be the last time."

Sera watched shadows pass behind his eyes as he thought. The lightheartedness of a moment ago had passed, leaving his troubles etched in the hard lines of his body. Outlined by the bright morning light from his position on the top rail, he looked like he belonged painted on the ceiling of a cathedral. An angel who had defected to the dark side.

"All right, I got one." His far-off voice startled her out of her daydream. "My father drove me down here one afternoon when I was thirteen. Even let me sit in the front seat." He pointed to a spot beyond her shoulder. "There was a group of high school kids hanging out, smoking, whatever. He told me to get out of the car and pick a fight with the biggest one. Wouldn't let me get back in the car until I did it. Until I won."

Sera was certain if she moved, her body would splinter in half. Anger coursed through her veins at the idea of a father treating his child so callously. She felt pity for the little boy, too, but she held on to the anger because if he saw her pity, he'd hate it. "Did you win?"

"No. I rode the subway home with two busted eyes that day. So he brought me back the following week. And the week after that. Until he could point out anyone on the beach and I could take them." He gave a quick shake of his head. "But I haven't lost a fair fight since then, so lesson learned, right?"

"Fair fight? *None* of that was fair." When he merely stared off into the distance, she drew in a deep breath to calm herself down. It didn't work. Her hands were shaking in her lap with the desire to break a commandment on his behalf. "Why did you tell me that?"

"To see if you'll leave." His hands clenched and unclenched on the rail. "Once you know I'm just a trained attack dog."

"Would you let me leave?"

"No." Stormy gray eyes found hers. "*No*."

In her old line of work, the ER had been a place where income brackets and political differences didn't matter. Making people better, that's what mattered. This need to care for Bowen went so far beyond a calling. It couldn't be controlled or reasoned with. It was necessity. Sharing his aches wasn't a burden, but a privilege. He'd just proven beyond a shadow of a doubt how vastly different their worlds had been growing up. How different they were *still*. She didn't care anymore if her pity was unwanted, though. She needed to touch him.

At the exact moment she launched herself from the bench toward Bowen, he dropped from the railing and met her halfway, their bodies colliding. His arms banded across her back, crushing her to his chest. Her chin fit just right into the notch of his neck. They held each other and swayed for a while, ignoring the curious looks of people walking past. She could only hold tight and hope the simple act of her being there helped in some way.

Suddenly, Bowen's body started shaking. It alarmed her at first until she realized he was laughing. "What?"

"You're not even going to believe me."

After everything he'd just told her? "Try me."

He gripped her shoulders and turned her around slowly. "Don't gawk, Ladybug."

"I don't gaw—" She never finished her sentence. Walking down the boardwalk, looking righteous and militant, was a pack of nuns. "No way."

"Way."

She dropped back onto the bench in a fit of laughter, Bowen

watching her with an amused expression. Sera hid her face in her hands, hoping the nuns would pass by quickly, but somehow knew Bowen wouldn't be able to let that happen. And she was right. As the nuns drew even with their bench, he let out a loud whistle.

"Sisters." He leaned back on the railing like a lazy cat and threw them a wink. "You're looking extra lovely today. Put in a good word with the big guy for me, would ya?"

As Sera buried her face back in her hands with a groan, she swore she heard one of them giggle.

CHAPTER THIRTEEN

I want to stay just like this forever. With Sera leaning against the railing in front of Bowen, wind lifting her hair off her shoulders, carrying her scent up to his nose. If only he weren't shielding her back with his body on the off chance someone decided to take a shot at her, it would be perfect. An ache sprang to life behind his eyes at the thought of her being hit, falling to the ground, while he stood there helpless. It was fast becoming his worst nightmare, one replaying itself over and over since this morning.

Connor hadn't followed them, he'd made sure of it. But he still didn't plan on taking any chances with Sera's life. What conclusions had the guy drawn from what he'd seen? If Bowen had judged Connor correctly, he didn't miss a thing. His other judgment, that Connor wouldn't do anything to harm Sera after she'd saved his life...he wasn't so sure about that anymore. Working for a man like Hogan, hell, being *related* to him, would harden a man over time. To go from the military to street muscle meant he'd done something to fall far. Despite his good gut feeling about the guy, Bowen had never trusted him. He didn't trust anybody. But now, after that look Connor had given him as he drove past, he'd graduated to a direct threat.

He'd been frantic to get her out of his neighborhood. Then as they drove down the parkway, he'd experienced the pressing urge to keep driving. Past Coney Island, out of Brooklyn. If he thought she wouldn't object, he might have actually done it. After seeing Connor this morning, he'd almost called Troy back and begged him to come get Sera out. To put her in a safe house somewhere no one could find her; screw the precious ledger the commissioner wanted. Then he'd realized what that meant. It meant they'd take her away from him. Forever. When it came down to it, would he keep her in jeopardy just to keep her in Brooklyn a little longer? God, he didn't know. The thought of not having her within reach caused nausea to rise in his throat. She was heaven propped against his chest, such a contrast to the cold metal of the gun at the small of his back. Two sides of the same coin. Good and evil. Which was he?

When Bowen heard the food stands and amusement park rides open behind them, he took her hand and walked her toward a warehouse-size building in the center of the attractions. With the beach getting busier, he wanted to get her indoors.

"Where are you taking me?"

"Don't you trust me?"

"Yes."

He squeezed her hand in thanks, trying not to think about what would happen to that trust when she found out he was keeping such a huge secret from her. As soon as the four walls of the massive video arcade surrounded them, a little bit of his tension faded. "How do you feel about air hockey?"

A mischievous smile played around her lips, making him want to kiss the breath out of her. "Oh, I feel pretty good about it."

Twenty minutes later, they were tied at two games apiece. He could not wipe the stupid grin off his face. She'd turned out to be a little competitor, his Sera. Having ditched school as a kid in favor of the arcade countless times, he'd played more than his fair share of air hockey. Fighting had kicked his reflexes up another notch, making him unbeatable. Sera was giving him a legitimate run for his money, and he wasn't taking it easy on her.

"Who taught you how to play? Don't tell me the nuns, I won't believe you."

Her smile was so gorgeous it made his stomach ache. "My brother and I used to play. When my...family came to visit us at school. They'd take us to lunch and the arcade. Had to drag us away from the table."

"Visit you?" He dropped two quarters into the slot. "How far away was college?"

She didn't answer right away. "Massachusetts. From third grade up, actually. At least for me. My brother was older."

"What?" When his fingers started to hurt, he realized he was squeezing the mallet in his hand. "Why would they send you that far away?"

"I don't want to talk about it." She put on a brave smile. "Anyway, I can just tell you're stalling to delay your inevitable loss."

All this time, he'd pictured her childhood filled with barbecues and pet kittens. Knowing it wasn't, knowing she'd been sent away and left on her own, reminded him he didn't know enough about her. And if he asked, all he would get was her cover story, which he'd already memorized. She wouldn't tell him anything about her parents, her upbringing. Suddenly it felt unacceptable that he didn't know every single detail about her.

She tapped her mallet against her thigh, those big brown

eyes practically begging him for a distraction from the subject. "Bowen?"

"You're right." He cleared the rust out of his throat. "I'm shaking in my boots, Ladybug."

"Are you patronizing me now? That's not a good strategy with me."

"I'll have to remember that." He sent the puck flying across the table. "I'm all about strategy when it comes to you."

"Is that right? You seem to be doing well so far."

"I can do even better."

Jesus, he didn't even know if they were talking about the same thing anymore, but the challenge in her voice was making his dick hard. Every time she slapped the puck back in his direction, her tits bounced underneath her dress. Her white teeth were sunk into that full lower lip as she bent over the table. It was a fucking shame he wasn't standing behind her. The backs of her thighs would be exposed, flashing every time her hips bumped the table. Dammit, he couldn't concentrate anymore.

Right on cue, she scored on him. "Hey, you want to wake up and give me a decent game?"

God, she was cute. "I wanted you to get at least one point before I smoked you."

"All right, big talker. Show, don't tell."

Taking advantage of her distraction, he knocked the puck off the rail and scored, laughing at her look of outrage. "Whoever wins picks what we do next."

"That's a pretty broad wager."

"Take it or leave it."

"I'll take it."

Yes, you will. With what he had in mind, no way was he losing. She put up a good fight, but in the end, he won by two points. No sooner had the puck been swallowed by the machine, Bowen circled the table and dragged her up against him. Both hands went to her ass, depositing her on the edge of the table. Her head tipped back as he kissed her, as if she'd expected it. Had been dying for it, just like him. They were in a dark corner of the mostly empty arcade, but he needed to get her somewhere more private. Pulling away wasn't easy when his body demanded he step between those thighs and take the hard, driving fuck he needed.

He jerked away from her with a growl. "Come on, my choice." After checking to make sure no one was watching, he tugged her off the table and led her across the arcade to the photo booth he'd spotted while they played.

"Bowen." She tried to slow him down. "I don't like having my picture taken."

Right. Probably rule number one for an undercover cop. Still, he needed something he could use to remember today. So if one day he woke up and she wasn't there, he would know she hadn't been a dream. They stopped outside the booth. "Make an exception for me?"

She looked conflicted, but eventually nodded once. Without giving her a chance to change her mind, he ducked and led her inside, closing the curtain behind them. When she dug into her pocket for change, he shook his head.

"Not yet, sweetheart." He sat down on the stool and settled her on his lap facing away from him, loving the little gasp she let slip when her ass pressed down against his erection. Desperate to taste her skin, he wrapped her hair around his fist and tilted her head to the side, tongue licking up the side of her neck to taste ocean air and sunlight. When he snapped his teeth down on her ear, she jumped a little and came down hard on his cock, making his vision dull. "Feel me? I need to be sucked off again by that pretty pink mouth. You going to do it for me again later?"

Her breath rushed out. "Yes. I want to."

"Loved how I tasted, didn't you?" He placed a hand on the inside of her knee, drawing slow patterns with his fingers. "Don't worry, you'll taste it again soon. If I wasn't dying to touch between your legs, I'd put you on your knees right now and tell you to open your mouth for it."

Her bare thighs rested on his, so when he spread his legs, the space between her legs widened, too, giving him ample access. He could tell having her legs open wide excited her; the hips suddenly writhing in his lap told him so.

"Quit it, baby," he growled at her neck. "I'm already fucking insane for you. Don't make it worse."

"Touch me, please."

Christ, he couldn't deny her anything under normal circumstances, but when she begged in that husky voice, the need to please her became his sole mission in life. His hand traveled the remaining distance to the barrier of her panties, cupping her and squeezing once. She moaned and tossed her head back to rest on his shoulder, thighs flexing on top of his. He opened his mouth against her ear and breathed with her, his fingers slipping beneath the cotton of her underwear.

What he found made his cock swell painfully in his jeans. "Jesus. How long has your pussy been this wet?"

"I-I don't know."

His tongue teased her earlobe. "Who made it wet?"

"*You.*" She whimpered. "You did."

"Why? How?" He didn't ask out of vanity. No, he needed to know so he could keep doing it. Find out what turned her on and become the only one who did it right. He expected her to say *the way you touch me.* Or *it happens when you kiss my neck.* But he never expected the actual answer she gave.

"You don't have to do anything." Lust-drugged eyes met his as she lifted her hands, sliding her fingers into his hair. "It's just you. Being with you. Everything about you does this to me."

His heart rate skyrocketed, pounding furiously against his rib cage, trying to free itself so it could lie bleeding at her feet. He opened his mouth, but no words came out. She'd opened a hole in his chest and if he thought too hard about what she'd said, it might bury him alive. "Tell me I'm your man, Sera," he demanded.

"You're my man," she rasped, rocking her hips. "*Please*, Bowen."

"I love turning you into a little beggar." He hated himself for needing to make this about sex, but it couldn't be helped. That was where his confidence lay. Not in beautiful words or promises. The things she deserved. Swallowing the lump in his throat, he traced her damp seam with his middle finger. "What were you thinking about? That day at the beach, looking at those shirtless motherfuckers?"

"I...nothing. I don't know."

"Nothing?" Bowen knew his jealousy was irrational. It didn't matter. Every emotion amplified itself where she was concerned. "Were you hoping they'd try to get under your hiked-up uniform skirt? Were you hoping they'd do this?" He pushed his middle finger past her entrance, both of them groaning in the enclosed space of the photo booth. "Answer me."

"No. I promise."

He pumped his finger in and out slowly. "You wouldn't lie to me, would you, Sera?"

Frantically, she shook her head.

"Who's the only one who gets under your skirt?"

"You. Just you."

"That's right." He started rolling his hips in time with his fingers, the weight of her gorgeous ass on his lap driving him crazy. If she weren't a virgin, he would be balls-deep right now. No question. She'd be feeling every inch of his frustration. Knowing he didn't have much longer before he lost his tenuous hold on control, he brushed his thumb over her clit, making her moan. "Who touches you here?"

"Y-ou do, Bowen." Her thighs clenched around his hands. "Oh, *God*."

He turned his head and captured her mouth in a wild kiss. A kiss so raw and sexual, it shattered something inside him. Fire licked over his skin, engulfing him until he couldn't see his way free. He ached. He ached so bad. For more. Everything. Touching her with his hand suddenly wasn't enough. He needed more. *No, no, you can't. You can't have her, you bastard. Especially here, like this.* But he needed *something*, needed to get closer. Before he knew his own intentions, he surged off the stool and pushed her against the wall of the photo booth, already tugging the panties down her legs.

"Baby, you trust me?" He barely recognized his own voice. "Please say yes."

"Yes."

He'd never seen anything in his life as hot as Sera, hands braced on the wall, underwear around her knees. The sound of the zipper of his jeans being pulled down made her moan and that reaction somehow drove his already blistering need higher. "Push your ass up and spread your legs," he directed her. "I won't take you, but when you come I need to feel it where I hurt."

When her sweet ass perked up, Bowen gave in to the urge to smack it. Would have done it again, but her hands were flexing impatiently on the wall, desperate noises falling from her lips. He couldn't leave her unfinished any longer. It was killing him. He took his heavy arousal in his hand, gritting his teeth as he led it between her legs. When his hard length slipped against her bare pussy, without a single barrier between them, his knees almost gave out. He had to do this quick or being inside her would become a necessity.

"Bowen, hurry. Please."

"Shh. I'm going to take care of you so good. You fucking *know* I am." He found her clit with the head of his cock and picked up where his hand had left off, rubbing quick, tight circles around her sensitive nub. It felt like heaven and hell. The most painful torture he could have devised for himself and yet he would kill anyone who tried to stop this from happening. "Come on, I want to feel that wet little shake of yours. The one I tasted with my mouth last night. Tasted so damn good, baby."

"Oh, God...I'm going to—"

"Good girl, let it go. All over your man."

Bowen got a hand over her mouth just in time to catch her hoarse cry. Pride and pain dueled inside him, common sense trying to battle its way to the surface. The job was done for him when he heard loud talking outside the booth. Immediately, his hands flew to Sera, tugging her panties back into place. Then in a movement so painful he wanted to shout every obscenity in the book, he zipped his jeans back into place over his raging erection. Drawing in deep breaths, he fell back onto the stool, taking Sera with him.

Just as two preteen boys yanked open the curtain.

"We'll be out in a minute." He jerked his thumb at them. "Scram."

The curtain fell back down, but not before he heard, "Bro, they was totally screwing in there."

I wish, kid.

Bowen turned back to find Sera watching him, chewing on her bottom lip. "You okay?"

His breath shuddered out. "I'm pretty damn far from okay, Ladybug."

Sera's lips trembled, he suspected with the need to laugh. Instead, she reached into her purse and removed a couple dollar bills, feeding them into the slot.

"Smile."

CHAPTER FOURTEEN

By the time Bowen and Sera dragged themselves away from the boardwalk, the sun had started dipping low in the distance, forming light patterns on the water. They'd collected so many tickets from winning arcade games, they'd started looping them around their necks like scarves. After lugging the tangled heaps to the counter, they'd agreed to exchange the tickets for the ugliest prize they could find, making Bowen the proud new owner of a fringed leather vest that said "Greased Lightning" on the back.

He never wanted to leave. As they drove back toward Bensonhurst, reality intruding with every mile, he wanted to whip the car around and go back to Coney Island. He wanted to stay there in the sunshine with Sera playing stupid games and riding kiddie rides they were way too old to ride. For this one too-brief day, he'd been someone else. Someone better. But as soon as the streets became familiar again, passing along the outside of his window, he turned back into his father, heir to the criminal throne. A throne of garbage and barbed wire. One he didn't want, but didn't know how to separate from.

As they pulled up in front of his building, his cell phone

buzzed in the cupholder. He checked the screen and cursed. Wayne. The last person he wanted to talk to with Sera sitting beside him, head lolling against the seat drowsily. Trusting him to get her home safe. All day long, they'd been a normal couple, but answering this call would end that with a quickness. Still, Wayne never let himself be avoided for long, and speaking to him over the phone was better than in person.

He pressed the talk button with a sigh. "Yeah?"

Loud music and voices greeted him before the older man spoke. "Now, that ain't no way to answer the phone."

Bowen ignored the pinch of irritation. He'd stopped taking Wayne's bullshit last time they spoke, and he couldn't take a step back now. "Hell, I probably use the wrong fork in restaurants, too, Wayne. Is this a fucking etiquette lesson? I'm busy."

An extended silence passed. "Busy doing what?"

"Practicing my origami." He closed his eyes when Sera shifted uncomfortably in the passenger seat, the perfect ease between them ruined. "What's it to you?"

Wayne's humorous chuckle reached down the phone, sounding like a warning. "I'm down at Marco's with some of the boys. You've got to show your face once in a while, kid. They need a leader. When they don't have one, they get restless and start acting on their own. You know what I'm saying?"

Bowen knew all too well what Wayne meant. The local guys who'd first been employed by his father, and now him, needed babysitting around the clock. They didn't have jobs to keep them occupied, and spending time with their families didn't exactly appear to be a priority. No, they weren't the type to sit tight and wait for a call about a job. They felt the constant need to prove themselves. Bowen was ashamed to admit he might have felt that at one time in his life, when he'd been too young to know better. Not now.

He had two options. Leave Sera here and hope Connor wasn't watching, waiting for Bowen to leave her alone so he could potentially carry out Hogan's orders. Or he could bring her along with him to Marco's.

Fuck, he hated either option.

Painfully aware of Wayne waiting on the line, he looked over at Sera. She gave him a steady half smile that warmed him immediately. Dammit, he couldn't leave her alone. The entire time he was gone, he'd be going out of his mind worrying about her. Worried he might come home and find her hurt. Or worse.

No, that wouldn't work.

"Be there in a while," he snapped into the phone, hanging it up before Wayne could reply. Sera laid her hand on top of his and it suddenly occurred to him she would want this. If given the choice, she would want to come tonight and absorb as much as she could. About him, his associates.

"Bowen?" Her soft voice soothed him even in the midst of his chaotic thoughts. "What's wrong?"

He stared out the windshield. "Will you go somewhere with me?"

"Is it going to be as fun as the beach?"

"No, Ladybug."

She nodded, as if she'd already known the answer. "Yeah, I'll go."

They drove in silence the ten blocks to Marco's and he parked in his usual spot. Without asking her, she waited until he came around to the passenger door to help her out. Sera was smart. She had to know the kind of danger she was in. Not for the first time, he wished he hadn't agreed to keep his involvement from her. He hated having anything between them. With a few words, he could ensure she trusted him without question. The relief that would bring was tempting as hell, especially when they were walking into the dragon's den.

But the commissioner's words echoed in his head. *She's got nothing to lose. No care for her own well-being.* Bowen didn't necessarily believe she'd be reckless, but the horror of Sera being in danger kept the truth sealed tight. Anything to keep her from being hurt.

He took her hand and led her into dark, boisterous Marco's. The place had been a restaurant at one time, with a connected lounge and bar area. Residents of the neighborhood who had been patronizing the eatery since they were children had stopped coming in for dinner eventually, turned off by the rough crowd that now frequented the bar and lounge. If a night went by where a fight didn't break out, the owners chalked it up to a full moon. At one time, before he'd even reached the legal drinking age, he'd been the instigator of most of those fights.

Several men puffed on lit cigarettes and cigars at the bar, clearly not giving a fuck about the law. Why would they when they broke more serious ones on a weekly basis? The smoke hanging in the air, the vile words being shouted, they never usually fazed him. With Sera walking beside him, holding his hand, they made him sick. These disgusting people would infect her. Hell, he would, too. Wasn't he the reason she was here tonight in the first place?

Heads turned at their entrance; conversations quieted. The reaction he typically received, but tonight it was more out of curiosity than respect. They were looking at Sera. Not blatantly checking her out—they knew better than that. He knew what they were thinking, though. Since when does Bowen Driscol walk into Marco's holding some girl's hand? Since when does he *begin* the night with a chick, instead of his usual process of picking one to leave with?

"Bowen." A hand slapped down on his shoulder. The gold

ring winking up at him would have told him it was Wayne if the voice hadn't tipped him off. Automatically, he jerked Sera into his side, mentally cursing when Wayne raised an eyebrow at the action. "You going to introduce me?"

Sera reached out to shake his hand. "I'm Sera."

Bowen's skin crawled as Wayne wrapped his hand around hers. "Not your usual type, is she, kid?"

"Is there a reason you're talking about her like she's not standing there?"

"I was getting to it," Wayne returned smoothly. "Where do you come from, Sera?"

"Lancaster, Pennsylvania," she answered casually. "Moved here a few months back."

He appeared to weigh her answer. "Can't say I don't find it odd that you chose this section of Brooklyn to relocate." His eye twitched. "But who am I to judge?"

Bowen's jaw felt ready to shatter. "I was wondering the same thing."

Wayne ignored him. "It's a pleasure, young lady. Sort of feels like we already know each other. After all, I've held your panties in my hand."

A blast of pure rage catapulted through Bowen's body. Knowing every eye in the room was trained on him, he repositioned his body so only Wayne could see his face. "This is your last warning, old man. If you disrespect her again, I'll forget all about your relationship with my father. To be honest, my memory is already pretty goddamn foggy. Watch. Yourself."

Irritation flared in Wayne's expression. "Feels like I'm having déjà vu. I remember when your whore mother showed up and Lenny went soft. Took years to pull his head out of his ass. By then, we had to start from fucking scratch. All over some pussy," he spat.

It didn't matter Bowen had a non-relationship with his mother—the insult made him livid. Worse, it had been an implied insult toward Sera. His hands curled into fists and his vision dulled with red haze. Somewhere in the back of his mind, he knew Wayne was provoking him on purpose, though. Why? The wild card was the only thing holding him back. No chances. He couldn't take any chances when he had Sera with him. Instead, he concentrated on the feeling of her fingers twining with his, the way she squeezed him as if she knew what an effort it cost him not to go for Wayne's throat.

"Did you call me down here to relive your glory days? I'm not feeling all that nostalgic."

Wayne looked surprised over Bowen's restraint. "No, actually. We got something to discuss. Privately."

"Not happening tonight."

"S'gotta be tonight." His lips curled into a smile as he glanced at Sera. "You don't mind. Do you, sweet thing?"

Calm down. He wants you to snap. Wants to remind you who you are, that you'll never be normal. That you'll never be anything but a violent temper on legs. With Sera beside him, though, he felt like more than that. He was her protector. Still, if he blew Wayne off now, it would come back to bite him in the ass. With everyone watching their every move, he couldn't blow off business for a girl. Word would spread he'd gone soft and it would only be a matter of time before someone tried to create a new job opportunity for himself by eliminating the competition. Him.

Bowen leaned down to talk in Sera's ear. "Can you sit at the bar for a few minutes? I won't be long."

She nodded, reassurance in her brown eyes. "I'll be fine. Go ahead."

"Great." Wayne snorted. "Now we've got permission."

Ignoring the comment, Bowen led Sera to the bar and boosted her onto a seat. The bartender came over immediately. A dirty martini. It had to be the last drink he would expect her to order, but that contradiction somehow made complete sense. An angel sitting at a bar full of scum, trying to blend in. God, he wanted to take her home.

"Don't go anywhere, okay? No one will bother you if you stay put."

She traced a circle on the bar. "Why won't they bother me?"

Why was she asking when she already knew? Did she need to be reassured or was she asking because she wasn't supposed to know? "They've seen you with me. They know what will happen if I come back and someone has made the mistake of talking to you."

"Just someone talking to me would bother you?"

"Sera, I'm wishing they were all fucking blind right now." Underneath the bar, he laid a hand on her bare knee. "If I didn't think seeing the sexy way you kiss would interest them more, I would take your mouth right now. I'd fuck it with mine, to remind them who you're with." He grazed her ear with his stubbled cheek. "But once they see the way that mouth moves, I'll have to fight them off, won't I, baby?"

He watched the pulse flutter at her neck. "No fighting, please. Not for me."

Bowen pulled back to study her adamant expression. She didn't like the idea of him fighting, looked distinctly upset about the possibility. "If I did fight for you, it would be the first time I'd ever used my fists for something worthwhile."

Guilt shone briefly in her eyes.

"I'll be right back." He gave a warning look to every male within spitting distance. "Be good."

CHAPTER FIFTEEN

Sera took a sip of her martini and tried not to gag. It tasted exactly as the name implied. Dirty, like it had gone past its expiration date or been left in the sun too long. Aware of the attention being paid to her, she didn't so much as flinch as the liquid burned down her throat. God, she'd kill for a Snapple to rid herself of the taste.

She noticed a group of men sending her covert glances. They looked drunk and bored, a dangerous combination. In fact, she had a suspicion they were nominating someone to come talk to her. She didn't want to see how that would go over when Bowen came back.

It would be foolish of her not to believe he'd meant every word. His jealousy, his possessive attitude concerning her, only grew by the hour. And in turn, so did her desire for it to *keep* growing, which didn't make any sense when the thought of him fighting bothered her immensely. When Bowen kissed her, when he talked to her as if it were them versus the world, she wanted it to be true. The more time she spent with him only made her confidence grow that he was the man she'd never known enough to hope for. He didn't belong in this world. He was a victim of his circumstances.

Could she save him as she'd resolved to do, or was she a victim of her circumstances, same as him? Were they doomed to part ways as enemies once this ended?

Today had been incredible. Possibly even the best day of her life. When they'd just been two people without deadlines or agendas coloring the air around them, she'd been Sera with him, not a nurse, or a cop, or a grieving sister. Just herself. After the strictness of boarding school and not knowing how to connect with her uncle on the odd occasion she saw him, being herself had been impossible. She didn't know who she was. How ironic that while pretending to be someone else, she finally felt comfortable in her own skin.

"Buy you your next drink?"

The words were slurred to her right, issued from the apparent nominee of Drunk and Bored Central. She smiled politely and shook her head, already having learned while waitressing that reasoning with a drunk man usually meant a convoluted or inappropriate response.

"Bowen and I are friends. He won't mind."

"If that were true, I think you know he would."

"You talk pretty."

Berating herself for opening her mouth, she scanned the bar for Bowen, but hadn't seen him since he disappeared into the back room a few minutes ago. A group of young women standing outside the ladies' room caught her eye, though. The last thing she wanted was Bowen to come back and find this guy talking to her, and the nearby ladies' room looked safe and close enough.

She slid off her stool. "Excuse me."

Trying to blend into the wall, she got in line behind the group of women, her eyes immediately tearing up as their abundance of flowery perfume hit her. They sent her a few furtive looks, then lowered their voices and huddled closer. Fortunately, they appeared to have knocked back a few drinks, much like everyone else in Marco's. Their voices weren't half as quiet as they seemed to think.

Walks in here like she's the first lady of the United States or something.

Maybe, but he *won't be the president for long.*

Thinks he's better than everyone…we'll see who's better real soon.

He's gone soft. Now there's something I never thought I'd say that about Bowen Driscol.

My Nicky says after that score on the ninth, everything is going to change.

Denial thundered through Sera as she absorbed their snidely whispered words, the implications of them. The ninth… the ninth. She'd overheard that same date mentioned in the hallway above Rush when Hogan was still in town. Combined with the women's conversation, it could only mean one thing. Bowen and his crew were involved in whatever Hogan had planned for May ninth. It connected the dots, finally answering the question as to why Bowen and Hogan were associating. But now a bigger, horrifying picture came into sharp focus.

They planned to take Bowen out.

The shaking started in her knees and moved up, higher until she trembled against the wall. Paralyzed, her heart seized in her chest at the image of a vibrant Bowen lying lifeless on the sidewalk. The trained fighting hands that painted murals and brought her body to life, never to be used again. Until hearing his life was in jeopardy, she hadn't known exactly how deep she'd let herself sink.

No, she couldn't let it happen. She hadn't been able to save her brother, but she could do something about this.

A sparkly pink cell phone twinkled at her from inside one of women's purses. She murmured a quick prayer and asked forgiveness for stealing. Possibly coveting, too. Then she snatched the phone out of the purse. While they were engrossed in a conversation that had turned to which bar they would head to next, Sera slipped away. Even as she made sure to maintain a casual air while walking through the packed bar, she knew Bowen would be back any minute and she needed to be quick. She didn't even want to envision what he would do if he came back and found her gone, although since every eye in the place was watching her leave, he'd have no trouble locating her. Hopefully they would assume she was popping out for a cigarette, instead of making the phone call that would save Bowen's life. A phone call that could very well put the kibosh on her investigation.

Thankfully she found the sidewalk outside Marco's empty. It wouldn't stay that way for long, though, so she needed to get her nerves under control. The jig would be up once she placed the call. Her uncle would know what, exactly, she'd done without his permission. Would attempt to convince her it was an overzealous crusade, possibly even try to bring her out against her will.

Didn't matter. Bowen's *life* was at stake. Her choice was clear. Sera centered herself with a deep inhale and dialed her uncle's desk line at the precinct. On a weeknight, he would be working late, probably getting ready to order Chinese takeout for anyone working overtime.

True to form, he answered on the first ring. "Newsom."

The phone felt heavy in her hand. "Uncle. It's me."

Silence. "Seraphina. What the hell is going on?"

Something in his tone felt off, but she didn't have time to mull it over. "I don't have a lot of time, so try to keep the lecturing to a minimum." When she tossed a look at the entrance to Marco's, a car idling at the curb caught her eye. She squinted to make out the driver, surprised to find Connor watching her. Her hand went up automatically in greeting, but he didn't return it. An uncomfortable feeling spread in her midsection when he pulled away and turned the corner at the end of the block without so much as acknowledging her.

"Sera." Her uncle's impatient voice brought her back to the present. "You take last-minute personal vacation time the *week* before Colin's birthday and don't even check in? Where are you? I demand a goddamn *answer*."

"I didn't plan this around Colin's birthday, but..." She closed her eyes. "It's fitting because I'm undercover with Hogan." The line crackled with static, but her uncle said nothing. No shouting, like she'd expected. "The ledger. I've seen him with it. We know he's good for my brother's—*your nephew's*—murder." A touch of hysteria changed her pitch. "So I'm here to get what we need. Everyone else seems to have forgotten what he did. Not me. Not—"

"Seraphina." His voice was cold. "Do you have any idea how reckless you're being?"

She waited for the order to come home, but it never came. *Think about it later. Protect Bowen.* "May ninth," she rushed to say. "I don't know what the date means, but something substantial is happening. Enough to warrant an increase in bodies around Hogan...put him on edge. I would increase surveillance of the usual locations in North Brooklyn." A lump stuck in her throat. "South Brooklyn, too. I'd suggest putting out some feelers or tapping any low-level informants you have. I'm working on nailing down specifics."

His anger crackled down the line. "I'm just supposed to

respond with 'how high' when you say 'jump'? This department didn't even *approve* this vigilante investigation."

"Bowen Driscol is involved," she added, before she could talk herself out of it.

"Really," he answered slowly.

Again, not the reaction she'd been expecting. "Yes."

A laughing couple spilled out onto the sidewalk, holding each other up. Sera walked a little farther away, ducking just inside the alleyway running alongside Marco's. "Listen, I know it's asking a lot under the circumstances, but I need a favor. Just agree to it without any questions. Can you do that?"

"That's asking quite a lot from someone like me. I could have your badge for this stunt, young lady."

Her shoulders tightened at the condescending endearment, but she had to let it slide. She needed Bowen taken off the street and arguing wouldn't accomplish that outcome for her. Furthermore, she'd known going into this her badge would be in jeopardy, but relating that to her uncle would only exacerbate his anger. "Just agree to it. I wouldn't ask if it wasn't extremely important."

A long-suffering sigh greeted her. "What is it?"

Relief rushed through her. "Pick up Bowen Driscol for something, anything, on the afternoon of the ninth. Whatever is going down, he can't be there. They're planning a hit. I only want him kept overnight. No longer."

Silence. "Since when do you concern yourself with the livelihood of criminals?"

Since I fell for one. "Isn't it our job to protect people? Would you willingly send a man into a situation when you knew his life was in danger?"

He scoffed. "Sera, you're too idealistic for this job. Just like I've always said." A loud slam reverberated down the line. "I should pull you out of there tonight. Find a safe house and keep you out of sight until the job can be done *right*."

"You wouldn't." The hard edge to her voice surprised even her. "You want Hogan too badly and I'm close enough to get him. And we both know this job should have been done by now." She reeled back her irritation. "Will you pick up Bowen on the ninth or not?"

"Yes," he returned in a clipped tone. "Get what we need, Sera, so we can have this done. This is completely unorthodox and I'm worried about you."

"I'm a capable officer. Please treat me like one." She pinched the bridge of her nose. "I have to go."

"You have one more night, Sera. *One*. No exceptions. I'll wait for your call."

She hung up, emotions warring inside her, the most annoying of which was the unwanted warmth she got knowing her uncle was worried. He'd taken her father's place at such a young age, but had never shown her anything resembling fatherly concern. Right now, when fear was creeping in, she wanted to bask in it. *No time.*

A car pulled up at the curb, interrupting her thoughts. One glance at the occupants of the vehicle had her turning on a heel, heading back toward Marco's at a brisk clip. There were four men, none that she recognized. A single glance at them told her she needed to be inside before they exited the car. One of them tapped a baseball bat on the dashboard, his mouth stretching into a smile as he looked her over. A whisper of apprehension moved up her spine, intuition telling her they'd come to Marco's to start trouble and she was in the wrong place at the wrong time.

Before she could reach the entrance, two of them jumped out of the passenger side and lunged in front of her, blocking her progress. The first thing she noticed were their injuries. Swollen purple discoloration under one man's eye. Another's arm wrapped in a plaster cast. It set off warning bells. "Where you going so fast, cutie?"

"Excuse me." A third man circled up behind her, so she pressed her back to the wall. "Let me by."

The man holding the baseball bat ignored her. "You belong to one of the assholes inside? That's bad luck for you."

Crap. Just as she'd feared, they weren't from this neighborhood, which meant they'd likely come to retaliate for something. It came back to her then. Bowen's conversation with Wayne the day he came to the apartment. His subsequent disappearance while she waitressed at Rush. These men were here to issue payback, and now her impulsive butt was caught in the cross fire. She knew how to handle herself, but there were too many of them and they all had weapons. Silently, she begged someone, anyone, to walk out the door and interrupt.

"I don't belong to anyone." She shrank back on purpose, appealing to their overblown arrogance, while also making sure they underestimated her. If their goal was to get her into that car, she would fight them with every ounce of strength in her body. Having surprise on her side would come in handy. "Please, just let me go."

The man holding the bat laughed and ran the coarse wood up the inside of her leg. "Oh, you definitely belong to somebody. You think he'll miss you?"

Before the bat could reach the apex of her thighs, she smacked it away. Knowing the attempt might be useless, she tried to pass one more time. Purple Eye snaked a hand around her elbow and yanked her to a halt. "We were parked down the block and saw you walk in with Driscol. Get in the fucking car."

Someone inside the car pushed open the back door, letting

out a whoop. "Our turn to send the message, isn't it? Come on in, girl. I'll keep you warm for him."

Sera breathed deeply as they propelled her toward the car, putting up only a token resistance. As soon as they were under the false impression that she would be coming without a fight, the hand on her elbow loosened. That's when she acted.

She snatched the baseball bat out of the man's hands, swinging it in a large arc to give herself some room to evaluate. Two of them jumped back, having been caught off guard, but it connected with Purple Eye's rib cage. He let out a vile curse and went down on one knee, allowing Sera a few precious seconds to focus on the other two men. The man wearing a cast on his arm circled up behind her, actually laughing at her attempts to fight them off. Trying to keep an eye on both men, she backed up a little, waiting to see who would come at her first. Unfortunately, the more she backed up, the farther she got from Marco's, so she couldn't let herself get too far.

"He should have taken better care of this one. She's spirited."

"Yeah, too bad," the man in the cast spat. "Let's go, girl. Only a matter of time, anyway."

Laughter poured from inside the car, as if the occupant couldn't believe his friends' inability to subdue her. It visibly pissed them off. Purple Eye launched himself from the ground and barreled straight for her. She brought the bat down hard, but he dodged it and wrapped a meaty arm around her waist. Not wasting a second, she brought her foot down on his instep and threw her head back, connecting with his nose. The two other men converged on her, just as Purple Eye's arm fell away with a shout of pain.

"*Bitch.*"

The bat was ripped from her hands to clatter on the ground a few yards away. Saying another quick prayer that someone would come out of Marco's, she threw a punch at the closest man, satisfied when she felt the crunch under her fist. She didn't have much time to celebrate landing a decent blow, though. A hand wrapped around her throat from behind, squeezing tight enough to cut off her air. Reflexively, her fingers tried to pry the hand away, but she couldn't get a grip. Her vision began to flare in tiny spots as air ran scarce. She had to make a move. Now. After taking a second to judge where his body was positioned so she could inflict the most damage, Sera got ready to let her body go limp. When she caught him off guard, she'd spin and go for his testicles. Three…two…

Smash. The front door to Marco's flew open, hitting the side of the building with enough force to splinter the wood. Through her dimming eyesight, Sera made out several men's silhouettes, including Bowen's, before his ferocious, earsplitting shout of denial rent the air around her. It startled the man choking her enough that he eased up on the pressure, allowing her to suck precious oxygen into her lungs. She caught herself just before her knees met the concrete, but her relief quickly gave way to horror.

Guns were drawn in quick succession, from both crews. Bowen held one in his outstretched hand. Sera didn't know what was worse, the inevitable gunfire or Bowen's expression. She barely recognized him. Never in her life had she seen someone so capable of murder, his body drawn tight, pupils dilated. Everyone in the vicinity sensed it, too. Each and every eye trained on him, waiting for him to react.

No. Sera wanted to rail over the unfairness. She'd been trying to save his life and in the process, she'd put him in a situation where he could very well commit murder. In front of her, an undercover cop. *Don't let it happen.* "Bowen," she whispered, taking a hesitant step toward him.

His haunted gaze made her flinch. She could see the emo-
tional battle taking place on his face. Finger poised on the trigger, he clearly wanted to fire on the man who'd been holding
her. Without saying a word, he tore his attention away from her,
indicating her captor with a nod of his head. "He doesn't go
anywhere."

Sera shivered under the iciness of his order. As she watched,
the group of men behind Bowen converged on the car, keeping
their weapons trained on the intruders. Two of Bowen's guys
lowered their weapons in favor of wrestling her captor to the
ground. His friends watched helplessly, unable to lower their
weapons and help their friend or they would risk being shot.
Finally, one of them cursed and shoved his gun into the waistband of his jeans, the others quickly following suit. They piled
back into the car, leaving their friend behind as they peeled
away from the curb.

Bowen jerked his chin at two men in his crew. "Follow them.
This ends tonight."

As they jogged off to follow Bowen's dictate, he sauntered
forward. Almost as an afterthought, he picked the bat up off
the ground and went toward the man who'd been left behind.
Dozens of patrons had spilled from Marco's to witness the
action, and they all watched in rapt silence now as Bowen
tapped the bat against his palm. Every tap felt like a physical
blow to Sera, who wanted desperately to wrap her arms around
him and beg him to stop, but she couldn't move. This man, this
frozen, rage-filled version of Bowen...she didn't know him.

He came to a stop directly over the left-behind crew
member, twirling the bat in his hand. His gaze met hers for
a brief, heavy second before he raised the bat and brought it
down with enough force to make her gasp and jump back. Her
heart raced out of control, breath shallow in her ears. She was

terrified to watch, to see the death her decision had caused.

The bat connected with the sidewalk beside the man's head, sending shards of wood in every direction. Some members of the crowd reacted with relief, others with disappointment. The latter made her sick even as thankfulness swamped her. He hadn't done it.

Her stunning relief was short-lived. Bowen crouched down and looked the cowering man square in the eye. "*You*. Are a dead man." Slowly and purposefully, he rose to his feet and held out a hand to her, his attitude daring her not to take it. She swallowed the hard lump in her throat and slipped her fingers against his cool palm, resisting the urge to snatch her hand back when she heard his low growl. One second she had both feet planted on the ground, the next he'd swung her up into his arms to carry her toward his car. She mentally begged him to look her in the eye as he settled her into the passenger seat and shut the door. Through the closed window, she heard him shout to his men, his words falling like boulders on her chest.

"You know where to take him. I'll be there as soon as I can."

His order left no doubt as to what would happen when he got there. He planned to kill the man for what he'd done.

Sera vowed then and there she would do everything in her power to stop him.

CHAPTER SIXTEEN

Twice in his life, he'd been scared.

The first time, his father had pointed a gun at Ruby. He'd been on the floor with a freshly broken arm, too far away to get between his sister and the bullet. From his position, he'd watched resignation transform her features, features so similar to his. It had been such an obvious acceptance of her own death, he'd almost looked away so it wouldn't be etched on his memory, but somehow he'd forced himself to continue watching. Somehow it would mean she didn't die alone. *So unfair*, he remembered thinking. After the close calls and scrapes they'd been in, she wouldn't even get the chance to fight. All of it, all these individual catastrophes, took place within his mind in one second. The longest second of his life.

Until tonight.

He hated the feeling of fear. It slithered like a living thing through his veins, trying to shut him down. Out of self-preservation, he allowed the fear to close himself off to anything but burning, festering anger. He welcomed it. Let it become comfortable and focused on it. Anything that would block out the image of Sera being choked, feet dangling in the air, hands clawing at her neck. If he let himself dwell on it, he knew with 100 percent certainty his world would implode.

The anger had a few different shapes, the first of which was directed at himself. He shouldn't have left her alone, knowing she would take any opportunity to further her investigation. It had been a poor decision and he'd nearly paid for it the worst way possible. Losing—

No. Don't think about it. Stay focused.

Anger. Anger at *Sera*. If he let himself feel it, maybe he could battle this need to pull the car over and drag her into his lap. Rock her. Smell her hair. Tell her what a crazy, stupid, maddening, beautiful girl she was. Shout at her. Kiss her. Shake her. Demand she hold him until this block of ice inside him melted and he stopped feeling shaky.

He wouldn't let himself, though. It was vital he keep his rage, hold on to it like a precious gift. Whenever she touched him, he lost the grip on his darker self. The self that had finally made an appearance tonight, much to the delight of his crew of assholes. Even Wayne had been smugly satisfied to see him promising violence and retribution. While Bowen might regret giving the man what he wanted tomorrow, tonight he couldn't give a shit. This hot, pumping anger needed an outlet and it would be unleashed on the man who'd put his hands on Sera.

At the reminder of what he'd seen as he walked out of the restaurant, his grip tightened on the wheel, making the car swerve. In the seat beside him, Sera's hand flew to her throat. That's when he noticed the red marks. Just over her windpipe, five fingerprints that had to have been digging into her hard, for a good while, to leave those kinds of marks behind. He stared at them, letting them fuel his anger, ignoring the brown eyes trying to get his attention. If he looked into her eyes, knowing he'd almost lost the chance to ever do so again, he would lose

it. He would *fucking* lose it. After what felt like an hour-long
drive, but in reality had only been three minutes, he pulled up in
front of his building. He took a moment as he rounded the car
to scan the block for Connor's car, but didn't see him.

Dammit, there were too many threats. Too many ways she
could get hurt. As soon as he took care of business tonight, he
was calling this shit off. Either the cops came and got her the
hell out of Brooklyn tomorrow or he would get her out himself.
He didn't know how he would accomplish it when she would
fight him every step of the way, but it would be done. Pain
lanced his stomach at the realization he wouldn't see her again
once they took her. God, he wanted to keep her. Wanted to lock
them both in his apartment and never leave, except maybe for
church. Whatever it took to keep her happy. But he knew his
stupid fantasy would never come true. It couldn't, because of
who they were and the damn countdown clock hovering over
their heads. Trying to make it come true would be selfish and
could get her killed.

Making sure not to look directly at Sera, he helped her
from the passenger seat and hustled her toward the building.
They were inside his apartment in under a minute, safe inside
four walls, but he rejected the feeling of calm. If he narrowed
his concentration down into one neat funnel, he could get out
of there without touching her to reassure himself she was all
right. If he let that happen, he didn't know if he could stop.

Leaving her standing just inside the locked door, he flew
around the apartment checking and double-checking no one
had broken in. Her gaze stayed with him the entire time. It drew
him, tempted him to lose himself inside it, but he staunchly
refused. Once he'd checked every square inch of the apartment,
he took her arm and led her into his bedroom. He wanted to
watch her, gauge her reaction to his private space. Instead, he

went to his closet and crouched down, so he could punch in the combination to his safe.

"Do you know how to use a gun?" he asked, trying to keep the sarcasm out of his voice. Of course she did, but he wanted her to lie. He wanted to throw fuel onto his fire. Another deception from her would do the trick.

"Yes."

His hand froze in the action of removing his Glock from the safe, something warm and unwanted expanding in his chest. That single truthful word doused his desire for her to lie. *Tell me everything, baby. Please, no more hiding.* "Really. Care to tell me how?"

"Bowen, please. Will you just look at me?"

He could feel her standing behind him. "You will stay in this room, with the door locked, until I come back. Anyone tries to get in that isn't me, you shoot them, Sera. Tell me you understand. Tell me you'll *listen* this time."

When he stood to face her, she was entirely too close. Close enough to grab. To taste. His bed was only a few short steps away, covers still rumpled and unmade from this morning. The mural depicting death and destruction on the wall behind his bed outlined her body, hitting home just how much danger existed around her. His danger. His world.

Bowen kept his gaze glued firmly above her head, pretending fascination with some invisible spot that didn't exist. "I'm waiting for an answer." He heard her deep intake of breath. She moved closer and everything inside him seized. "*Don't.*" Don't what? He had no idea what he was asking her not to do, only knew it would break him.

Obviously deciding to ignore his request, she laid a hand on his chest, immediately making him shudder from head to toe. He closed his eyes defensively as her hand traced over his chest, up his neck and into his hair. Oh, God, he wanted to fall at her feet. Frantically, he searched in the darkness for his anger and gripped it like a lifeline.

When she laid her lips against his neck, that lifeline was ripped from his hands. "Please, don't leave me. Please stay." Unable to speak, he shook his head, but it only caused her lips to drag along the heated skin of his neck. A groan left him before he could stop it. The battle to remain detached growing weak with the sound of her voice. "I'm scared. Stay with me."

No. Oh, Jesus. She'd said the one thing that could topple the reinforced steel barrier he'd built. At that moment, the only thing that kept it standing was the chance she could be playing him. Was she really scared or did she just want him to stay? He made the mistake of finally looking into her addictive brown eyes and felt irreparable cracks forming in his wall. Fear. She *was* scared. With the acknowledgment of that came the need to protect. To erase the fear. He tried to hold it back, to remember what needed to be done tonight. Retribution. Payback. He needed to punish the men responsible for the fear.

Her lips brushed over his, once, twice. She disentangled the hand she'd twined in his hair, letting it coast down his body and linger at his belt buckle. His body felt ready to snap with the tension, the anticipation of something he didn't have the right to want.

"I have to *go*, Sera."

Her breath raced past her lips. "Where are you going?"

"You know where I'm going. Don't make me say it." *Fuck.* Her eyes were wet. It stripped him bare. The emotions he'd been holding at bay came rushing in from all sides and he fell back a step, reaching deep to find his determination and coming up empty. Frustration welled in its place, laced with the helplessness he'd felt earlier. "You have any idea what could have happened to you?" He was shouting but couldn't find the will to care. "What if I hadn't gotten to you in time? If I'd been one minute later, Sera. *One fucking minute*!"

"I know, I—"

"You would have been *gone*. I wouldn't have known where to look. By the time I found you—" He broke off, not able to put the horrifying images into words. "Goddammit, I'm so mad at you. I'm so *mad*, but all I can think about is how bad I need to fuck you sideways."

Admitting it out loud sent blood rushing to his groin. As if he'd made taking her inevitable just by vocalizing the suppressed need. It shouldn't happen, *couldn't* happen, not when he had this much chaos knocking around inside him looking for a way out. Her glazed-over expression, the parting of those damp, pink lips, did nothing to ease the growing ache, however. Nor did it help matters when she stepped closer, sexual intention plain in her every movement.

"The first night we met, you said you didn't fuck around with virgins."

He'd never heard her curse before and that tiny corruption shouldn't have turned him on, but it did. All the resisting he'd done since meeting her had caused a painful buildup of hot, surging desire and hearing the word "fuck" falling from her sexy mouth made him want to do just that. *No, you can't. Don't do it.* "I did say that, baby. And I meant it."

When she curled her fingers in the hem of her dress and drew it up over her head, revealing her sweet, supple body covered by two scraps of fabric, every ounce of self-control within him vanished. "Good, Bowen. Then let's stop fucking around."

Sera felt bold.

Bowen's gaze raked over her, lingering at the tops of her thighs, the place where they met between her legs. His chest rose and fell with accelerated breaths, hands fisting and releasing at his sides. Color appeared in his cheekbones, making him appear feverish. She almost had him. While this might have started as a desperate attempt to keep him from leaving and doing something he would regret, saving him from himself, it had turned into intense physical need. A need to be joined with him, connected in that final way. To reach where they'd been headed since the beginning.

Determination humming in her bloodstream, she unhooked her bra and dropped it to the floor. His mouth worked as he devoured the sight of her exposed breasts, teeth sinking into his lower lip with a raspy, masculine moan.

"Ah, God. You hot fucking girl." He gripped himself through his jeans. "You like seeing this? You like knowing I'm obsessed with something I can't have?"

She went closer, slipping her hands underneath his shirt and running her fingernails up his ridged abdomen. His muscles contracted beneath her fingers, making her feel powerful. This strikingly beautiful man miraculously couldn't resist her. Oh, Lord, she didn't want him to. The inevitability of what she was embarking on made every pulse point in her body hammer, concentrated mostly between her legs. "I only like knowing what I do to you because the other half isn't true." She lowered her hand to palm and squeeze his straining arousal through his jeans. "You can have me. Now."

His hand flew up to cover hers, as if he meant to remove her touch. Instead, he tightened her hold and helped her squeeze, his voice deepening on words that didn't make sense to anyone but her. "Good, ah, that's fucking good. Rub it up and down now. *Yes.* You make it like that, baby. You make it hurt so bad, don't you? I want to shove it right into your slicked-up pussy, Sera, but I can't. I *can't.*"

How could he still attempt to stop this when she felt so out of control? Her body trembled with the constant surges of heat stealing her sanity. To try to deny it seemed more criminal than any dark deeds in his past. To hell with the consequences of her actions. For once, she didn't care. She just needed *him.* He obviously needed her, too.

"Why can't you?" She went up on her toes and licked into his eager mouth for a kiss, distracting him while she unfastened his belt and unzipped his jeans. "Tell me."

Her hand found his erection and grasped it firmly, forcing a hungry growl past his lips. Almost angrily, he clasped her face in his hands, his radiating intensity stealing her breath. "Can't you see this is the last thing keeping me decent? I don't have a fucking shred of honor, except for this *one thing.* Leaving you untouched is all I've got left. All I can give you." He shook her gently. "Do better than me."

A sob wrenched free of her throat. Her chest verged on cracking wide open to toss out her sore heart. Part of her wished it would so she wouldn't feel the sharp, painful damage his words caused. She wouldn't let him go on feeling as if he were unworthy. This misconception wouldn't stand. That familiar need to *fix* roared to the surface, made so much stronger by her feelings for him. Feelings that were flooding her, finding their way to every corner and putting down roots.

She could feel his desire in her hand, hear it in every shuddering breath. It wouldn't take much to shake his control. Her hand began stroking him as she pushed up for another searing kiss. This time, though, she didn't end it. Her tongue wrestled with his, savoring every noise of suffering that came from him.

Triumph made her lightheaded when he took charge of the kiss. One hand sank into her hair as his mouth punished hers with rough, wet kisses. He dropped his other hand to her bottom, delving inside the cotton of her underwear to cup and knead. An incessant pulse beat between her thighs, dampness spreading, heating.

When he pulled away to draw air, she got a split-second glimpse of his frenzied expression before he dived back in, kissing her with enough force to knock her back a step. She kept the momentum going, relieved when he followed her progress toward the bed, never letting up on his assault of her mouth. Using what little functioning brainpower she had left, Sera shoved the jeans down his hips, excitement drumming through her when he stepped out of them.

She fell back onto the bed in time to watch him strip his shirt over his head. The action left his hair standing on end, creating such a mind-numbingly sexy effect, she had to press her legs together to ease the throb. Such a hefty amount of danger radiated from him, a Hail Mary involuntarily popped into her head before she shoved the prayer aside. No room for that here. Not with this gorgeous man staring down at her as if he were deciding exactly where to start.

She'd only just reached out for him when he fell on her with a harsh curse, wedging his hips between her thighs and finding her mouth again. "Same as last time, okay?" His Brooklyn accent had grown thicker. "I get to pretend I'm fucking your tight-as-hell pussy and you get to come inside those lily-white panties. Ready for it, baby?"

"*No.*" The word burst past her lips. If he started doing this his way, she would get lost. He needed to be inside her. The way she felt about him made anything less feel like a sham. Something unworthy of them. Bowen looked down at her, sweat dotting his forehead, as if he couldn't believe she'd put the brakes on, but when she reached down and started to peel off her panties, recognition dawned.

"Ah, please. Come on, sweetheart, don—" A savage shout erupted from his lips when the length of his erection slipped against her naked core. He shifted his hips as if he had no choice, working himself closer. "Jesus. Jesus Christ. You get so wet. All for me. Right, Sera? Say it."

"All for you." Sensing him about to give in, she found his ass with her hands and hauled him closer, the friction making them both cry out. "I'm all for you. Have me, Bowen."

His strong arms shook on either side of her, perspiration beading on his shoulders. "Please," he growled through clenched teeth. "I can't hold out. Need to fuck you so bad. So hard."

"Yes." She wrapped her legs around his waist, using all her strength to bring him close. "I want you to."

He pressed their damp foreheads together, warm breath fanning her face. "The idea of hurting you makes me crazy," he said in a harsh whisper. "I've got a little too much crazy in me already tonight. I don't think I could go easy. I know I can't."

"Bowen." Her fingers threaded themselves through his hair. "You're hurting me more by saying no."

The flare in his eyes told her he didn't like hearing that. Hated it, possibly. A beat passed where she could practically see the wheels spinning in his head. Then he kissed her hard once and reversed their positions. She went from flat on her back to straddling his waist, looking down at the most breathtakingly handsome, insanely complicated man she'd ever met. His cheekbones were high with color, slate-colored eyes blazing with lust.

"It has to be this way, Sera. Otherwise you'll end up with your ankles behind my neck, screaming while I pound you." His teeth sank into his bottom lip. "And that's just how it'll start. When I feel myself coming, I'd hold it back. I'd flip you onto your hands and knees and start all over." He ran his hands up her rib cage to grasp her breasts. "On second thought, maybe you'd like that. Catholic girls spend a lot of time kneeling already, don't they?"

Oh, wow. Why wasn't she taking offense? Why did his taunt only make her infinitely hotter? She planted both hands on his shoulders and slid up his thick erection, then worked her way back down with little writhing motions of her hips. His sharp curses and quick intakes of breath told her he liked it, so she did it again. "I think I like it this way, actually," she gasped.

He fisted her hair in his hands, dragged her down to his chest to ravage her mouth. "Tell me again that it hurts when I don't fuck you. Make it okay for me, Sera."

"It hurts." She rubbed her breasts against his muscular upper body. "It *hurts.*"

Bowen inched them up the bed and grabbed hold of the wrought iron headboard with both hands. "I'm going to stay still as long as I can to let you get used to me. But…ah, baby, I'll be going crazy for you to ride it hard. Try to move as much as you can, okay?" His hands flexed and tightened in a white-knuckle hold. "There's no going back after this. Are you sure?"

"Yes. I want this, Bowen. You."

His eyes burned. "I can't go back, either, Sera. Not once I have you."

She dragged her fingertips down his naked body. Watching for his reaction, she took his hardness in her hands and guided him between her legs, moaning at the slippery contact.

"Wait." Looking as though he were in severe pain, he jerked his chin toward the bedside table. "Condom. In the drawer. *God,* please hurry."

Silently berating herself for not even sparing a thought for protection, she leaned over Bowen and opened the drawer, impatient to get back to touching him. As she drew out a foil packet, his tongue swirled enticingly over her nipple before sucking it hard into his mouth. He drew so deeply on her, she cried out and nearly collapsed. Her hands flew to the headboard for balance, sensation rocketing through her body. Between her thighs, she could feel him pressing at her entrance, thick and huge.

"Give it." He snatched the condom out of her hand, ripping it open with his teeth. His gaze burned into hers as he rolled it on in one smooth motion. "Let's get me inside you before I fucking die. How does that sound?"

She nodded shakily. "Good."

Bowen's hands went back to their death grip on the headboard and she took him in her hand once more. His jaw went slack as she squeezed him once, twice. "Rub me against your clit, baby. I own that spot, don't I? Use me to touch it."

Her thighs shook as she followed his instructions, shallow breaths echoing in her ears. It only took a matter of seconds for the emptiness to take up residence in her belly. That need to be filled she'd always experienced with him. "I can't…I want—"

"I know what you want. Take it."

Need him as close as possible. Need all of him. Not giving herself a second longer to psyche herself out, she pushed the head past her entrance and sank down with one hard push. A shockwave of pain reverberated through her, making her cry out.

"*FUCK.*" Bowen threw his head back on the pillow, neck and arm muscles straining. He slammed the headboard against the wall with his hands, nostrils flaring as he sucked in several deep breaths. "*Christ*, Sera," he grated. "Are you trying to kill me?"

"Hmm." She tried to answer his question, but her sole focus was the gradual lessening of pain. The worst was beginning to dull, leaving behind only the pressure of him inside her, the need to test the feeling. Slowly, she circled her hips, gasping when her clitoris grazed the base of his erection. Pleasure sizzled across her nerve endings. "Oh, G-God. I think I can move now."

"Good girl." A low, primal groan broke from his lips. "Find where it feels good and I'll find a way to make it better for you. You trust me?"

"*Yes.*" When she leaned forward and braced her hands on either side of his head, more of the discomfort fled. Her lips hovered just above Bowen's as she rocked her hips up and back, grinding down where their bodies joined. In the beginning it felt good...then it started to feel *great*. The pressure stopped feeling like a hindrance to her movements as she worked her sensitive flesh against his, finding the perfect angle. Beneath her, Bowen watched her under heavy eyelids, his body flexing with the effort to keep his hold on the headboard. He looked ready to shatter and for some inexplicable reason, that turned her on even more. She wanted to shatter him. Wanted them to shatter together. She planted her hands on his chest and increased her pace, bucking her hips one minute and circling slowly the next.

"Fuck. I have to touch you." One hand left the headboard to grab hold of her bottom, goading her into moving faster. With the other, he reached between their writhing bodies to stroke her clitoris with his thumb. She cried out as a tightening in her abdomen started, working its way lower, encompassing her thighs and the suddenly needy place between them. "Don't stop, Sera. Give it up to me. Give it *up*."

Instinct took over, making it her mission to find out where this ache ended. It was unlike anything she'd ever felt, stronger than any pleasure she'd found on her own. She was suspended over the edge of release, but felt suddenly unsure about taking the leap. This would change something inside her. She could feel that with perfect certainty, yet she couldn't deny it, either. Her confusion escaped in the form of a whimper.

Bowen jackknifed into a sitting position, as if propelled by her chaotic thoughts. His mouth found hers for a hard kiss, the rough hand on her backside forcing her to slow down. "Hey, you look at me. I don't know where you went, but get the hell back here. *Now.* You don't get to drive me out of my mind, then disappear. I'll drag you back kicking and screaming."

Having his warmth pressed against her, his mouth so close, sent reassurance pouring over her, bringing with it a renewed heat. Even the course, blunt way he spoke to her boosted her confidence and once again, she started to roll her hips, desperate to find the edge again. His answering groan sizzled through her bloodstream.

"I'm driving you out of your mind?" she whispered.

"You like hearing that, don't you?" He bit her bottom lip and tugged. "Does it make you hot to know how fucked up I am over you? Over this pussy?"

Her hips pumped faster, of their own accord. "Yes."

Bowen wrapped her hair in his fist and tugged her close, so he could speak against her ear, hot breath sending a shiver down her neck. "You don't fuck like no virgin, Sera. You don't get on your knees like one, either." He leaned back slightly, thrusting up into her at a new angle that made her head spin. His expression was pure lust, the filthy kind that she didn't realize she'd been craving. "If you weren't choking the hell out of my cock, I wouldn't believe it. You a natural, baby? A tight little natural?"

She moaned loudly and let her head fall back. The need for relief came charging back, her mind going blank except for

Bowen and the promise that he could provide it. She arched her back and widened her thighs, riding up and down on his slick, rigid length. One calloused hand palmed her breasts, squeezing, before his greedy mouth found her nipples. He growled as he licked and sucked, sending the final dart of pleasure through her she needed to climax. It felt like drowning and being rescued at the same time. Not being able to breathe, but somehow her lungs had never been so full. Bowen's hands on her backside urged her to ride it out fast and hard, as he drove himself up high and deep with forceful thrusts, making her scream.

Bowen crushed her to his chest, barking a curse as he came apart beneath her. His teeth raked down her neck, his powerful body shaking in time with hers. "God, Sera…baby, it's so good. So fucking perfect. Mine now. My girl."

She wrapped her arms around his neck and held him tight, still attempting to catch her breath. "Yes, your girl."

He rocked them for a while, a move she wouldn't have expected from Bowen, but somehow felt completely necessary. She couldn't fathom ever leaving that position, his warmth, the smoky masculine scent he carried with him. The reality of their situation tried to intrude, but she pushed it away in favor of savoring the moment, their bodies molded together.

It was hard to say when reality started creeping back in. Perhaps with the tightening of Bowen's shoulders, his prolonged silence. The way he went still, stiller than she'd ever seen him. Panic invaded her, horror that she'd seen this for something it wasn't. Minutes ticked by as she tried to summon the courage to move, to face whatever change had come over him. Dreading what she would find on his face, she slowly lifted her head and found his icy stare back in place, the one he'd worn after the scene outside Marco's.

"Bowen?"

He nodded once, but didn't meet her eyes. "Remember what I said. You stay in this room with the door locked. Anyone tries to come in, you shoot them. Tell me you understand, Sera."

She flinched over the detachment in his voice. "You're leaving now? After…"

Finally, he looked at her. What she saw caused the blood to drain from her face. Pure, lethal determination. "Did you think if we slept together, it would make me *less* eager to kill for you?" He leaned in and captured her mouth for a thorough, possessive kiss. One that brought back the throbbing between her legs. "If that was your goal, it backfired. I've had you now. Made you mine. The one who tried to take you away from me is going to pay."

CHAPTER SEVENTEEN

Sera.

S Bowen woke up with a head filled with sand.

His body ached for reasons he couldn't remember and the hardwood floor he lay sprawled on wasn't helping matters. Sunshine blinded him, sending splitting pain through his skull. As soon as the light vanished, his memory returned with the force of a tsunami, rushing in like moving cement. He shot up into a sitting position and immediately regretted the action as his stomach pitched. His hands rose to clutch his head and he saw the blood. So much blood.

No. Not blood. Paint.

He'd come home and found Sera asleep in the guest bed, looking so beautiful he could have stood there staring at her for the rest of his life. Watching her chest rise and fall underneath her halo, where she belonged. He had no idea how long he stood there before returning to his room to paint. And drink. God yes, he'd drank. Enough so he wouldn't have to think about what he'd done. Her face when she realized he was leaving her, abandoning her after what she'd given him.

Now that he was thinking semi-clearly, his head free of blinding vengeance, he recognized his massive mistake. He'd proven himself unworthy of her. Something he'd already known with absolute certainty, but she'd seemed willing to ignore. There would be no ignoring it now. She'd given him the best night of his life and he'd squandered it by letting his inner demons get the better of him.

How he'd managed to pull himself away from her, he still didn't quite understand. Hell, he couldn't *remember*. After she'd wrecked him for any other experience life had to offer, his protective nature had swelled inside him, cutting everything else off. In his arms, he'd been holding the most precious thing in the universe and instead of enjoying it, instead of holding her through the night as he should have done, he'd only been capable of picturing that man's hands around her throat. He'd thought about what they would have done to her, how they would have hurt her, and his mind had gone berserk.

God, he'd give anything to go back in time and sleep beside her. To tuck her against him and keep her warm, make her feel safe. What if he never got that chance again? He *shouldn't* get that chance. If she gave it to him, he'd probably attempt to talk her out of it, then beg for the opportunity anyway. Jesus Christ. What a pathetic fuck he was turning out to be. After drinking himself into oblivion, he'd stumbled out of his room and parked himself in front of her bedroom door like a guard dog, which is where he still lay. He needed to clean himself up before she came out, maybe put on some coffee. She liked coffee. Maybe that would at least get her talking to him.

But…what then? Hadn't he decided last night he would call Troy and demand they come get her, whether she'd secured the ledger or not? There were too many threats around her, including himself, as was proven last night. As long as she stuck around, his enemies were her enemies. He'd made it obvious to anyone with a pair of eyes she was important to him, and someone would eventually get the balls to use her against him again.

A new pounding took up residence in his temples at the idea. Right now, she was safely tucked in bed, right where he wanted her, *needed* her, to be. She was scheduled to work tonight at Rush, but there had to be a way to keep her away from the place. Just one more day. Please God, he just wanted one more day with her.

His hand went to the guest room doorknob without any conscious thought. The sudden need to see her sleeping peacefully, unharmed, wouldn't leave him. As quietly as possible, he turned the knob and pushed open the door.

Gone.

Bowen's knees buckled under him. He grabbed the doorframe for balance as denial went off like firecrackers in his already-pounding head. The bed was unmade; her clothes were still there. She hadn't planned on leaving for good. Had someone come in and taken her while he lay passed out on the floor, unable to intervene? *No, please. No.*

Calm down. She could still be here. He stomped toward the bathroom and nearly ripped the door off the hinges to get a look inside. Lights off. Empty. He spun in a circle, searching through the apartment, seeing no sign of her.

Commanding himself to focus, he dialed Troy's Manhattan cell phone number. He answered on the first ring, the sounds of the precinct behind him. "What is it?"

"*Did you take her?*" he shouted. "*Did you take her from me?*"

A long pause on the other end had Bowen pulling his hair out. Finally, Troy spoke. "Calm down and explain yourself. Sera's *gone?*"

Red danced in front of his eyes. "Don't play dumb with me, you asshole. Where the hell is she? No cops. I told you no cops…

that it had to be on my terms." He couldn't swallow, couldn't get a decent breath. "She wouldn't just leave. I told her. I told her there was no going back."

"You're not making any sense, man." Troy blew out a breath. "Look, I have no reason to lie. We've heard nothing from her."

Bowen barely registered Troy's assurances over the buzzing in his brain. She hadn't called in. She wasn't here. He hadn't kept her safe. Failed. Oh, God, he'd failed her.

"*Mr. Driscol.*"

Not Troy's voice. Someone else's. Newsom? Based on the impatience in his tone, he'd been trying to get his attention for a while. Bowen almost felt too numb to respond. "What."

"I have an idea where she might have gone."

Sera stared blankly across the empty field, watching a plastic Ziploc bag float around in the wind. She pulled up the hood of her sweatshirt and drew her knees up to her chest, ignoring the creaking of the ancient bench beneath her. She'd come here before, but there had always been families, teenagers playing soccer, senior citizens walking in groups.

That hum of activity had made the park where Colin had been shot seem less desolate, more redeemable. Possibly because of the slight chill in the air, the only thing inhabiting the field today was garbage. A forgotten sweatshirt. A cracked Frisbee. It made the park, the last place where her brother had drawn breath, unbearable.

Black spots winked inside her vision, a product of her lack of sleep. Bowen had left. Just…left. She had no recollection of how long she'd sat on his bed feeling raw and exposed, convinced he would come back and hold her, before dragging herself to the guest room. No. He'd chosen retaliation. The pipe dream that she could save him had cracked and flooded her insides. Eventually, the flood turned to a block of ice so thick she wasn't sure it would ever thaw.

Around three in the morning, Bowen had crashed into the apartment. She'd heard him come into her room but pretended to be asleep, terrified to see the evidence of what he'd done in her name. Hours later, she'd heard him through the door, mumbling her name, saying it like a curse, a prayer, accompanied by the disctinct sound of a glass bottle clinking on the floor. The healer inside her had still wanted to go to him. Hold him. By morning, though, she'd managed to steel herself against the urge, stepping over him and his empty liquor bottle in the darkness, and leaving before she broke down and indulged the impulse.

No longer.

Her brother would have been twenty-nine today, and what gift had she given him? She'd allowed herself to get swept up in a man and forgotten about his justice. The future he'd been denied. Selfish. She'd been selfish. Worse, she'd been wrong about the man who caused the lapse. After last night, even thinking his name hurt. She'd let him distract her from the needs of her family, she'd trusted him, given him a part of herself, and he'd disappointed her. Honestly, she deserved it. She deserved to feel as though her chest had been chiseled into and ripped wide open. Her uncle hadn't trusted her to do this job, to avenge Colin, and she'd proven him right.

Not anymore. She would do whatever it took to make up for her lapse in judgment. With so many eyes on her, it would be risky, but no other options existed. She would *not* be the failure her uncle expected her to be. Her brother's death would not be in vain, no matter what mistakes he'd made or payouts he'd taken. She had to believe if he were still alive, he would have corrected his mistakes. Now she had to do it for him.

Tonight's waitressing shift at Rush would be her final chance, and she wouldn't waste it.

Right now, she needed to go back to...Bowen's, much as it would kill her to be around him when her feelings still existed. They *more* than existed, they crowded her insides, making it hard to breath. She thought she'd known him, swore a different man lived beneath the violent facade, but he'd proved her wrong. No longer could she trust him or let herself be sucked in by the magnetic pull in his direction.

Sera dropped her feet to the ground and stood, but something kept her from leaving. Before she knew her own intention, she began walking through the park, picking up trash. She tossed an empty juice box, a candy bar wrapper, and two paper plates into the garbage can, then went back for more. A little bit of pressure that had been building in her head since last night eased, the routine giving her purpose, comforting her. Her brother's grave had been too far, considering she only had public transport at her disposal, so instead of leaving flowers, she could do this instead. She could make this place a little less miserable.

Every few minutes, Sera scanned the surrounding area. She was a good distance away from Bensonhurst and she still carried the gun Bowen had given her, but that didn't mean someone hadn't spotted her. After the way Connor had ignored her as he drove past last night, she knew he didn't trust her. Another person she'd had a positive gut feeling about that turned out to be wrong. It called her decision-making ability into question. A tiny voice in her head whispered *your uncle is right.* She quickly buried the recurring thought when a car roared into the parking lot behind her, sending her heart into her throat.

Very slightly, she turned, careful to keep her face hidden underneath the hood. The aluminum can she held in her hand dropped to the ground when she saw Bowen coming toward her. Warning bells went off. Not only because of the wild look in his eye, but the fact that he was there in the first place. She hadn't told him anything about Colin. At least, nothing that would lead him here. Unless...

Unless he'd already known her brother had been killed here.

Sera's stomach bottomed out, possibilities whipping through her head. Flashing images of their exchanges came back to her with disorienting speed, refusing to make sense. How had he known to come here? To this *exact* park on this *exact* day? Her brother had died here and he'd known to come. Which meant... he knew about Colin. *Her.* He knew *her* identity.

Sera held back a sob. How long had he known and kept it from her? Furthermore, did his knowledge of this place mean he'd been here before?

Oh, God, had he been involved in her brother's death?

With that final sickening possibility coating her brain like molasses, Sera started to run. *Think, think.* She couldn't pull out her gun in broad daylight, not this close to the street, but she wanted to. Wanted to point it at him and demand the truth of what had happened. She let out a frustrated noise when she realized that even with all the doubt, all the questions circling him, the idea of pointing a gun at him felt abhorrently wrong.

"*Sera.*" Bowen gave chase behind her. "Don't you run from me."

Ignoring him, she sprinted from the park to the sidewalk across the street. This neighborhood had been thriving at one time, but construction developments had halted only halfway finished thanks to the weak economy. She ducked inside one of those empty concrete structures, jumping over stray cinder blocks, abandoned tools, and overgrown weeds. Not far behind, she could hear his feet hitting the pavement, his constant calling of her name. As soon as she was out of view of the street, she drew her gun and waited for him to enter the building.

Seconds behind her, he entered the near-darkness and came to an abrupt halt. His gaze landed on the gun and then rose to meet hers. She refused to acknowledge the pain she saw there. "Ladybug, put the gun down."

"No. You put *yours* on the ground."

Without hesitating, he put one hand up, slowly reaching behind him with the other to remove the gun at the small of his back. He laid it down on the ground and kicked it away, never removing his steady attention from her. "Now put yours down so we can talk."

"How did you know where to find me?" she asked, horrified to hear her teeth chattering.

His hesitation hit her like a physical blow. For the first time since meeting him, she felt as though she didn't know him at all. He was everything his police file proclaimed him to be.

"*Answer me*," she shouted, the gun blurring in front of her. "How did you know? Were you here that night...did you—"

"*Jesus*." His voice packed a raw punch. "Do it. Pull the trigger right now. It'll be better than hearing the rest of what you were going to say."

Sera shook her head. "Stop. Just stop."

"Stop *what*?"

"Saying things like that to me. Pretending I mean something to you, when you've been lying to me since the beginning." Her extended arm started to shake. "Haven't you?"

"No more than you've been lying to me, Seraphina," he returned, gravely.

Everything inside her seized at the use of her full name. Confirmation of what she'd already suspected, that he'd known her identity since the beginning. Had he just been humoring her, so secure in his own criminal immortality that he hadn't found her a threat? The idea hurt worse than she could have imagined. She thought back to last night, how he'd waited to exact revenge, instead of doing it in front of her, so she'd have no way to prove his guilt. He'd known.

"You still haven't answered me," she said, her voice barely above a whisper. She needed this final nail in his coffin, so she could maybe one day put him behind her. "How did you find me?"

His jaw flexed. "Commissioner Newsom told me where you were."

Her arm went limp, the gun dropping to her side. Every available breath in her body fled, driven away by confusion. "What?" she wheezed.

He took a step toward her, cursing when she backed up. "It's complicated, Sera, and I can't think straight enough to explain when you're looking at me like I'm a monster."

"Aren't you?"

Pain blanketed his features. "Only half of me. The half I never wanted you to see."

"Stop talking in code and explain yourself," she demanded. The implications of his words were refusing to register. Bowen and her uncle. Her uncle and Bowen.

Bowen dragged agitated hands through his hair, drawing her attention to the kaleidoscope of colors coating his fingers and knuckles. Had he been *painting* inside his bedroom last night? Such an absurd thing to be curious over when her world was crumbling around her, but for some reason it seemed important.

"Ruby's boyfriend, Troy," he said. "He's a detective. When you went solo and dropped out of sight, they pulled him in. The police don't like his connection to me, but they live with it. Especially this time, when they needed to use it. Use me."

He paused for a moment, no idea he'd just broken something inside her. Her uncle had known her plans this whole time? Why had he pretended otherwise? Humoring her. He'd been humoring her, all the while keeping tabs on his incapable niece.

"They asked me to keep you safe. To help get you out."

Undiluted exhaustion swamped her. No confidence. Not one person in this world believed in her. "And you just agreed? What did they offer you?"

He laughed without humor. "They offered to make my life hell if I didn't play along. My sister's life." With renewed determination, he prowled toward her. "I didn't want to do it until I saw your picture. But I would have walked through fire after I did." His eyes searched her face as if committing it to memory. "Before I even met you, I'd started falling for you, Sera. Believe me or don't believe me. I'm not sure if it matters anymore. Not if you think I'm a monster." He took a deep breath. "But I need you to know that I'm fucked for life over you."

No, she wouldn't let those words penetrate the hard shell she'd begun to form. "So you didn't do it to get the cops off your back. You did it to get *me* onto *mine*."

Her words broke his stride, made him flinch. "Don't you talk about us like that."

"What *us*?" Her temper sizzled. She'd been played, not just by Bowen, but her uncle, the police department. She must be a laughingstock if they'd sent in a known felon to rescue her. This entire time, she'd been playing a part and Bowen had known the truth. What kind of fantasy world had she been living in?

The kind of world where the police commissioner's niece goes on dates with the leader of a racketeering operation. So *stupid.* "There was never an *us*. I was undercover and they made sure you were convenient." She applied the gun's safety and let it drop to her side. "Does the commissioner know he sent in a murderer to save me?"

CHAPTER EIGHTEEN

Sera stared out the passenger side window of Bowen's car as they drove back to Bensonhurst, marveling at how completely she'd been flipped on her head since yesterday. She'd sat in this exact spot, still warm from the beach. Sleepily satisfied from Bowen's touch and wondering what they'd have for dinner.

Beside her, Bowen steered the car through narrow Brooklyn streets, his face inscrutable. Thankfully, he hadn't spoken a word since they'd revealed themselves at the construction site. She didn't want him to open his mouth and drop more words on her head. Words that perpetuated even more doubt where too much already existed. She didn't want to know how he felt about her. She didn't want to hope he'd meant what he'd said. That kind of thinking had already been proved useless by their mutual lies. Perhaps he didn't have an inkling of her insecurities where her uncle was concerned, but he'd still been a part of the deceit. He'd let her carry on like a wayward child with a babysitter. In her mind, that in itself was unforgivable. Nothing he could say would negate those deceptions or change who they were, so his silence, *both* of their silences, was for the best. She just needed to make her shift at Rush *count* tonight and this would be over.

Any longer and her uncle would swoop in and shut her down.

In the console between their seats, Bowen's cell phone vibrated and danced in the cupholder. As if on autopilot, he picked the phone up and held it to his ear.

"Yeah, Wayne." He listened for a moment. "Fine, I'll get it done." Another lengthy pause. "Well, it shouldn't surprise you that I'm handling business. The guy knew what would happen if he didn't pay." They pulled to a stop at a red light. "No, I'll do it on my own. Yeah, I'm sure."

Trying not to let her alarm show at the deadness in his voice or what he'd said, Sera waited for him to explain, but he stayed silent. "Where are we going?"

"Quick stop." His lips barely moved. "Won't take long."

The uncomfortable feeling in her chest increased as they pulled up in front of a run-down white house. A dirty FOR SALE sign hung at an angle in the yard and one of the steps leading to the porch had completely caved in. She didn't know what kind of business Bowen planned on handling, but he didn't seem in good shape for much of anything at the moment. It shouldn't concern her, not after what she'd just found out, but it did. A lot. She hated the idea of him walking into a potentially dangerous situation, especially alone, in a frame of mind she couldn't read.

Up until this point, he'd at least made a token effort to hide his illegal activities from her. The fact that he seemed to have given up on that score…frankly, it scared her.

"Don't go in there."

He gave no sign that he'd heard her. "Stay in the car. Don't get out for any reason."

"*Please.*"

Without so much as a glance in her direction, he climbed out of the car and slammed the door. He moved with graceful purpose toward the house, rapping quickly on the door twice.

Sera held her breath, her heartbeat echoing in her ears. Everything inside her screamed at her to stop him, but she also felt glued to the seat, as if watching a horrible accident in progress. A minute passed before the door opened a crack. She barely glimpsed the man's pale, panicked face before Bowen wedged his foot inside the crack and muscled his way into the house, locking a hand around the man's throat as he went.

No. The house's front door thumped shut with a hollow noise and the only audible sound was her shaky inhales. Was this some kind of challenge? *Go ahead and try to stop me, cop.* Sera didn't think so. His move seemed desperate, born of the frustration she'd caused.

She flashed back to the previous night, when he'd held her in his arms like a treasured possession. *I'm fucked for life,* he'd said back at the construction site. A hard lump formed in her throat at the memory of his face, the torture written all over it. No, this reckless behavior was something else. Something that both of them could later regret. Bowen, because he wasn't thinking clearly, and her, for once again sitting back and watching the action take place around her. She needed to *do* something.

Decision made, she double-checked the weapon tucked into the deep pocket of her coat and left the car, careful to close the door gently behind her. Midmorning on a weekday, the street stood empty, the blue-collar residents long since having left for work. She moved swiftly on the cracked cement surrounding the house, locating a window that would allow her a glimpse inside. Using an overturned bucket for extra height, she boosted herself up and peered through the filthy window. What she saw nearly made her body shut down.

Bowen stood in front of the man who'd answered the door, face covered in blood. He swayed a little on his feet, eyes glassy and unfocused. The man stood with hands fisted at his sides, still looking terrified. It made no sense when he was clearly the one inflicting injury. He shook his head and tried to step back from Bowen, but Bowen only followed. Then his mouth moved and Sera read the four words on his lips with dawning horror.

Hit me again. More.

He wanted to be hit. Wanted the pain. Tears blurred her vision as she scrambled off the bucket. Responsibility for his pain bogged her down as she sprinted for the door. If she wasn't responsible, at the very least, her uncle owned the burden. But no, this was *her*. She'd done this.

When she reached the door and heard a sickening thud on the other side, she wasted no time throwing open the unlocked door, letting it slam against the inside wall. Her hand itched to draw her weapon, but the white-faced man wasn't armed. To her shock, she still wanted to retaliate against the man who continued to pummel Bowen with his fists, even knowing Bowen was asking him for it.

"Get away from him." The man appeared slightly dazed as his attention flew to her, but he didn't move to follow her order. "I said, get the fuck away from him!"

Bowen weaved on his feet as the man jumped back. "Get back in the car, Ladybug."

The use of her nickname, slurred and flat, sliced like a knife through her heart. Swallowing the fear of seeing his bloodied face up close, she closed the distance between them and slipped her hand around his elbow. "Come on. I'm not getting back in the car without you."

"Not done here."

"Yes, you are." She pulled him around to face her, wincing at the cut under his eye pouring blood. His lips were lacerated in two spots. The eye that had already been blackened when she met him was now swollen shut. Tears clogged her throat.

"Dammit, Bowen. Dammit."

"I hate it when you curse…you're too good. My girl is too good." He cupped her cheek and swayed toward her. "But you're not my girl, are you? I dreamed it?"

She felt on the verge of collapse, under his weight, his words, but she needed to focus on getting him out of there. "No, you didn't dream it. Let's go home."

"Home. I like you saying that." He pierced her with his one good eye. "I didn't do it. Last night…that guy who tried to take you away from me. I couldn't do it."

Sera should have felt surprise. Or relief. Remembering the state he'd been in leaving the apartment last night, it didn't seem possible he'd left the man alive. Yet she believed him wholeheartedly.

"Why didn't you do it?" she whispered, aware of the other man still standing close by.

"I don't know." His throat muscles worked. "I wanted you to be proud of me or something."

She scrubbed a hand over her hollow-feeling chest. "I am. I'm proud of you."

Finally, he let her lead him toward the door. Before they walked out, he turned to the man who'd been pounding him with fists only minutes ago. "The debt is squashed."

The man deflated. "Thanks, man."

Bowen shook his head. "No more. Lose your money somewhere else. I don't want it."

'm proud of you.

Bowen focused on those words, let them mingle with the pain in his jaw, his head. No one had ever said that to him. He never realized it until he heard them. He'd done something right. It wouldn't make a difference now, but at least she didn't think he was a total monster. Part of him wished he were still standing in that house, fists connecting with his face. He'd craved that pain, found it beautiful as long as it distracted him from the image of her running away from him. Pointing a gun at him and calling him a murderer. Hating him.

He'd only meant to let the guy get one good shot at him, but it felt so damn good to feel something other than loss. *There is no us.*

She would leave as soon as this investigation wrapped, leaving him with the knowledge of her and no way to achieve the contentment she provided ever again. In his mind, she might as well have already walked out the door. It made him feel sick and raw and frantic. Made him want to beg her to turn the car around so he could seek out more of the reality-blurring pain.

Sera took a left, steering the car toward his block. "Why didn't you tell me you were working with the police?"

Her question dragged him back from his helpless rage, but didn't detract from it. Too much of it existed. He could feel it gathering, expanding, multiplying inside him. *She's leaving. She's as good as gone.* "Why would I do that, huh? So you'd know you're safe with one of the good guys?" He pulled at his hair, bitterness lacing his tone. "I'm not a good guy. I might not be the guy who killed your brother, but I'm closer to their kind than I am to yours."

When she flinched beside him, he wanted to throw himself out of the moving vehicle, but managed to remain in his seat. After a heavy silence, she spoke quietly. "Is that the only reason? This could have been much easier if I'd known you were on my side."

No way would Bowen tell her what his other orders had

been. Remove the ledger from her possession, take it to the commissioner. He couldn't do it, anyway. Couldn't take away her chance to prove herself. More importantly, the ledger was her ticket out. The ticket he'd never been given, but always wanted. She'd be gone from him, but at least she'd be safe.

He breathed through the agony of knowing he'd be without her soon. When she saw his name among the other criminals in Hogan's ledger book, she'd be thankful. "Keeping it to myself wasn't a suggestion, it was an order. They threatened me if I did otherwise. Didn't think you would appreciate the help and would do something rash." He stared at her until she gave him her attention. "You won't be, by the way. Doing something rash."

"You don't get to tell me what to do. If you'd been honest in the beginning, things might have been different." She drifted to a stop outside his building and put the car in park. "It's up to me to fail or succeed. Not you."

Frustration burned in his gut. At Sera, for not realizing the kind of danger that surrounded her. At himself, for hearing the truth in her words and wishing he'd come clean on day one. She'd deserved that much from him. "Fail or succeed," he scoffed. "You realize what failure means? They're not going to let you waltz out of Brooklyn. Not after how close you were. Not after what—" He cut himself off, remembering she knew none of this. Knowing it would drive an even bigger wedge between them.

"After what?"

His jaw flexed. "You overheard something important. A date." He watched the wheels turning behind her eyes, waited to see if she would pretend ignorance and prove she still didn't trust him.

She tugged the keys out of the ignition and handed them over. "I don't remember hearing anything about a date. Who told you I did?"

Based on her expression, she already knew, but wanted to hear him say it. "Connor. You're marked, Sera. Hogan doesn't like loose ends."

"Connor." A touch of hurt flashed over her features. "I wonder why he didn't just take care of me last night and be done with it."

Bowen went still. "Last night?"

She glanced at him warily. "He was outside Marco's, right before...it happened."

Two threats against her. Not one. He'd been inside with Wayne, discussing the offer of protection for a new neighborhood business, while she'd been outside exposed to two chances of death. His fists shook in his lap with the need to break something. Not trusting himself to speak, he climbed out of the car. As he walked to her side, he scanned the street for anything unusual before helping her stiff form from the driver's side. He thought he saw regret in her brown eyes as they looked over his battered face, then decided he'd imagined it.

A minute later, they were locked safely inside his apartment. He watched her from the kitchen as she paced, looking as though she were at a loss how to behave with him now that her identity was out in the open. Finally, she removed her sweatshirt and went into the guest bedroom.

He followed her, terrified he would round the corner to find her packing. Instead, he found her lying on the bed, staring up at the scales of justice. His body ached with the urge to crawl on top of her, kiss her body all over until she had no choice but to respond. "So what's the call, Sera? Let me help you or shut me out? I'm not going anywhere, so I'd suggest option two."

Just when he gave up on getting an answer, her voice broke the deafening silence. "When I was seven years old, about a year before my father died, my brother got to do a ride-along with him. He was ten at the time." She cleared the rust from her throat. "That morning, I begged to come along. I cried and pleaded until he finally gave in. I can still remember being so excited, so stunned he actually agreed." Slowly, she sat up, clasped her hands between her knees. "Then he left me with the dispatchers. All day. While my brother did the ride-along. They braided my hair."

His heart clenched thinking of her at seven. Left behind. While his childhood had been the exact opposite, he still understood the feeling of not belonging. "I'm sorry, Ladybug."

"Are you? I feel the same way right now as I did back then." She laughed under her breath. "When he came back, I told him I wanted to be a cop. That I would be the *best* cop. He told me he liked my braid."

How can I not touch her when she looks so sad? This is killing me. Everything hurts. "I wish I wasn't a part of making you feel this way. You have no idea how bad I wish for that. But I can't pretend I don't understand that need to protect you."

"Help me understand." Her gaze pleaded with him. "Do I come across so helpless?"

"Not helpless, baby." The right words eluded him, so he just told the truth. "I don't know how to explain it. I want to walk beside you everywhere and absorb anything bad, so it won't touch you. Won't change you, make you like me."

He saw moisture in her eyes and wondered if he would ever stop putting it there. When she stood and came toward him, he held his breath, praying she would touch him. Just before their bodies met, she stopped, taking in the injuries to his face. "This isn't the first time you've done this to yourself, is it?" She reached up to test his eye, but he leaned into her palm instead. "You told me you never lose a fight, so I wondered why you were always banged up. Tell me why you do this."

Bowen swallowed heavily, afraid if he moved, her touch would go away. "I don't know. I do it so I don't feel numb like the rest of them. I do it to feel. I do it *not* to feel. Take your pick."

She couldn't hide her distress. "There are other ways to feel, Bowen."

"Yeah?" He knew she hadn't meant it to sound sexual, but he'd never been able to resist going down that road in his mind with her. Especially when she stood so close, worrying about him. Touching him. Acting on its own, his hand settled on her hip, massaging circles into the sensitive area with his thumb. "You want to help me feel, Sera?"

CHAPTER NINETEEN

Sera's pulse danced, every muscle below her waist pulling taut. Logic shouted in her ear to step back, away from this man. This damaged complication of a man whose world she could never live in. Nor could he ever live in hers. She needed to *listen* this time. Her body had been making too many decisions lately, and while the need to soothe his pain was a living, breathing demand inside her, she couldn't give in. Oh, but she desperately wanted to. He could be her lifeboat as the storm of emotions raged around her, through her. Grief for her brother on his birthday, anger at her uncle for not believing in her, tempered with embarrassment she hated feeling. Fear of what the night would bring. Bowen would demand all her concentration and for a while, it would be perfect. Amazing. Until it ended and things were twice as knotted as when they began.

With a near-paralyzing case of reluctance, Sera stepped out of his reach, dislodging the hand on her hip. "You should go wash off that blood."

"You should come help me."

His thickened voice was so full of intention it made her stomach flutter. "No, Bowen."

She noticed an immediate change in his demeanor. He went from seductive bad boy to self-assured ladies' man before she could blink. He'd seen the evidence on her face that she still desired him. The confidence that knowledge provided combined with the sting of her rejection was responsible for his attitude change, she knew that for certain. She felt a frisson of alarm, wondering how he would use the attraction. Right now, he just looked downright irritable, but there was also intention in the hard set of his jaw.

"We don't have to fuck, Sera. But you're coming to shower with me." When she stared at him in openmouthed shock, he gave her a tight smile. "I told you. Nothing rash. Since you haven't agreed to let me help you, you're not leaving my sight. I'm not coming out of the bathroom and finding you gone."

"I'm not showering with you," she scoffed.

He shrugged. "Then the blood stays." Without another word, he walked out of her bedroom. A second later, she heard the unmistakable sound of him lighting a match, the smell of cigarette smoke permeating the air. After the morning she'd had, the blatant challenge he presented proved too much to resist. Doing her best to look casual, she followed him out into the kitchen and picked up his pack of cigarettes where it sat on the counter. As he watched her suspiciously, she flicked on one of the stove burners and lit the end, lifted the cigarette to her lips, and took a deep pull before it could go out. The smoke felt like fire pouring down her throat, but somehow she managed not to cough. Instead, she blew a steady exhale of smoke in his direction.

"What the hell are you doing?" he demanded angrily. "Put that out."

"Why?"

"It's bad for you." When she took another puff, he growled.

"Knock it off, Sera."

"No. Every time you smoke a cigarette, I'm going to smoke one, too." Sera knew this little act of rebellion was childish, but God, it felt fantastic. She'd been protected her whole life, learning so young that acting out only made things worse for herself. Well, right about now, things were about as worse as they could get, so she might as well go for broke. Bowen had just gotten finished telling her how *good* she was. How he wanted to absorb all the bad. This was her way of telling him she didn't need it.

Before she could take her third drag from the cigarette, Bowen tossed his own into the sink and advanced on her. The cigarette was plucked from her fingers on the way to her lips and held up between his fingertips. "If that's the case, I'll never touch another one in my goddamn life."

Having his vibrating intensity so close heated her head to toe. She tried to back up but her hips hit the counter. "Right." Her laughter sounded breathless. "I doubt it's that easy."

"You don't think so?" He lifted the edge of his shirt so she could see his ridged abdomen, the smooth skin interrupted by scars every few inches. A now-familiar feeling of dread kicked up a fuss in her stomach. "You want to know how important it is to me that nothing bad touches you? This'll be my reminder."

He ground out the lit cigarette on his stomach.

Sera screamed a denial, making a frantic attempt to stop him, but it was too late. His hand fell away and she could see the charred ring of flesh just above the waistband of his jeans. She slumped against the counter, watching in disbelief as he flicked the cigarette butt into the sink without taking his eyes off her. Not once. He hadn't even flinched once.

Suddenly furious, she shoved against his chest, but he didn't budge. "Stop using me as an excuse to hurt yourself, *dammit.*

What is wrong with you?"

"That's the million-dollar question, isn't it?"

The black smoking hole on his stomach, the blood on his face, it became insufferable. She needed it gone, *now*. Whether or not his behavior had been rational, she needed every reminder of what she'd driven him to do gone. Seeing him in pain when she could stop it went against everything in her nature. With a groan of frustration, she took his hand and dragged him toward the bathroom, making a valiant attempt to ignore the victory that flashed in his eyes. It made her question his sanity, yes, but she was also grateful for that look. It would give her a reason to resist him. Today, in this moment, she would not give in. No matter how much willpower it took.

She flipped on the light as they entered the small bathroom, having to tug her hand away when he didn't let her go immediately. Seeing them in the mirror, his taller, more muscular frame inches behind her, watching her as if his heart were in his throat, made her determination waver all too soon. Closing herself off to the emotions, she turned on the shower taps and found a lukewarm temperature in deference to his fresh wound.

A glance in the mirror showed him stripping his shirt over his head and tossing it on the floor. His hands went to the fly of his jeans then, but she refused to turn around completely, as if watching him disrobe in the mirror would somehow affect her less. How he could make every pulse point in her body pound while covered in blood and a self-inflicted wound staring her in the face, she had no idea. But if the power he had over her body continued to be this potent, after everything they'd faced since last night, it would never go away.

Doesn't change anything. "Get in," she instructed, cringing inwardly over the huskiness in her voice. Behind her, Bowen pushed his jeans and boxer briefs down in one quick movement and stepped out of them, revealing his too-beautiful body. Despite all the scars, the bruises, the blood, she'd never seen anyone so magnificent. "I'm not going to stand here all day."

One edge of his lips tugged up, but it looked unnatural thanks to his cuts. "I thought you were a nurse, Seraphina. Where's your bedside manner?"

"Do you think it's funny?" Swallowing her nerves, she turned. "Throwing these things you knew all along about my life in my face?"

"No." His expression went from playful to fierce. "Nothing about this shit show is funny. Your life being in danger isn't funny. Knowing you're leaving. *Isn't. Funny.*"

His passionate speech sent her back a step, much to her irritation. "You're right, it's not. But it's reality."

Her words seemed to set him off. "And let's not forget you knew every gritty detail of my life, too, Sera. I saw the disgust in your eyes the second you found out my name. Found out whose hips you'd had your legs wrapped around, whose mouth your hot little tongue had been inside." He grabbed the shower curtain and yanked it aside. "You must hate wanting me. That should make me happy. All that bad I want to protect you from? I'm the fucking worst of it."

No, you're not! She wanted to shout and stomp and rail at him for having such a low, distorted opinion of himself, but she held back. Encouraging him would be a mistake because if he saw a crack in her resolve, he'd hammer away at it until she broke. She couldn't allow it. Someday soon, when this was over, she would break. That eventuality couldn't be avoided, but she could put it off. She could do it without him watching, dying to pick up her pieces.

He stepped under the spray, letting the water course down his chest, abdomen, legs. She waited for him to move the shower curtain back into place, but he didn't, giving her an up close view of him showering, lathering soap in his hands and scrubbing the blood from his face and neck. Moving lower to give attention to the cut muscles of his chest, soapy water flowing in patterns between the hard ridges. She tried to watch with the professional detachment of her past nurse self, but it failed miserably, slick heat settling between her legs instead. It was turning him on. Whatever he saw on her face, he liked it. He liked her witnessing this private ritual; she could see the excitement in his heavy-lidded gaze. Trying to maintain an impassive expression, she watched him move lower, lower, until he reached his aroused length. Until now, she'd kept herself from staring, but when he took it in his hand, she could no longer avoid looking. His eyes challenged her to look away as he braced a hand on the shower wall and started stroking himself.

"I might be bad for you, but I make you feel good, don't I, baby?"

Inside her bra, her nipples puckered so tight, she knew they were visible against her tank top. Her palms itched to run up her thighs, over her belly, to end at her breasts. She wanted to squeeze the sensitive buds, feel the answering tug between her legs.

He bit down on his bottom lip and hummed in his throat. "Tell you what I'm thinking about right now. I'm thinking about the way you leaned back last night and bucked those hips like a fucking pro." His eyes closed on a groan. "I have no idea how I held back so long…needed to come so bad inside my tight girl."

She shot her hand out to brace herself on the sink. His growled words were making her knees shake right along with her willpower. "Stop," she whispered, but could barely hear herself over the pounding shower spray. Her body willed her to climb into the shower and let him take her, hard enough to shake the memories of this morning loose.

"It's a good thing we wore that condom, Sera. It might have been the only thing keeping you off your back." His hand worked faster over his rigid flesh. "You know what I'm thinking about now, don't you? No barriers. Just me, buried deep and fucking you hard. I'd block those screams with my mouth until they had nowhere to go and you'd just have to work your motherfucking hips faster to make up for it. I saw you, baby. I saw how dirty you'd let me give it to you."

Her back hit the wall, chest rising and falling with shallow breaths. The urge to touch herself had never been so strong. It nearly overwhelmed her. She closed her eyes to block his image before she lost control, forgot why she'd decided to resist him in the first place. When the shower spray shut off, panic loomed. She heard him climb out, his wet footsteps stopping right in front of her. So close. Too close. Resolutely, she kept her eyes squeezed tightly shut, even as his body heat enveloped her, the fresh scent of his soap invaded her head. Above everything, she heard the slap of his hand working his erection, his raspy moans driving her toward insanity.

"That's how it's going to be, baby? You want it, but you're not going to take it?" Against her lips, she felt his tongue, licking slowly, sensually, across the slightly parted seam of her mouth. Nothing could stop her head from tipping back, seeking more contact. Damp air kissed her belly, telling her he'd lifted her shirt to bare her midriff. Smooth, wet flesh dragged over her belly and his uneven groan told her it had been his hard arousal. The hand holding the sink to keep her steady shook with the effort. Never in her life had she wanted anything more than she wanted Bowen in that moment. She wanted to climb his body and let him sink deep inside her, turning his words into reality. Just when she thought she would cave to the desire, he drew his lower body away from her. "You want to call this a win when we're both aching for it? That's just fine, Sera." His mouth grazed her ear. "Just remember one thing. No matter what happens or where you go, I had you first. I took up every tight inch of you. I watched you get off while you called me your man. Nothing, *nothing*, will ever change that. You might not want me, but I'll be your man until I die."

Her eyes flew open at his words, heart beating so out of control it was a wonder it stayed inside her rib cage. Jaw set, gaze on fire, he was a glowing brand burning his words into her skin where they'd be for all time. He seemed taller, broader in that moment, filling her entire vision. Inescapable. *Real.* Part of her, the part she'd let fall for him so fast, begged her to launch herself at him and return the promise. Yet even in her overwrought state, she knew she would regret it. It would be a promise she wouldn't keep and that would hurt even more.

His face grew shuttered the longer she stayed quiet, earnestness replaced by bitter acceptance. With a final once-over of her shuddering body, he whipped a towel off the metal rack and wrapped it around his waist.

"Tell you what, baby, I'm going to keep it hard for you. I want you to know it's there waiting."

He left the bathroom without a backward glance.

CHAPTER TWENTY

Bowen stared at Sera over the rim of his nonalcoholic beer. It tasted like shit, but what didn't taste like shit lately? On top of the slight hangover he was still nursing from last night, he didn't want his reflexes dulled, so he suffered through a long pull. His hand tightened on the glass when she dropped off a round of drinks to a table full of men who, in their inebriated state, couldn't help sending her appreciative looks.

She would make her move soon. He'd seen the glances she'd been throwing around the club to judge how much longer she should wait to head downstairs. As it got later, the music got louder and people stopped noticing how long she spent out of the dining room. Except for him. He noticed every single movement she made. Every breath, every hesitation, every gesture.

The torturous afternoon he'd spent painting so he wouldn't lose the battle with his urge to just fucking seduce her already, she'd spent plotting in the guest room. Knowing she was so close had wreaked havoc on his senses for five unbearable hours. He'd wanted that voice in his ear, begging him to fuck her faster, deeper. He still wanted it with a vengeance, but at this point he would settle for her simply talking to him, sharing her plans. After the shower that had resulted in this century's worst case of blue balls, they'd retreated to their corners and hadn't spoken since, except to decide what time he'd take her to work.

There was an unspoken agreement that tonight she would finish her investigation come hell or high water, but she obviously had no intention of involving him. So he was involving himself. He'd sit at the bar drinking shitty nonalcoholic beer until she needed him. A dozen different emotions battled for supremacy in his chest. Desire for her to succeed and prove herself in a way he'd never gotten the chance to experience. Self-disgust over a small hope that she didn't succeed and had to stay with him longer. Rage that she wouldn't involve him. Fear that she'd get hurt.

Not that he would allow that nightmarish outcome willingly, but what if she got caught in a cross fire? He bit his bottom lip to avoid asking the bartender for something stronger, to drown out the image of Sera in pain. In fifty years, even if he never saw her again after the dust settled, he knew that outcome would remain his worst nightmare. He'd told her as much this morning, ripped open his bleeding chest and let her see his bones. And she'd rejected him. It didn't matter that she still wanted him physically. Women had wanted him as long as he could remember. That didn't help him now, not with someone like Sera, who needed something more. Some*one* more.

As if she'd heard his thoughts from across the dining room, she slowly straightened from the table she served and looked at him. Just…looked. At first, he didn't know what she was trying to communicate to him, but it slowly dawned on him. Goodbye? This was her good-bye? It plowed through his chest like a freight train, sucked the oxygen from his lungs. He slipped off the stool, wanting, *needing*, to go to her, but she shook her head subtly, halting him in his tracks.

No, no. *No*. It couldn't end like this. What he'd said to her in the bathroom couldn't be how he left things. He couldn't live with that. Couldn't live with the memory of her cowering from his touch, as if he'd ever lift a finger to hurt her. But he had; he'd been hurting her by throwing their mutual attraction in her face. Challenging her to say no, even though he'd known it was the right thing for her to do.

He shook his head, trying to communicate his need to say a decent good-bye. Remind her that she'd live inside his head forever. But she broke their eye contact and disappeared into the kitchen. Bowen stood there frozen, torn between the need to go after her and common sense, which told him someone would notice if he followed her. A minute passed, maybe two, and he could already feel insanity creeping in. As if she'd dragged the light out along with her, leaving him standing in an awful red glow that felt more like a horror flick than real life.

"Driscol."

His last name being spoken behind him permeated the red fog. He wanted to turn and take a swing at whoever stood there, like a wounded animal. Then the voice registered and his blood ran cold. Connor. What were the odds that he would arrive just as Sera disappeared downstairs? He didn't have time to think about it, only knew he had to keep the man there. The chance he'd been waiting for to help Sera had presented itself. It would also prevent him from ever seeing her again. The irony of that made him want to bang his head against the bar.

"Connor." His voice sounded rusty. "Shouldn't you be hiding shirtless in the shadows somewhere?"

The other man eyed him suspiciously. "Union break."

Bowen nodded to the empty stool beside his own and gestured to the bartender. "You allowed to drink on the job?"

"Who gives a fuck?"

"Point taken."

They stayed silent as the bartender pulled a pint of beer for Connor and set it in front of him. Tension lay thick between them, but both were waiting for the other to acknowledge it. Bowen understood this dynamic. He had it with Wayne and his father. Passive-aggressive bullshit that passed for being friendly in Bensonhurst. But he'd never dealt with Connor before, a man who actually had something more than greed going on behind his eyes. He just didn't know what it was.

"Heard about what happened last night outside of Marco's," Connor said, taking a sip of his beer. "Also heard you let him off with a couple broken bones."

Remembering the sound those bones made as they broke, nausea rolled in Bowen's stomach. "What's it to you?"

Connor shrugged. "It's not like you to be so benevolent. That Sera's influence?"

Never going to see her again. Never again. "I don't like you saying her name."

"I don't care."

Bowen's fists started to shake, so he hid them under the bar. He didn't get challenged very often and he shouldn't let it stand, but he had Sera to think about. On top of it, there was something in Connor's tone that stopped his words from being a taunt. Almost as if he were amused. At least someone was. But he didn't like this asshole throwing him off guard, so he decide to surprise him. "Speaking of benevolent, I hear you starting working for your cousin, Hogan, just so he'd help pay off your mother's medical bills."

The beer paused halfway to Connor's mouth. "Mind telling me where you heard that?"

"I don't kiss and tell."

Connor's lips twitched, but Bowen could see murder in his eyes. "All right, you don't want to tell me who's been running their mouth, that's fine. I'll find out on my own." A tense pause ensued. "What about the nonalcoholic beer? You turning over a new leaf?"

"Just watching my waistline."

"Where's Sera?"

Gone. She's gone to me. The sickening thought rattled around his skull like dice, but he managed a casual laugh. "She's working, otherwise I wouldn't be here. The atmosphere isn't exactly captivating."

"I mean, where is she *now*?"

Bowen held the man's steady gaze. As far as he could tell, Connor hadn't glanced once at the dining room since walking into Rush. "If you have something to say to her, you'll say it to me first."

A muscle jumped in Connor's cheek. "My cousin will be back in the morning, a day ahead of schedule. He asked me to talk to you personally." He leaned in and lowered his voice. "Our contact overseas got in touch with Hogan. The shipment has been rescheduled for tomorrow night. It's risky, but he wants to stay the course. Same plan, different night. He wants to make sure you're still in. If not, we call it off and wait another month. We need your manpower."

The back of Bowen's neck tingled. It didn't sound right. "I'm just supposed to trust the word of this contact who I didn't speak to directly?"

Connor nodded, before pulling a slip of paper from his jacket and sliding it across the bar. "I told Hogan you'd ask, so here's his phone number. Do whatever you have to do and get back to me by tomorrow afternoon."

Bowen shoved the paper into his jeans pocket. Tomorrow.

He almost laughed. Tonight was a difficult enough concept to wrap his mind around. Tomorrow sounded like a far-off place when his present had just walked away from him without a backward glance.

"Driscol," Connor said, drawing him back before he could be sucked in permanently by the red fog. He jerked his head toward the dining room, where Sera had vanished from five minutes prior. "If you haven't already, I'd suggest handling this little matter before it's taken out of your hands."

Sera closed the drawer of Hogan's desk quietly, just in case anyone stood at the top of the staircase. When it jammed, she set down her flashlight on the desk to jiggle it carefully, not wanting to break anything that would be visible the first time Hogan came back. A piece of loose wood at the base of the drawer snagged the skin of her palm and she hissed. With a frown, she grabbed the flashlight and shone it on the source of her injury. The slat had come loose in one corner of the drawer. Something black and hard was visible through the crack.

She crouched down and gently pried the bottom away, eyebrows shooting up when a slim laptop slid free into her hands. A hidden laptop. Valuable information. There was no more time. Sitting down and searching through the device wasn't an option. Thinking quickly, she snatched a letter opener off the desk and used it to pry the cover off the underside of the laptop and remove the hard drive. With one more nervous glance at her watch, she shoved it into her back pocket and pulled out her cell phone.

A terse voice answered midway through the first ring.

"This is Officer Seraphina Newsom requesting my pickup.

I'm—"

The line went dead before she could relate her exact location.

Ignoring an odd foreboding in her stomach, Sera made sure nothing appeared out of order on Hogan's desk. She tucked the ledger book under her arm and turned to leave. Okay. She simply needed to walk up the stairs, through the kitchen and out into the alley. They'd hung up because they already knew where she was. That had to be it. Someone would be there within minutes for her in an unmarked vehicle. An officer who would take her to police headquarters and out of this neighborhood. Forever.

Her steps faltered when relief didn't come flooding in as expected. Not an ounce of triumph or pride came with finally having secured Hogan's list of financial transactions. Names, dates, locations that she'd now seen with her own eyes. It had the potential to crumble not only Hogan's enterprise from the inside, but other Brooklyn operations as well. Her uncle would finally be proud. The injustice of watching Hogan profit of others' loss would be over.

Bowen's face appeared in her mind, bringing with it stinging pain where the relief should have been. No, that couldn't be it. She wouldn't allow him to be the reason this accomplishment felt so hollow. So…nothing. This was her brother's murderer, and she had the tool with which to bring him down.

At the base of the stairs, she came to a dead stop. Using the dim bulb above her for light, she flipped open to the page where she'd seen her brother's name, the notations that indicated he'd been taking payouts. Taking a deep breath, she sat down on the bottom step and stared hard at the numbers, something she hadn't had the opportunity to do before. Colin had taken three thousand dollars a week for six months. A lot of money to a rookie cop. She could imagine him being tempted, but not actually taking it. But he had, for six whole months. Sera squinted down at the messy handwriting. At six months, the payments had stopped, indicated by a series of zeroes. She checked the dates. He'd stopped taking the payouts two months before he'd been killed.

Hope fluttered to life in her chest. Had he seen the error of his ways and changed course? It appeared so. Furthermore, it gave Hogan the motive to take out her brother. It wasn't much, but it gave her a jumping-off point.

Finally, she felt something akin to victory come to life inside her, but not as strongly as it should have. Bowen sat at the bar, right above her head. Now that the moment had arrived to walk away from him, she had no choice but to admit it felt horribly, painfully wrong. As if she would be leaving a piece of herself behind when she walked into that alley. The same alley where they'd listened to Mrs. Petricelli sing opera that first night. Right before he'd kissed her.

Digging deep, she found the will to secure the ledger book into the waistband of her skirt, tucking her shirt in over it. As she dragged herself up the stairs, her legs felt like they weighed a thousand pounds. She spotted the car as soon as she walked outside, down at the end of the alley, out of view of the residential buildings. As she made her way over at a quick jog, the tall, familiar figure huddled beside it brought her up short.

"Uncle?"

"Sera." His smile was brisk, but his eyes warmed. "Did you get what you were looking for?"

She nodded once, still reeling that he was the one to come get her. As a highly recognizable figure, he'd taken a huge, unnecessary risk. Why? A shiver moved up her spine as she continued toward the black sedan. "Yes, I got it."

"Good. Let me have it."

The ledger disappeared into the inside pocket of his over-coat the second she handed it over. For some odd reason she couldn't explain, she held on to the hard drive in her back pocket, some inner warning telling her not to give it up just yet.

He indicated the passenger side door. "Let's go home."

"Home?" Sera shook her head. "Don't you mean the precinct? It's protocol to debrief me immediately after—"

"It can wait until the morning." He shot a look down the alley. "Sera, it's very important you don't mention this book to anyone. Not until I've had a chance to look at it."

No, this was all wrong. They had to do this by the book or none of the evidence would be admissible in court. Not to mention, his edgy behavior was so unlike him. He shouldn't have come on his own when his niece had been involved in the investigation. How could he be objective? Nothing about this felt right.

The answer hit her with the force of a battering ram.

"You knew." Her voice rang in her ears. "About Colin. Are you trying to cover it up?" She sucked in a breath. "Is that why you refused to reopen the official investigation? You didn't want anyone to find out?"

He started to deny it, but whatever he read on her face prevented him. "We will talk about this later when I get you somewhere safe."

"I've been safe my whole life," she shot back. "So he took a few payouts. I didn't expect it of him, but he stopped. We could have kept it quiet."

"No. No, we couldn't." He sighed long and loud, pinching the bridge of his nose. "Those payouts trace back to me, Sera. This book…they're proof Hogan has been holding over my head for years. The information contained in here is the leverage I need to keep him from blackmailing me, again and again."

Her mind reeled. "Why take payouts? You don't need the money. I don't understand."

"Your brother kept the money, but I looked the other way. His partner came to me with a complaint and I swept it under the mat. Even found a way to get your brother's partner reassigned." Her uncle's face looked suddenly ancient, etched with regret. "Everything came to Colin too easy. He didn't understand the concept of consequences, and it finally caught up with him. I was wrong about which of you two was the cop in the family. I'm sorry, Sera."

Sera wanted to dwell on the apology, wanted to bask in her uncle's rare approval. It had been so damn long in coming, from him, from *anyone*. But she couldn't. Her brain had zeroed in on one thing he'd said, and with it the implications made her vision waver. *It finally caught up with him.* "The trial," she rasped. "Did you get him off because he had dirt on you? Evidence that you knew about the payouts?"

His silence was the only answer she needed. Sera staggered back from the car, feeling as if the fabric of her existence had been ripped in half. The standards she'd held herself to her entire life were suddenly meaningless, a crumbled foundation. Her uncle only watched her, hands propped on hips, looking ashamed. She'd never seen that look on her uncle's face before. It brought another horrible realization to the forefront of her mind.

"Did you..." she started in a small voice. "Did you *know* I was going undercover? Did you...*let* me so I'd do your dirty work for you?"

Again, he couldn't look directly at her. Coffin? Meet nail. "Get in the car. We'll talk about this at home." He jerked open the driver's side door. "Tomorrow we'll debrief you, then take you to a safe house. You'll stay there until this blows over, then we'll discuss more options."

Her life was once again being planned out for her, by a man she didn't even know. A man who'd let her brother's killer go free to save his own job, his own reputation. A man who would reassign an innocent officer to God-knew-where instead of doing the right thing. Worst of all, a man who would use his niece to further his own ends. No, she wasn't going anywhere with him. And suddenly, there was only one place in the world she wanted to be. At the thought of returning to Bowen, her heart starting beating for what felt like the first time that day. She'd judged him on a scale her uncle had created. A black-and-white scale that allowed for no gray area, but her uncle lived in the gray, just like Bowen. Only, one of them did it by choice, one had never been given a choice. Or a chance.

"Go without me. I'm not leaving."

He snorted. "That's not funny."

"Good. It wasn't a joke." She started walking backward toward Rush. "Leave before someone sees you."

"I'm not leaving without you. *Get in the car.*" She kept walking, drawing a vile curse she'd never expected to hear from him. "It's *him*, isn't it? Sera, you can't be serious. He's scum."

She paused her footsteps. "And yet you sent him in to babysit your niece?" When he had no answer, she laughed without humor. "That scum has taught me more about myself since I met him than you even bothered to do. You never gave me a home. But I think he might have."

He started to come after her, but jumped back into the shadows when a light came on in the apartment building, illuminating the alley. No way could the police commissioner be seen here, talking to her. Anyone with a television set would recognize him. With a final disgusted look in her direction, he tugged his jacket collar up around his neck. "This isn't over,

Sera. I won't let you ruin your life like this. I owe your father better than that."

"I owe him better than to turn out a liar." This was it. No going back. "My badge is at my apartment on my bedside table. You can shove it up your ass."

She had the satisfaction of watching his face pale. "You'll regret this."

"I only regret one thing tonight." *Leaving Bowen.* "You want my silence, Uncle? Let me go. Let Bowen go." She was taking a gamble that Bowen would want to disappear with her, but prayed he would. "You won't hear from us again."

He said nothing. Just clenched his jaw and ducked into the car.

Hidden in the shadows, Sera watched him drive down the alley and turn onto the street, red taillights disappearing around the corner. There should have been more of a sense of apprehension, or loss. She'd just chosen Bowen over family. Over potential safety. She could figure out the rest. They'd do it together.

I love him. Oh, God, I love him so much.

When the kitchen door slammed open and Bowen charged out, hands in his hair, looking in every direction with raw agony on his face, she knew she'd made the right call. Her entire being gravitated toward him. *Soothe him. Make him better.*

She ran toward him.

CHAPTER TWENTY-ONE

She's really gone.

When Connor left the club, he thought he might have had a chance to catch her. What would he have said? Please stay? I'm sorry I couldn't be what you need? He didn't know, hadn't been able to formulate a plan beyond seeing her one more time. But he hadn't made it. The alley was empty, except for a few stray patches of light. Feeling the world sway beneath his feet, he started to slide down the brick wall, wondering when he'd ever get the strength to stand again once he hit the ground.

"Bowen."

His heart lurched when Sera came into view, white light falling around her beautiful form, making him question if she was real or just a figment of his imagination.

Is this it? Insanity? If so, I could stay here.

No, she was running toward him, her mouth moving, saying his name. Standing very slowly in case sudden movements might send her away, he waited for her to get closer before he allowed himself to hope. Then she threw herself against him. His back hit the brick wall in the most welcome assurance of reality he could remember. When her mouth made contact with his, it brought everything into sharp focus. *Sera is here, kissing me. Make it last.*

He reversed their positions, trapping her against the wall with his hips, getting as close to her as humanly possible, groaning as her thighs wrapped around his waist where they belonged. "I thought you'd left already," he whispered at her lips. "I didn't think you'd let me say good-bye. How long do I have?"

"They already came to get me." Those perfect hands of hers slid into his hair. "I couldn't leave you. I couldn't go."

"What?" He hadn't heard her correctly. Or maybe he was still sitting on the ground, imagining this entire scene. "What do you mean, you couldn't leave me?"

"I'm staying, Bowen." She licked into his mouth for a dizzying kiss, which he returned like a starving man. "I need you."

Disbelief tried to overshadow the joy spiraling through him. How could this be happening? He didn't want to question it; he wanted to take this twist of fate he didn't deserve and run with it, but he couldn't, not completely. She'd given up a chance to be safe. For *him*. It tempered his happiness with worry. The responsibility to make sure she didn't regret it. His blood heated with possessiveness, the honor he'd been given to keep her safe. She'd picked him. This amazing girl had chosen him. Until she came to her senses, he would treasure every second.

She tugged at his hair with her fists. "Let me clarify. I need you *now*." Her hips writhed between him and the wall, hardening his cock with a swiftness that had him gasping into her delicious mouth. "Stop thinking, please."

"Not here, baby." He pressed higher between her thighs, negating his plea. The needy whimper that drifted from her lips sent blood rushing to his groin. He'd left himself unfinished this afternoon and the deprivation came back to bite him now. It would take an act of God to tear him away from her at that moment, and he still would still claw his way back for more. "Ah, God, don't let me fuck you in an alley, Ladybug."

"Yes. *Here.*" She reached down and tugged her own skirt higher on her thighs. Seeing how her desperation matched his own was a powerful realization. This wasn't just sex for her, either, thank Christ. In his chest, his heart raced out of control. "I can't wait," she moaned. "I need you so bad."

Her begging had the effect of a drug, whizzing along his nerve endings and making him hungry to get inside her. *Protect her*, a voice shouted from the back of his racing mind. Keeping her on the wall with his hips, he reached into his back pocket and ripped the single condom from his wallet. Her fingers were already on his belt, yanking leather through loops with shaky hands. It humbled him, her need. He'd never considered himself a lucky man, but right now, with Sera wanting him so bad, he didn't think anyone luckier had ever existed in this world.

She slipped her hand into his jeans and squeezed his erection, chasing away the last rational thought in his head. Growling into her frantic kiss, he reached between her legs and palmed her pussy. *Mine, mine, mine.*

"You still sore from your first time, baby?" He ripped her panties with a twist of his wrist. "That's not going to stop me from hitting it hard, you understand? I'm too far gone to fuck you easy. I might never be able to again."

"I understand," she breathed. "Just…*please.*"

He wedged the packaged condom between her teeth. "Wrap me up, then. Get your man ready to fuck. I want to see it."

Challenge in her eyes, she ripped the foil with her teeth and he had to bite his bottom lip to prevent a growl. Jesus, how had he ever lived without this girl? She made him feel so fucking alive, he didn't know how he withstood it. As she rolled the latex over his cock, he responded to her challenge by slipping his middle finger inside her, pushing it high and deep. It distracted her halfway through her task, her head falling forward into his shoulder with a hoarse cry.

"Better finish what you started, Sera. Unless this is enough for you." He withdrew his finger halfway and shoved it back in again and again, gritting his teeth at the feel of her tight, damp heat. Perfect. So goddamn perfect. He nudged her clit with his knuckle and felt her mouth open against his neck, her teeth rake his flesh. "Are my fingers enough for you?"

"Yes…no. I-I don't know." Her hands moved on his aching cock, rolling the condom on fully. It made him even hotter, watching her perform the task. Seeing her erratic movements, her rush to get him prepared to be inside her.

Bowen gripped her chin in his hand. He wanted her looking at him when he finally sank in. Inevitably, he would lose himself, and he needed her eyes to anchor him. "Tell your man how bad you need him. Tell him to give it to you hard."

"I need you, Bowen." Her eyes were clouded with lust. "Give it to me hard."

He rammed himself deep, driving her high against the wall. She screamed in her throat, the most erotic sound he'd ever heard, her lips shaking with the effort to keep quiet, keep them undiscovered. Even he had to put a leash on the need to shout, the feel of her made him feel so crazed. "Jesus, *fuck*. You tight-ass girl. I can't *breathe* when I'm inside you. I can't *think*."

Her ankles locked just above his ass, sinking him even deeper and drawing a groan from his mouth. "D-don't think, just move," she said shakily.

Knowing he was seconds from losing any semblance of control, he braced his arm between her back and the wall so she wouldn't get hurt. Then he flattened his free hand above her on the wall and started pumping his hips. He didn't start slow. Couldn't. His pace was merciless, giving them what they both needed.

"*Nobody* feels like you, baby," he groaned against her neck, before sinking his teeth into the sensitive skin. "I'm so fucking deep and it's not enough. It'll never be enough. I can't touch all of you at once and it drives me crazy. I need everything, always. More, *more*."

"You have me." Her voice shook with the force of his thrusts. "I'm here."

"You left." He pressed their foreheads together, focused on the brown eyes glazed with passion. "I watched you leave. Don't do that to me again."

"I won't." She whimpered as he increased his pace. "I promise."

His hips moved on their own, plowing into her with deep, savage thrusts. The force of his drives shook her locked ankles loose at his back, so her legs dangled on either side of him, suspended inches above the ground. She wrapped her arms around his neck tightly, her moans increasing in volume against his ear until he knew she was almost ready to come. He was overcome by the obsessive need for her to tighten up and shake around him, the way she'd done the first time. He needed to be what sent her there.

Bowen licked up the side of her neck and bit down on her earlobe. "You came back for me, Sera. You came back because I mean something to you and thank Christ for that." His hand left the wall to jerk her left leg up around his waist, and they both moaned at the new friction. "But there's another reason you came back and I'm fucking you with it right now. Isn't that right, beautiful? You love what I put between your legs. Admit it for me, part of the reason you came back is because you know you won't get this anywhere else. Not like I do it."

Her fingernails dug into the back of his neck; her thigh started to shake in his hand. "Yes. *Yes*, I need it."

"Nowhere else," he growled against her mouth. "Let's hear it."

"Nowhere else," she gasped, her pussy clenching around him so tight, nothing could stop him from ramming into her spasming flesh, over and over, unable to hold back an ounce of his strength. Electricity shot down his spine, into his lower back, between his legs. He momentarily panicked when his eyes went blind because he couldn't see her, so he concentrated on her fingers riffling through his hair, her clean scent.

Burying his face against her neck, he pushed deep inside her and let the mind-blowing orgasm drag him under. "Sera, Sera, *Sera*. Feels so fucking good, baby, take it. Take it all for me. See what you do to me? You and that sweet pussy? I can't *breathe*."

For long moments, he stayed like that, crushing their bodies together as his pulse returned to a semi-normal rhythm, since it never completely steadied with Sera around. Reality came back gradually, like a Polaroid coming into focus, but he was still afraid to move. Afraid he would step back to find himself huddled on the ground, imagining her. "You okay, Ladybug?" he mumbled and then held his breath, waiting to hear her voice.

Her open mouth pressed a kiss to his cheek. "I'm okay. I'm better than okay."

He pulled back to take in the sight of her flushed face. She looked as if she'd been attacked, and even knowing he'd put her in this state, even though she'd wanted it, he still felt irrational worry. "I wish I could tell you it won't be like this every time, but I can't. You do something to me, Sera. You change me and once that happens…I need that feeling too much to hold back."

"Bowen." She laid a finger over his lips. "Let's go home."

Oh, God. Was it possible for a man's heart to explode in his chest? "I like you saying that."

Hands brushing, mouths seeking, they pulled their clothing back into place. Alarm pricked the back of his neck when he realized they'd been vulnerable for—how long? Jesus, anything could have happened while he'd been lost in her. He needed to be more careful. Hogan was set to return early for the shipment tomorrow, and the threat to Sera would skyrocket.

Bowen would handle it. He *would*. He'd keep her safe, protect her with his life without a second thought. Could he finally walk away from Brooklyn? Yes. *Yes.* In a heartbeat. As long as he had her, anything was possible.

CHAPTER TWENTY-TWO

Walking into Bowen's apartment, Sera felt *resolved*. For the first time in recent memory, she'd made a decision based on *her* needs, not the needs of others. Making the decision to throw herself into his arms had been scary, until those arms had closed around her and his energy had wrapped her inside it. She craved the need he felt for her. She *wanted* him to need her, because with every second that passed, her own attachment cemented itself. As soon as everything was out in the open, no secrets littering the ground in front of them, the connection she felt to him could only strengthen.

She wasn't ready to think about what her actions meant. What repercussions they might have in regard to her future. One that now included Bowen. Her uncle, the serious problems presented by what she'd done...those would need to be dealt with. Soon. She hoped, *prayed*, Bowen would want to help her solve those problems. But not tonight. After what she'd learned from her uncle in the alley, her brain couldn't process any more. Months of preparation, years of pain, had been funneled into this mission to avenge her brother, and in the end, the whole thing had only been part of a cover-up to protect a corrupt man. A man she'd obviously never known. It had been one big illusion, a relationship she'd created with the charismatic man on television.

"Hey." Bowen tipped her chin up, a frown marring his brow. "What are you thinking about?"

"I'm thinking I'm hungry."

He focused on a spot past her shoulder. "You're not...you don't already regret—"

"No." She shook her head, laying a hand over his. "I just want to be here with you tonight. I don't want to think about anything else. Can we do that?"

Oh, boy. He wanted to argue. She could see it. Sera had no doubt that if he could pin her to the floor and demand to know every thought in her head, he would do it. Bowen didn't sit back and wait for explanations, and this was new to him. Instead of pressing, though, he squared his jaw and nodded. "I haven't been to the store in a while. Been a little distracted." He winked at her on the way to the refrigerator. "Egg sandwich? Or I can order something..."

"Egg sandwich, please." She leaned on the counter, utterly delighted to watch this rough-hewn man with visible battle scars cracking eggs into a bowl with enough masculine grace to flush her skin. As he performed the task, he threw her somber glances over his shoulder. Expecting her to disappear? How could she blame him? Her plan all along had been to disappear. Still was. Only now, she would ask him to find her worthy enough to follow. If he didn't, the loneliness would be vastly harder than before because she knew what it felt like, being with him.

"Ladybug." Sera jumped when she realized Bowen was leaning across the counter, face inches from hers. "I can get on board with your no-thinking rule, but you have to cooperate."

She picked up the sandwich. "Cooperating."

Bowen tucked into his own sandwich. "So I guess your waitressing career is over," he said between bites. "Good thing you have those law enforcement skills to fall back on." One end of his mouth ticked up, but his eyes were serious. His not-so-subtle way of asking if she intended to remain on the force? "Something tells me you won't get a good reference from Rush."

"Are you saying I'm not a good waitress?" she evaded.

"No. I'm saying you're a terrible one."

Determined to keep the mood light, she threw a balled-up napkin at him. "It's harder than it looks. I've had patients come into the ER less concerned about a broken leg than some customers in Rush are about their chicken wings."

"Wings are no joke."

"Hmm." She downed the last of her sandwich, feeling even more relaxed now that she had something in her stomach. "Anyway, you were my most belligerent customer and you didn't even order anything to eat."

"I wanted to. I wanted to watch you bring me dinner. Still do." He scrubbed a hand over his hair. "Jesus, that didn't sound so fucking crazy in my head."

"I'll make you dinner someday," she rushed to say, wanting to erase the sudden insecurity in his face. "I owe you for the egg sandwich."

"You never owe me for anything. Never." He took her plate and set it in the sink, along with his own. When he turned back to face her, he looked thoughtful. "Actually, there's one thing you can do for me. Come on."

She had no time to prepare before he dragged her toward his bedroom. "Subtlety isn't really your thing, you know that?" Not that she minded in the slightest. Already, goose bumps were forming on every inch of her skin, heavy heat trickling into her lower belly. Would she ever get used to him, the way he controlled the reactions of her body?

He stopped at his bedroom door and turned to her with a chastising look. "Get your head out of the gutter, baby. You Catholic girls and your filthy minds."

Her mouth dropped open, then snapped shut as he pulled her inside and flipped on the light. His murals were…gone. All of them. His walls had been painted a startling white, the evidence of his work strewn across the floor in the form of paint cans and spattered drop cloths. It looked like a tornado had whipped through the room and ripped all the color from the walls. No, not all the color. As Bowen moved farther into the room, she saw it. On the far wall, he'd painted a woman.

Her? It was…*her*.

Even though painted Sera was missing a mouth, it captured her eyes, her hair, with perfect detail. When she looked at it, she might as well have been looking in a mirror on her absolute best day. The way he saw her…it heightened what she knew actually existed. He'd painted her eyes as if they were weighed down with love, her hair floating out around her like a cloud.

Sera's throat tightened painfully. She could feel Bowen watching her, awaiting some sort of reaction, but she didn't know how to put her feelings into words. For his sake, she tried anyway. "It's beautiful. I wish you hadn't gotten rid of all the others, but it's so beautiful."

He ran his gaze along the bare walls, horror marring his features. "I couldn't have any of those things around you. They had to go."

"Oh." She wondered what he would do if she curled up on the floor and basked in those words for a while. "When did you do this?"

His booted feet made the floor creak as he closed the distance between them. "The night I…left you here. I came back and found you sleeping under your halo. But I couldn't sleep afterward, so I painted." He brushed a thumb over her bottom lip. "I should never have left that night. I'm so sorry."

Sera nodded, unable to speak for a moment. "It's okay. I'm starting to understand why you did." She leaned into his touch. "But next time you won't. You won't have to get that far before you realize you're better than that."

"Is it wrong if I let you go on thinking that?" he murmured. "Probably, but I'm going to anyway. Whatever will keep you here the longest."

If he continued speaking in such a manner, she would turn into a puddle. "Why don't I have a mouth? My painting, I mean."

"Huh?" It took his eyes a moment to refocus. "Oh, right. That's what I need your help with. I couldn't get your mouth right." He tugged her toward the wall. "Pose for me?"

She laughed as he bent his knees to study her lips. "How'd you get my eyes to look so accurate and you couldn't remember my mouth?"

"It's not that I can't remember it, Ladybug. I just..." He groaned in his throat. "When I look at your mouth, I want it *on* me. I'm not thinking about the gentle swell of your upper lip." His gray eyes twinkled, looking momentarily blue. "Disappointed you didn't hook up with a poet?"

"No," she answered, trying not to smile. "Poets are too tortured. Artists are much more well-adjusted."

"Ah, and I hooked up with a wiseass." He gripped her chin and tilted her head, still studying her mouth. It unnerved her, in a breathless, anticipatory kind of way. "You think maybe we could, I don't know, balance each other out?"

His gaze finally met hers with an intensity that shook her to the soles of her feet. She swallowed the knot in her throat. "Do we have a choice?"

"I don't." He released her chin and picked up a clean paint-brush. She watched as he mixed together red and beige on a wooden palette, so much concentration going into the task it felt necessary to remain silent. When he spoke again, his deep, husky tone breaking through the quiet of the bedroom actually startled her. "The first time we met, I thought you were wearing lipstick. But when I kissed you, it stayed on. No type of lipstick could have stayed on through that kiss." He sucked his bottom lip through his teeth. "They're pink, your lips. I've never seen that shade before, like maybe you just got finished sucking on some candy. Fuck, is that why they make me hot? I can't look at them without thinking of sucking?"

"I don't know." The words came out in a whoosh. She leaned back against the wall to the right of the painting, afraid whatever he said next might finally topple her. "I'm more of a savory girl. Like, you know, egg sandwiches..." *Oh, please, please shut up now.*

He dabbed the paintbrush into the paint, amusement tipping the edges of his sensual mouth. "Are you actually flustered, Ladybug? After I've made you come in a stairwell, a photo booth, an alleyway — "

"Point made. Just paint my mouth."

She watched his hand move, leaving a rosy shade of paint on the wall. Every few seconds, his gaze would flash to her mouth and each time felt like a bolt of lightning to her overwhelmed system. She found herself wanting him to look at her mouth, felt it parting of its own accord, her tongue slipping out to dampen her lips. A pulse beat at the base of her neck and the sound multiplied itself in her ears.

Finally, Bowen stopped looking away, obviously sensing the change in her. "Can you try not to look so goddamn fuckable for a second while I finish this? It's important to me, Sera."

The frustration in his tone cut through her haze of lust. "Why is it so important?"

With a curse, he dropped the palette and paintbrush, before planting his fists on either side of her head. He brought his face close enough to kiss her, then stopped. "I need something to prove you were here, all right? Are you happy?"

"No." His flinch sent her backtracking. "Being here with you makes me happy, Bowen. But I'm not happy you're so worried about me leaving."

He scoffed. "How can I be anything else when you won't talk to me? When you want to play this no-talking game?" His head dropped onto her shoulder. "You're here and I'm so fucking grateful for that, but I don't know *why* or what led to it. If I don't know those things, how can I make sure I keep doing them? You're making me crazy, Sera."

"I'm sorry. I don't mean to," she whispered, shaken by his passionate speech. The events of the night were right on the tip of her tongue. She'd been played, *used*, by her only remaining family. Her brother, the sibling she'd always looked up to, had been flawed in a way she'd never imagined. Nothing felt concrete except Bowen against her, and she wanted to lose herself in him. Forget everything, just for one night. Tomorrow, she'd find a way to trust again and tell him everything, but right now? Her insides felt raw.

She ducked under his arm and picked up the wet paintbrush, making sure enough rose-colored paint coated the end. Then she turned toward the wall and wrote, in giant letters, SERA WAS HERE. She started to set the brush back down, but changed her mind. Beneath it she continued with, BECAUSE OF BOWEN.

It wouldn't be enough for him, but she simply didn't have the words to give him tonight. His eyes were on her and she could feel them boring into her back. When she couldn't stand his silence anymore, she turned to face him.

Just in time to be dragged to the floor.

Her gasp of shock was swallowed by his mouth, but it turned into a moan when he settled himself fully on top of her. She'd never felt anything like it, the weight of a man, pressing her body down into the hard wood, with nowhere to go. It felt divine, intoxicating. It made her feel so perfectly feminine, she threw her head back and reveled in it.

Frantic to get closer, to feel *more*, she spread her legs and Bowen dropped into the cradle of her thighs with a groan, rocking into her center immediately. When he couldn't get close enough, he yanked her skirt higher and melted into her with a desperate noise.

"You're goddamn right you were here, Sera. You're every-where I look." He pushed two fingers past her lips, which she sucked deep into her mouth. Her boldness shocked him, she could tell by his sharp curse, the flash of heat in his eyes. "You know what happens when I see you get all flustered? When you're dying for a fuck, but don't know how to just *ask* for it? My cock gets so hard it hurts. Do you do it on purpose?"

With his fingers in her mouth, she couldn't speak, so she shook her head.

"No?" He withdrew his fingers and gave her a firm pump of his hips. "Tell me what you want, baby. Right now."

"I want you in my mouth." She said it without thinking. Having his fingers there had brought back the memory of him standing above her, his face tortured and fraught with pleasure at the same time he slid past her lips. The way he'd begged and shaken as he came had given her such an incredible feeling of power, she would have done anything at that moment to feel it again.

Bowen held his breath as if he couldn't quite believe she

were real, then he hardened his jaw and slowly dragged his cut body higher, higher, against hers. Muscles slid over curves, drawing panting breaths from both of them, until he could kneel above her. His knees were on either side of her head, straddling her, in the most intimate position she could have imagined.

Bowen undid his belt and unzipped his jeans with shaky hands. "You think I'm noble enough to say no to that? When I know what your mouth can do?" He freed himself from his jeans, biting his lip on a groan, and held his swollen flesh just above her parted lips. "If you want it so bad, baby, lick for it. The way you were licking those pretty lips when I was trying to concentrate. *Now*, Sera."

His desperation, his harsh words, flooded her with desire, and she didn't hesitate to do as he asked. She swirled her tongue around the head, then traveled lower to lick him slowly, base to tip. All the while, she kept her eyes trained on him, his throaty sounds and panting breaths ratcheting her desire up until her hands clawed at the powerful thighs bracketing her head.

"Ask for it, now." He rubbed the smooth head against the seam of her lips. "Say, please, Bowen. I want you to own my mouth. Make it yours."

She repeated the words back in a rush. Not wanting to wait another second to drive him out of his mind, she wrapped her hand around his arousal and guided him into her mouth. She pulled on him deeply, reacquainting herself with his taste, his texture, his size. Above her head, she heard his palms slap down on the floor, putting him on his hands and knees, with only his hardness making contact, dipping into her mouth. It felt illicit and wrong, but she raced toward the promise of a new experience with no fear. Fear didn't exist with Bowen.

"I'm only going to give you what I know you can take, baby." His voice sounded like gravel. "Tell me you trust me."

He lifted himself away long enough for her to answer. "I trust you, Bowen."

Slowly, he lowered his body again, his rigid length pushing through her lips. "Fuck, *fuck*. I shouldn't be doing this. Not with my girl." He pumped himself into her mouth with shallow thrusts, so much restraint behind them she knew what an effort he made to hold back. "Oh, God. Make me stop."

Instead, she tightened her lips around him and urged him deeper with a hand on his ass. Her eyes teared a little when he reached the back of her throat, but she took a deep breath through her nose as he withdrew, and focused on Bowen's reactions to what she was doing. Beneath her hands, his muscles flexed; filthy curses fell from his lips every time she sucked him deeper. It only served to drive her need to please higher until she'd taken all of him and he was able to enter her throat fully.

His inner thighs spasmed against her ears as he pushed deep and held. "Oh fuck, oh fuck, oh *fuck*. You've got all of me in that perfect mouth. I can't...I'm dying." He drew back and slid himself into her throat again with a choked curse. Then again. And again, until it turned rhythmic. "Eyes on your man while you take it, baby. Show me you want it. Show me you want to be as ruined as I am."

Ruined. Yes, she wanted to be ruined. With him. Forever. Keeping their gazes locked, she dug her nails into his thighs and swallowed around his rigid flesh. His entire body jerked, shuddered. One strong hand slipped on the hardwood floor, forcing him to catch his weight on an elbow, hips never ceasing in their movements.

"Touch yourself, baby," he said, voice cracking. "Get ready for me, because I am about to fuck you out of your mind."

Anticipation went wild in her belly, and she didn't hesitate to follow his command. Her hand slipped down between her thighs and tugged aside her panties. Dampness greeted her, but she didn't feel an ounce of surprise. Her body flamed, crying out for relief from the heat that continued to build like an inferno. Bowen pushed into her mouth one final time, and then withdrew with a hissed breath, his erection in his fist.

He dragged himself down her body, removing his shirt as he went to reveal a wall of mouthwatering muscle. Sera had no time to prepare herself before he flipped her over onto her stomach and yanked her hips up, putting them level with his own. She heard the metallic rip of the condom wrapper and a grunt as he rolled on their protection. "Hang on. This is going to be rough."

"Yes, I want it. *Please.*"

In one dizzying movement, he yanked aside her panties and rammed himself deep. He tested the angle once, twice, then drove deep once more. She felt his hands at her knees, yanking her legs wider. "You want it hard? Give me some room to work then, baby."

A calloused hand gripped the back of her neck, urging her cheek down onto the floor. The position pushed her bottom high in the air, leaving her open to receive his savage thrusts. "Look at you, skirt up around your waist, still wearing your cock-teasing panties while I satisfy that pussy."

"Oh, God," she gasped. Pressure built in her stomach, between her thighs. Close. So close. "Bowen, *please.*"

"You like it rough, Sera?" He anchored a fist in her hair and quickened his pace. "Did you think I could give it to you any other way after you let me fuck your mouth?"

"No. Yes." Release screamed closer. "Don't stop, *don't stop.*"

He increased his pace with a growl that told her he was close, too. Knowing his edge loomed sent her spiraling, sobbing into the hard floor as pleasure overtook her. He sank deep one final time, shaking against her as he came, a litany of curses echoing through the room.

When she expected him to collapse onto her back, he surprised her by turning her around and gathering her close, so close she could hardly breathe. His mouth moved in her hair, hands stroking along every inch of her skin. Twice, she sensed him start to speak, then stop. Finally, he picked her up and settled her into his bed without losing contact. After he disposed of their protection in the bedside wastebasket, they lay there in a sweaty tangle of limbs, regaining their bearings for a time. It wasn't long before she fell asleep, lulled by the sound of Bowen's heartbeat knocking in his chest.

CHAPTER TWENTY-THREE

*S*eraphina.

Bowen sprang awake in bed, his lungs seizing with the need for oxygen. *Breathe, breathe.* No, he wouldn't allow himself a breath until he touched Sera. His hands tore through the tangle of sheets, searching for her mass of brown hair. No matter that he could feel warm, naked skin pressed against him, after the things he'd dreamed, he needed to get eyes on her.

There. She was there. Air infiltrated his chest, twining with something far more drastic than relief. *I love her. I love her too much.* The realization didn't come as a surprise. He'd seen this coming since the first night. Maybe he hadn't allowed himself to acknowledge it because she'd always planned on leaving. Now that she didn't want to leave, the emotions he'd kept at bay came flooding in until his heart bobbed among them like a buoy.

She practically glowed in the predawn light filtering in through his single window. Her mouth, that *unbelievable* mouth, grew stubborn when she slept, lips pursed as if ready to argue. Damn, he liked that. He wanted to kiss her mouth until it softened for him, but then he'd lose this chance to savor waking up with her in his bed for the first time. Hair he'd abused with his hands all night, directing her up, down, sideways, lay in a tumble on his pillow. He'd been rough as hell with her, but at some point during the night, he'd stopped feeling like a corrupter of innocence. It might have had something to do with Sera's confidence growing every time he took her. She'd learned quickly how to turn him into a begging mess. As if he hadn't been one for her all along.

Is this how you like me to touch you, Bowen?

Faster?

Like this?

You feel so good. So hard.

Can I please put you in my mouth again?

Apparently he'd done *something* right in his life. As an added bonus, this beautiful, caring, intelligent girl whom he'd walk through fire for also *loved* giving him head. Go fucking figure.

Loath to wake her but physically incapable of not touching her, he ran his thumb over her arched eyebrow and watched the stubbornness fade from her mouth. One gorgeous brown eye popped open, followed by the other. She woke up one eye at a time. He loved knowing that about her. Wanted to know everything. He *would* know everything, starting today.

No more secrets, no more pretending the obstacles between them didn't exist. Every moment they spent tiptoeing through this minefield surrounding them, she was in danger. She wanted to stay with him and she would get what she wanted. Simple as that. The fact that her presence in his life would make it worth living came secondary. As her face transformed with sleepy awareness, he wondered if she knew. That he loved her. Would kill for her. That even though her naked breasts were making his dick hard, he simultaneously wanted to hide her under the covers and guard her.

"Too much, Sera. You make me feel too much."

Her smile dipped at the edges. "Is that a bad thing?"

"No." He pressed his lips to her forehead. "Not as long as you're with me to shoulder some of it. Sometimes I get worried I'm not enough to carry it all."

"You're not the only one who feels too much." Her gaze searched his. "You have to help me, too."

A dizzying rush of love careered through him. He couldn't see anything but her, felt nothing but her body beneath him, molding to his so perfectly. *Perfect. This is perfect.* He took her wrists and pinned them above her head on the pillow. "Then let me ease you now, baby."

A shrill series of beeps broke the spell she'd placed him under. It took Bowen a moment to place the sound, his head was so fogged with Sera. His phone. It vibrated and danced on the side table next to his bed. Lust slowly dissipated at the implications of a 6:00 a.m. phone call. No good news came this early in the morning. Sera's soft form tensing beneath him told Bowen she'd come to the same conclusion.

Knowing he'd never be able to concentrate while lying cradled between her thighs, he reluctantly sat up and snatched up the phone. When he read the caller ID, it felt as though he'd been kicked in the ribs. *Rikers Island correctional facility.* "Hello?"

"Bowen Driscol?"

A man's clipped voice. Not his father's, as he'd been expecting. What did it mean that someone else was calling? "One and the same," he answered slowly.

"Your father has been taken to the infirmary. We're obligated to inform the closest family member." The caller paused, as if letting that news sink in. It didn't. "Details aren't available right now, but we do know he had an altercation with another prisoner. His wounds are serious enough that you should try to make it here as soon as possible."

"Fine." He hung up the phone and breathed deeply through his nose, trying not to lose the contents of his stomach. His mind whirled, trying to find detachment so he could get to his feet and move. But all he could come up with was guilt. In order to protect his sister, he'd played a part in putting his father away. A small part, but a part nonetheless. Now Lenny could die because of it. No matter that their relationship bordered on hostile. They were still blood.

Sera rubbed circles into his back, her lack of questions telling him she'd heard everything. "Bowen," she said, softly. "Get dressed. I'll come with you."

He shot to his feet, already trying to come up with an alternative. Her safety came before everything else. Yes, even Lenny. "Are you out of your mind?" In the dimness, he searched for the jeans he'd discarded the night before, tugging them on with jerky movements. "Even if the idea of you in that place didn't make me feel sick, I can't bring an undercover cop around my father. Not to mention every other motherfucker who's taken a shiv this week. What if someone recognized you?"

"No one will recognize me." She rose from the bed, her naked body still flushed from his touch. He had to pause in the act of dragging on his T-shirt to watch her approach, she was so goddamn beautiful. How could this girl be in his room? Listening to his foul words and still wanting him?

"You're not coming with me."

She obviously wanted to argue, wheels turning behind her expressive eyes. "You realize the only other option is to leave me alone here?"

"No, it's not," he bit off. "I'll take you to Troy and Ruby."

Fear coated her expression. *Fear?* His body had a physical

reaction to seeing it on her face. "No, Bowen. No cops."

"What happened last night, Ladybug?" He had to work to keep his voice even. "Before you came back to me?"

She looked down at the ground, obviously still not ready to talk about it. Her unwillingness to confide in him hurt. Badly. He watched as she changed tactics, tried to distract him. Even though he knew her game, he also knew it would work. She slipped her arms around his neck and held him tight. "No one can protect me like you. If you want me to stay in the car, I will, okay? I don't want to be pawned off on someone else."

Her compact curves felt too good against his, her confidence in him heady. Did he want to leave her side for one single second? Hell no. She would be safest with him. And if he allowed himself to see reason, the parking lot of a correctional institution might be safer for her than Bensonhurst right now.

"All right." His fingers traced down the slope of her back. "Go ahead and take a shower. Much as I like having my scent all over you, I want you comfortable."

"Bowen," she murmured into his chest. "Today. We'll talk about everything today, okay? That's a promise."

He forced himself to release her, watching until she disappeared into the bathroom.

Bowen walked down the hallway of the infirmary, where the harried nurse had directed him. He didn't spend a lot of time in hospitals, but he imagined the Rikers Island infirmary looked nothing like the fancy Manhattan ones most men his age went to to visit their fathers. Lenny would hate being here, would consider any kind of care performed on his behalf as a weakness. A lessening of his manhood. The number of times he'd resisted medical attention reminded Bowen he'd inherited at least a small part of Lenny. Right at this moment, with his potential fate staring him in the face, it was an unwelcome thought.

To his left, two male nurses who looked more like nightclub bouncers played checkers. They eyed him lazily as he passed, as if they knew something he didn't. It made him itch between his shoulder blades, urged him to turn around and leave this place so he could focus on getting Sera somewhere safe. Somewhere they could be together without looking over their shoulders as they walked down the street.

He stopped in front of the hospital room door he'd been sent to, bracing himself for what he would see on the other side. A man who had once been his hero and tormentor, hooked up to machines?

Bowen pushed open the door and came to a halt. Lenny sat in a chair wearing street clothes, cursing at the remote control he had pointed at the television. The picture of health, not a sign of injury marred his robust frame. First came the relief, but rage followed closely on its heels.

"Took you long enough," Lenny remarked casually, without even bothering to look at him. "Chrissakes, daytime television sucks. You know what I miss most about being on the outside? HBO. Miss it even more than you, in case you were wondering."

"I wasn't." Bowen yanked the door closed behind him. "What the fuck is this?"

"This? This is a favor I called in." Lenny tossed the remote onto the unused hospital bed. "I knew I wouldn't get you down here any other way. Still got a soft spot for your old man?"

"Maybe I just came down to make sure you were dead."

"And if I wasn't? Were you going to finish the job?" Lenny laughed. "Sorry to disappoint. The only thing capable of killing me on the inside is the food."

Bowen crossed his arms impatiently. "Explain yourself or I'm out. A reunion wasn't on my to-do list for the day."

"What was on your to-do list, son? Besides the waitress." He used his fingers to symbolize quotation marks as he said the word "waitress." White-hot heat punctured Bowen's chest, traveling down his entire body. Panic, fury, denial hit him, one by one. When Lenny laughed, Bowen knew the fire burning out of control inside him was showing on his face. How much did his father know? Did he know Sera was a cop? Or was it merely speculation passed on from a suspicious Wayne?

He had to play this exactly right. "Let me ask you a question. When did you and Wayne become so fascinated by what chick I'm bagging?"

Lenny stood slowly, his trademark scorn contorting his features. *There he is, my father. This is him, not the affable joker I walked in on.* "I'll tell you when. Since you let a man get away with a blatant show of disrespect. Let him come into our neighborhood and spit where you live. And you let him *walk*?"

Bowen said nothing. Lenny was referring to the night he'd gone to retaliate for what had happened outside Marco's. The night Sera had come dangerously close to being taken. Hurt. Ironically, he never wanted to kill a man as much as he had that night, but the promise of her goodness had miraculously pulled him back.

"*Jesus.*" Lenny paced. "You know what they're saying about you?"

"You think I give a fuck?" Bowen shot back. "We could have had this little heart-to-heart over the phone."

"No, we couldn't have. I needed to look you in the face to make sure you understand."

"Understand what exactly?"

Lenny came closer, bringing them toe to toe. "I won't be in here forever. Oh, no. When I get out, if my operation has been taken over by some muscle-head with shit for brains, I will make you sorry." He swiped a hand over his mouth. "Those men won't listen to Wayne. He doesn't have the fight to back up his mouth. Not like you."

"Be careful, there might have been a compliment in there somewhere."

"What do you want? A dad who takes you to Mets games? Teaches you how to marinate a steak?" He spat on the floor. "I taught you more valuable lessons. How to fight. How to make money. You should be grateful."

"Yeah?" Bowen laughed under his breath. "That's going to be a tough card to find on Father's Day. Dad, thanks for giving me the ability to put someone in a coma."

Lenny stared up at the ceiling, as if imploring it for patience. That made two of them. "Listen to me," his father enunciated through clenched teeth. "I brought you down here to talk some goddamn sense into you. Whoever this girl is, she damn sure ain't worth giving up what you help me build. Sometimes one gets under your skin and makes you question yourself. Take it from the man who was fucked over by your whore mother. They're all the same. So do us all a favor and stop thinking with your dick."

Even against his iron will, a niggle of doubt arose at Lenny's warning. The mention of his mother had done it. The memory of Pamela leaving, tossing him to the wolves, where he'd remained his entire life. He tried to focus on Sera's image to eradicate the doubt, but he only managed to temporarily subdue it. There were far too many uncertainties between them still, blanks she refused to fill in. His father might be an asshole, a criminal to the bone, but there was truth in his voice. Leftover pain, even, from what Pamela had put him through.

"I see I finally made an impact."

The smugness in Lenny's tone pulled Bowen from his disturbing thoughts. "Are we done here? I've got better things to do."

His father gestured toward the door. "Don't be a stranger."

Bowen walked back out of the infirmary through the security check he'd passed through on the way in, raising his arms so they could pat him down again. He wondered fleetingly which one of the employees Lenny had called in the favor on, but his thoughts immediately went back to Sera. What his father had said…he wouldn't let it apply to Sera and him. The connection between them was real. It made him feel whole. If he could believe her, it made *her* feel whole, too. Dammit. *If* he could believe her? *No*, Lenny wouldn't have power over his mind like this. He wouldn't let him. A vision of Sera's smiling face burrowing into his pillow drifted though his head. Once he saw her, touched her, the doubt would cease to exist. He just had to have faith.

As he exited the facility, the phone in his pocket vibrated. He continued walking as he drew it out, needing to bring Sera into view where she sat in his car. When he saw her pretty face smiling back at him through the windshield, a sense of calm settled over him. Everything would be all right. She was here with him now and he should be ashamed of himself for questioning her. For letting Lenny get the upper hand.

He held up his finger to let her know he'd be a minute and answered the phone. "Yeah."

"Mr. Driscol." Newsom. "Is Sera with you?"

"Yes," he answered without hesitation. "She's safe for now. But we need—"

"*I'll* tell you what we need."

Summoning patience he didn't have, Bowen slid a hand through his hair. "You know, I have to be honest, Commissioner. I've had about enough of that for one morning."

"She wants you arrested, Driscol."

Unexpected pain twisted in his chest. Careful to keep his features schooled, Bowen peered through the windshield at Sera. She looked back at him curiously, not an ounce of guile on her face. Could he believe it? He tried to keep the dam from bursting, but it gave way and the doubt rushed in, pulling him under. "Why?"

"She found out about the shipment you're waiting on, Hogan's involvement, all of it. She called me and told me to get your worthless ass off the street." Some papers shifted in the background. "You know Sera well enough by now to know she wouldn't leave this unfinished. Why else would my own niece refuse to be picked up last night?"

Niece. His body went numb, as if his broken heart had sent him into blessed shock. Everything clicked in his head, making perfect sense. This was why she hadn't confided anything in him. Why she'd come back last night. Not because she wanted to be with him. She'd just been biding her time until they could get him into handcuffs. He made eye contact with her through the glass and felt her suck the last of his soul away. In a way, he felt relieved. No soul, no way to hurt. He couldn't survive this with any part of himself intact.

Very quietly, but very potently, the numbness turned ugly. He craved the ugly, wanted it to stomp out all the beauty he'd stupidly allowed himself to believe in.

"Why are you calling to warn me?"

"I owe you for keeping her safe until we could wrap it up properly." Newsom paused. "I need you to get her to the precinct immediately. Drop Sera off and go on your way. Even exchange.

Her for your freedom."

Bowen almost laughed out loud. Freedom. From what? "Then tomorrow you'll pinch Hogan at the shipment and it'll all be over, huh? Your *niece* gets her man and everyone goes home happy?"

Newsom was quiet a moment. "If you're thinking about tipping them off, I'd reconsider."

"You have my word. No tip-offs."

He wouldn't have to. They'd moved the shipment to tonight.

CHAPTER TWENTY-FOUR

Something was terribly wrong.

Bowen hadn't spoken to her since leaving the infirmary. She'd chalked his silence up to his father's condition, but instinct told her she was missing something. Whereas Bowen normally radiated energy, always jiggling a leg, tapping a finger, or harassing his hair, now he appeared...vacant. The man who'd jogged back to the car twice to kiss her before entering the infirmary had vanished and been replaced by a shell. For all she knew his father hadn't made it and he just needed time to process it before talking to her. Having lost her brother and working as an ER nurse, she knew better than most that everyone processed grief differently.

She took a deep breath and laid her hand on top of his where it rested on his thigh. Cold. Unmoving. He made no move to hold her hand, didn't even acknowledge her touch. After the night they'd shared, touching each other without cease, his lack of recognition set off alarm bells.

A glance out the window had her doing a double take. Why were they in Manhattan? Yellow cabs zipped past, bicycle deliverymen weaved through the steady traffic, skyscrapers towered over them on either side of the street. After being in Brooklyn so long, it felt like she'd been transported to a different planet. She'd been so focused on Bowen and his odd behavior that she hadn't realized they weren't driving back toward Bensonhurst.

"Is everything all right?"

A muscle ticked in his cheek. "Fine. I just thought we'd go for a drive. Get out of Brooklyn for a while."

His flat, emotionless voice made her want to tug her hand away, but she kept it there determinedly. "Whatever you need. We can go somewhere and talk—"

He laughed, but it sounded nothing like his usual amused chuckle. Harsh, sarcastic. "Now she wants to talk. How about we just pull over and fuck, instead, baby? You seem to prefer that to talking."

She ripped her hand away and watched his cold hand curl into a fist. "What is wrong with you?" When he said nothing, she pressed. "Did something happen to your father?"

"Lenny is the picture of health." He whipped the wheel for a right turn, making the tires squeal. "In fact, I might go see him more often. Can't put a price tag on fatherly advice. Right, Seraphina?"

She flinched at the way he said her name, like a curse. Bowen's detachment was slowly dissipating, being replaced by something darker. His eyes were glassy and unfocused, his voice sounding unnaturally strained. This change in attitude might have something to do with his father, but something else was in play. That phone call. It had to be the phone call he'd taken just before he'd gotten into the car. A pit formed in her stomach.

"Who were you on the phone with?"

He ignored her question. "It must have pissed you off. Knowing what I am and wanting me anyway." His hands flexed on the steering wheel. "You weren't faking it in bed, I know that much. You were too wet for it."

"Stop it," she shouted. "Bowen, whatever you're thinking about me, it's wrong. You just have to talk to me. We'll figure this out."

"Talk to me, talk to me." He took another hard corner. "My, how the tables have turned."

The resignation in his voice reached across the car to slap her. Before she could recover, he'd thrown the car into park. She only had a moment to register the industrial-type commercial store before he opened the passenger-side door and pulled her out. Taken off guard, she clutched his shoulders for balance, bringing their faces close. His angry countenance slipped for a split second and she glimpsed utter misery behind his gray eyes. It cut through every raging emotion in her chest, made her ache to take away his pain. She reached up to cup his cheek, but he caught her wrist before she could make contact.

"*Don't.*"

Sera's knees almost buckled under the weight of that single word. "You're scaring me," she whispered. "This isn't you."

"Oh, God, please just drop the act." His head dropped forward, hair obscuring his face. "I can't take anymore."

"W-what act?" Her mind whirled at the implication of that statement. When he wouldn't answer her, she had no choice but to follow him in a daze as he led her to a metal door, located in an alcove on the side of what looked to be some kind converted factory. Confusion and panic assailed her. This man was unrecognizable to her, and his tight grip on her wrist did nothing to alleviate her worry. He hadn't told her where they were going. A wild card was in play that he wouldn't share with her. She couldn't just walk in there with him. Not with so many unknowns lying between them. Not until he calmed down enough to listen.

Bowen pounded on the metal door with his fist. Seeing he was momentarily distracted, she tried to wrench her hand free. Midmorning in Manhattan, people were rushing to work around them, ignoring everything but the sidewalk in front of them and their cell phones. Bowen's eyes shot wide, as if he couldn't believe she was trying to get away from him, but he didn't release her wrist. Instead, he yanked her back up against him.

"Let me go," she demanded.

He searched her face. "Why? What are you worried about?"

When she tried to free herself with a twist of her arm, she watched something inside him break. It made her go completely still, breath trapped in her lungs. An answering rupture in her own body occurred, swift and painful.

Looking wild, he gripped her shoulders and shook her. "*You think I could hurt you?*" His voice had risen to a shout, bringing people to a stop on the sidewalk around them. "I fucking *love* you, Sera. You can do anything to me. *Anything.* Lie to me, lock me up, treat me like a monster, and I will still fucking love you. And you're *killing* me."

Her body went limp, his words on repeat in her head. *I love you. I love you.* It was all she could hear, her heart rejoicing and breaking at the same time. Finding out he loved her shouldn't feel like a tragedy, but it did. And she still had no idea *why*, dammit. Oh, God, she loved him back. If she could still feel this overwhelming, consuming pull toward him when he stood in front of her, stripped bare, with all his faults in plain view, these feelings would never, ever go away.

A throat cleared in the doorway and Sera turned to find a familiar girl standing there. In her muddled state, it took a moment to place her. Ruby. Bowen's sister looked between them, her expression leaving no room for doubt she'd heard every shouted word. She laid a hand on Bowen's shoulder and he turned his tortured expression on her, making her visibly flinch.

"Come on." Ruby nudged Bowen gently. "Let's get you off the street."

Sera grabbed Bowen's arm as he turned to follow Ruby inside, but he pulled away. "Come on, Sera." His outburst seemed to have sucked the remaining life out of him. "Let's make this quick."

She didn't pause to take in her surroundings as she followed him inside, only registering the smell of wood, sawdust, oil. Her full attention was centered on Bowen's stiff back. Then he started talking and her world came to a grinding halt.

"Give me a head start, then call Troy. Tell him Sera is here and to come pick her up. He needs to take her directly to the station. To her uncle, the fucking *police commissioner*." He pulled at his hair as he addressed a horrified Ruby. "All right? Can you do that for me?"

Devastation rolled over Sera in a wave. *You can lie to me, lock me up...* Lock me up. She thought of her uncle in the alley last night, his parting words of "this isn't over." Bowen thought she wanted him locked up and there was only one way he could have come to that conclusion. That had been her uncle on the phone. She'd never been so sure of anything in her life. For the first time, it occurred to her she had reason to be scared of her uncle. He would sabotage her life, the lives of others, to protect his prestigious position.

And Bowen was sending her right into his hands, where her future would be his to dictate. Where he would find a way to keep her quiet about what she knew.

No, this couldn't be happening. She should have told Bowen everything last night. The conversation between him and her uncle had mentally sent him packing, out of her reach. Made him incapable of being reasonable. She could see it in his jerky movements, the thousand-yard stare he kept directing at her. Could she even get through to him at this point? Or had every ounce of trust between them been destroyed?

"Bowen." She planted herself in front of him, but he fixated on some spot on the wall behind her. "You don't know what you're doing. There so much you don't know, about my brother—"

"Did you tell your *uncle* you wanted me arrested?"

She swallowed hard. No more lies. "Yes, but obviously not for the reason you think."

He'd stopped listening after she confirmed it, his expression slamming shut, jaw hardening. She opened her mouth to keep going, to explain she only wanted him safe from the men who wanted him gone, even though his face told her nothing she said would get through. Before she could speak, he silenced her with his mouth.

Yes, yes, yes. If he wouldn't listen to her, this was her only hope. He couldn't kiss her and not realize how she felt. She went up on her toes, threaded her fingers through his haphazard hair, and put her soul into the kiss. A broken noise in the back of his throat wrenched her heart in two, but she kept kissing his mouth, hoping to get past the wall he'd built. He framed her face with his hands and kissed her back with an aching thoroughness. A different kind of kiss. No less passionate than before, but he wouldn't give himself over to her completely. With a final blast of dread, she realized it felt like good-bye.

One hand dropped from her face to take her wrist. Before she could process what he intended to do, her hand had been secured to the wall. She broke away with a gasp, her gaze flying upward to see what he'd done. No. *No.* He'd attached her to some kind of rack with an industrial-sized zip tie. A rack full of pool sticks. What was this place?

"Let me go. *Please.* You don't know what you're doing." She implored him with her eyes. His breathing was labored, eyes more tortured than before. She'd been damned since last night, hadn't she? Damned by her silence. A sob worked its way free of her throat. "Bowen—"

He clapped a hand over her mouth. "I don't blame you, Ladybug. You did the right thing. I'm going to go somewhere I can't hurt anyone else. Didn't I tell you I'd always give you what you want?" He tucked a hair behind her ear. "No smoking, okay? Ever. You promised. And stay out of dark alleys from now on. I won't be there to keep you safe." His voice shook on the last word. As if he couldn't help it, he pressed a final kiss to the center of her forehead. "You were the best part of my life, Sera. Even if it wasn't real."

She couldn't see him through the tears clouding her vision, the denial rising in her throat. Defeat, thick and abhorrent, crashed into her as he turned and walked away. In a move of desperation, she reached out to grab him, but her imprisoned wrist prevented her and she only caught air. She'd lost. Somehow all the hope and resolve between them last night and this morning had been ripped to shreds. Helplessness shone through it all, the pain of knowing anything she said right now would be construed as a lie.

"Please don't go," she tried to scream, but it came out sounding strangled. "You asked me so many times if I trusted you. I said yes and I meant it. Give me the same trust now."

Bowen ignored her once again, pointing a finger at Ruby. "You tell Troy that if anything happens to her, I will burn that precinct to the ground. *Tell him.*"

Sera swiped at her eyes, turning her attention to Ruby. Bowen's sister looked visibly shaken, tears coursing down her own cheeks. "*I'll tell him,*" she shouted back, when he refused to budge without an answer. "You're about to do something stupid, aren't you? Ask me for help. Just ask and I'll give it."

The door slamming was his only answer. He hadn't even looked back.

Sera sank to the ground, dimly registering another woman walking out of the back room. Bowen's mother. Her face appeared stricken, but Sera couldn't summon the will to care. So much unbearable pressure existed in her chest, she couldn't believe it hadn't cracked wide open yet so her insides could spill out. Any second, though, it would happen. She'd welcome it. Anything, *anything*, had to be better than this freezing sensation. Loss. She'd lost him. He'd left her in danger. *He* was in danger. And he had no idea.

When Ruby reached into her pocket and drew out a cell phone, Sera came out of her stupor with a burst of adrenaline. "*No.* No, wait. Don't make the call yet."

Ruby spared her a disgusted glance. "I don't break my word. Not to him."

"You make that call, you'll get him killed."

She stopped dialing. "Explain. Quickly. Just because my boyfriend's a cop doesn't mean I trust all of you. From what I heard, you set him up."

Sera stood on wobbly legs, taking in her surroundings vaguely. Pool sticks. Everywhere. They were in some kind of factory. "I wasn't setting him up, I was trying to save his life." She sucked in a breath, gesturing toward the door. "I couldn't get him to listen to me. He wasn't in his right mind."

The other girl considered her closely. "I've never seen him act like that," she admitted softly. "He wasn't…there."

More cold permeated her, making her feel brittle. Somehow that frozen feeling gave her a moment of clarity. She wouldn't let anything happen to him. No way in hell. She'd broken him, and she would fix him. Fix herself. This entire situation. Responsibility weighed heavily on her shoulders, but she accepted it gladly. It gave her something to focus on.

"Call Troy," she directed Ruby, grateful for the steel in her voice. "Ask him to come here without letting anyone know. Just ask him for ten minutes to hear me out." She tested the zip tie holding her hostage, had the feeling she'd be in it until they believed her. "I have a plan."

CHAPTER TWENTY-FIVE

Bowen stared through unseeing eyes as the crates containing stolen computer hardware were loaded into the backs of rented vans. Some had been provided by Hogan, some by him and his men. They worked in complete silence, tension thick in the air. Nighttime had fallen hours earlier, but to Bowen it had been dark much longer. His body felt tired, as if he'd expended actual, physical energy trying to block out thoughts of Sera and her betrayal. Had it even been a betrayal? He'd known she was a cop since the beginning. There'd been a dawning apprehension when she wouldn't talk to him, let him help her with his eyes wide open. Maybe he deserved to feel like this. Like someone had taken a sledgehammer to his ribs and left him to rot.

God, he was one pathetic son of a bitch. He should be thinking about getting the stolen merchandise to the distributer in Queens, out of his hands. All he could think of was her. Was she safe? Had her feelings been genuine or had it all been in his fucked-up brain? Perhaps he'd taken one too many punches and these were the gruesome side effects. Seeing things that weren't there. Hoping for a future that was laughable for someone like him. His future had been mapped out before he entered this world. It had been stupid of him to lose sight of that.

An image of Sera sitting on his windowsill, bathed in sunshine as she sipped coffee, hit him hard and it took an effort not to double over and shout until his vocal cords gave out. On its heels followed the sensation of her fingers sifting through his hair, the husky sound of her voice telling him he felt so good inside her. How long? How long could he live like this? A hole gaped in his chest, yawning wider by the moment. He knew if she were standing in front of him just then, he would beg her to let him try again. Beg her to come with him when he left Brooklyn.

He had to leave. For so many reasons, not the least of which was the beautiful girl he'd left tied to a pool stick rack this morning. No, there was more. The end was coming. A tingling at the back of his neck that didn't go away anymore. It had graduated to a roaring in his ears, and combined with his grief over losing Sera, threatened to kill him on its own. An invisible weapon, instead of a real one. Part of him would rather take the bullet he suspected he had coming than to let this gut-wrenching feeling drag him under. It would be quicker and less painful. Merciful, really.

Ten yards away, Hogan blew warm air into his hands and rubbed them together, nighttime having brought a cold front. Beside him stood Connor and two other men Bowen knew only by sight. Wayne stood by the van with a clipboard, making sure they were receiving their fair share of the merchandise, but Bowen could feel the constant glances in his direction. Wayne's edginess should have made him nervous, warned him to be on guard, but he couldn't steer himself in that direction. It was hard enough to stand there acting like a normal, functioning human being when all he wanted to do was give up.

There. Now that he'd allowed the thought loose inside his

head, it ran wild. His plan involved him driving to Queens tonight with Wayne, getting paid for the score, taking his cut, and giving the rest to Wayne. From there, he would go...where? God, anywhere. It hadn't mattered when he'd formulated the plan in a fit of restlessness. Now he didn't know if he could execute it. Since he could remember, his life had felt like one endless tightrope walk, and now that he'd finally lost his balance and fallen, there didn't seem like any point in getting back up. Not without her.

His heart squeezed in his chest, so goddamn hard he had to suck in a breath. Distraction. He needed a distraction fast or he would self-destruct. Bowen cleared his throat and walked toward Hogan. "All done here. Same time next month?" There wouldn't be a next time for him, not if he got out of town as planned, but letting anyone know would be suicide.

"Yeah, about that..."

Behind Bowen, there was a series of doors slamming, then all four vans peeled out, leaving him standing alone on the dock with Hogan and Connor. Wayne had come to stand behind him. *Behind* him, not beside him. Three against one. It hit him immediately and with zero shock. This was it. Finally. He was about to die. Jesus, he was fucking relieved. He wouldn't have to live with these thoughts much longer, these memories. Although right now, when presented with the prospect of his own death, it felt like a travesty that any memory of Sera would go unremembered. That they would die with him. He wished he could have had a little bit longer to paint them on his walls, to keep them alive the only way he knew how.

Bowen nodded once, letting them know he knew what was happening. If he was going out tonight, he'd go out with his pride. "Let's not draw this out, Hogan. Don't take this the wrong way, but your voice isn't the last thing I want to hear."

Cold gunmetal pressed against the back of his head. "How about mine, kid?"

"Even less." Bowen shifted on the balls of his feet, body tensing. *Interesting.* Some part of him wasn't entirely resigned to his fate. His fighter's nature was rising to the surface, a knee-jerk reaction to being threatened. All of a sudden, he was back in his father's car in Coney Island, scanning the beach through eyes swollen shut, being forced to pick out an opponent. Digging deep inside and finding a spark among the ashes, he fanned it to life. He could hear his father's voice, shouting at him, telling him to suck it up. Then he saw Sera. *Sera, Sera, Sera.* How could he go without knowing she was okay? *No*, he couldn't. Not without seeing it with his own eyes. Even just to catch one final look at her from a distance. "Hey, Wayne. Can we avoid the head? I know this is a hit and there's a tradition you want to uphold, but there's no reason to fuck up my hair."

Wayne growled and shoved the barrel against his head, but Bowen refused to wince. Not with Hogan watching him with a smug expression. "You little fuck. I should have done this a long time ago. Your father thinks I'm weak? That I can't do better than some pussy-whipped *painter*? He's in for a surprise when he gets out."

"Don't forget balloons and a cake. The man has a thing for coconut."

As expected, Wayne now felt the need to get in his face. For a split second, the gun dislodged from his skull and Bowen took advantage. He ducked low and spun, reaching up to knock the weapon from Wayne's hand. It went skidding across the pavement, but Bowen didn't take time to see where it stopped. He was too busy drawing the weapon tucked into the back of his jeans. The one Wayne had been too cocky to remove.

The whites of Wayne's eyes stood out in the near-darkness.

Slowly, his hands went up but the sneer on his face remained in place.

"Looks like this painter got the drop on you, old man."

"Not on me," Hogan drawled.

Bowen saw Hogan point the gun at him out of the corner of his eye and braced himself. When the bullet didn't immediately come, he started talking. "You think South Brooklyn will be easier to deal with if Wayne's running things? You're wrong. This is a mistake, Hogan."

Hogan laughed. "I'm seeing a much bigger picture, my friend. Tonight's deal is two for the price of one. After tonight, I won't be dealing with either one of you. Just myself."

So he planned on putting them both down and running both territories. From the panicked expression on Wayne's face, he'd been confident in his alliance with Hogan. The gun in Bowen's hand pointing toward Wayne became irrelevant. Hogan would only laugh if he pulled the trigger. It would make things easier for him.

Anger flooded Bowen. No. *No.* He'd only just decided to *live.* He needed to see Sera again, find a way to immortalize the memories in his head, and this motherfucker was trying to take that chance away. There didn't appear to be a damn thing he could do about it, either. No way of negotiating when a man's greed outweighed his conscience.

"Where's the girl, Driscol?"

Every muscle in his body seized, but he showed no reaction to the question. "There's been more than one girl this week. You'll have to be more specific."

"You're not as good a liar as you think." Hogan used his thumb to cock his gun. "There's some important shit missing from my office and I'm missing a waitress. Where the fuck is she?"

"Even if I could tell you, you're planning on shooting me

anyway. I'm not exactly swimming in motivation here, man."

Hogan bared his teeth. "I'm going to find her, you know. I won't stop looking. There's nowhere they can put her that's out of my reach. And when I find the bitch, I'm going to tell her you sent me."

When Hogan aimed the gun at his head, Bowen already felt dead and buried, those final words being the nail in his coffin. He would be leaving her in danger, at the mercy of the same criminals he'd been appointed to protect her from, and the ineptitude of the cops who would have the job going forward. Finding the image of her face, he closed his eyes and focused on it. It took him a moment for Hogan's outraged curse to break through to him.

"What the fuck are you doing?"

Bowen looked on in shock at Connor pressing a gun to the back of Hogan's head. "I second that," Bowen muttered, relief and confusion joining forces in his chest.

"Sorry, cousin," Connor said. "Nothing personal. Just put the gun down nice and slow."

After a brief hesitation, Hogan lowered the gun with a low expletive. "After what I did for you? For your mother? You bastard."

Connor's laugh sounded cold. "We both know I've paid that debt ten times over."

"I'm going to kill you," Hogan grated.

"You're welcome to try."

Sirens.

Breathless seconds passed as all four men exchanged looks. Hogan looked like a trapped rat, while Connor didn't even react, simply keeping the gun trained on his cousin. Wayne, old school to the bone, made a run for the shadows, disappearing from sight almost immediately. Bowen had never run a day in his life, so he stayed still and watched the half dozen NYPD squad cars approach with something akin to fascination. Until he saw Sera step out of one of them. His eyes greedily took in the sight of her, even as he registered the gun in her hand. The badge at her hip. Her professional clothing so different from the dresses she wore in his memory. When several officers approached them, weapons drawn, Connor finally dropped the gun and knelt, hands over his head, as did Hogan. Bowen was pushed to his knees, his gaze still locked on Sera as they cuffed him.

Shame ripped him wide open. No, she couldn't see him like this. Now, *now*, he truly wished he were dead. Troy came up behind her and laid a comforting hand on her shoulder. Seeing anyone besides himself comfort her finally succeeded in breaking him.

"Is this what you wanted, Sera?"

Even from this distance, he could see the tear roll down her cheek, and it sent him struggling against his handcuffs, blood rolling down the palms of his hands.

"Get her out of here," he shouted at Troy, who made no move to follow his order. "I said, get her the *fuck* out of here!"

Finally, Troy yanked opened the door of his squad car and eased Sera down into the driver's seat, closing the door behind her. He could still see her face through the window, though, forcing him to squeeze his eyes shut defensively as they led him to one of the waiting cars. His fighter's instinct took on a different form then. Knowing he couldn't use his fists to get free this time, it took pity on him and numbed his mind. It shut him down so he couldn't feel a thing. Red and blue flashing lights blurred together and he concentrated on them, trying not to dwell on the fact that the only girl he'd ever loved had just taken away his freedom. How he should hate her for it, but could only lament the fact that he'd never hold her again.

CHAPTER TWENTY-SIX

Sera watched Bowen through the two-way glass. Being this close to him made her sore, aching heart race in her chest. Her hands pressed against the cool surface, itching to touch him and explain everything, but after his behavior at the docks, they'd barred her from the interrogation room, thinking her presence would only send him into a rage. She hated knowing they were right. The disappointment on his face when he'd seen her standing there, the *misery*, she'd never recover from it.

Now he sat slumped in a hard metal chair, staring at an invisible spot on the wall. His hair stood at a hundred different angles; blood circled his wrists, making him look like a battered angel. Beside him, Connor sat looking as though he were late for another, more important, appointment. Coolly detached, but impatient, while Bowen's lights had gone out completely, like someone had turned off his switch. No, *she'd* knocked them out. She could only hope when he heard the truth, he would forgive her. That he would understand. And if he didn't, she'd already made up her mind to barge in there and scream her head off until he did. She would summon every saint in her arsenal for aid in tearing through his wall and bringing him back to her. Saint Monica, possibly. Wasn't she known as the saint of persistence? Or was she the patron saint of arthritis?

Focus, Sera.

Since Troy had been the one at her side during the mad rush to bring her new plan to fruition this afternoon, the one who would fix the problems her silence had created, he would be the one addressing Bowen and Connor. Right on cue, the interrogation room door opened and shut, Troy walking in and taking a seat across from the two men. Bowen didn't make any move to acknowledge him. Connor tipped his chin up once and crossed his arms over his big chest, as if to say *about time.*

Troy cleared his throat and flipped open the file he'd been carrying. "You've probably assumed by now that we intercepted the stolen equipment, along with several of your accomplices, including Wayne Gibbs. Trevor Hogan has already lawyered up. It shouldn't surprise you to know they've implicated you both, in addition to themselves. So much for taking one for the team, huh?"

Connor split a look between Troy and Bowen. "Come on, man. You some kind of masochist or something? Put the guy out of his misery."

Troy closed the file with a sigh. "Bowen, you awake? I'm not going through this twice."

Bowen held up his middle finger.

"Great. Thanks for joining us." Troy nodded toward Connor. "We brought in Mr. Bannon this afternoon and made him an offer. I've been given permission by the newly appointed commissioner to make you the same one."

Confusion flared in Bowen's eyes. "All this song and dance better have a point."

"Let me start from the beginning," Troy said. "Through the information Sera collected in Hogan's office, she discovered that her brother had been taking payouts from Hogan before his death. Her uncle was aware of it and covered it up. Hogan had a financial paper trail to back that up."

"*What?*" Bowen sat up straighter in his chair as if he'd been reanimated. Sera watched as the wheels started turning in his head. "Are you telling me he knew Sera was going to put herself in danger? Hoping she'd find what he needed?"

"Yes." Troy shot to his feet at the same time Bowen did, holding up a hand to ward him off. "*We* weren't told the truth. Newsom had already destroyed the ledger Sera retrieved by the time we found out. Luckily, Sera had recovered a hard drive off Hogan's laptop and kept it to herself, instead of turning it over. It forced Newsom to make a full confession and as of an hour ago, he has been relieved of his position." Troy paused. "He had already confessed to Sera last night. It's why she wouldn't go with him. And rightly so since he was willing to protect himself at all costs."

"I…" Bowen's jaw clenched. His fists shook at his sides. Even without those visible signs of rage, Sera could tell how much effort it cost him to remain in control. "I tied her up and left her for you. For *him*. You're telling me I left her…unsafe?"

Troy hedged. "She was technically never in danger. As soon as you left her with Ruby, they called me and told me everything. I contacted the deputy commissioner immediately." He lowered himself back into his chair. "We brought in Mr. Bannon and asked him to cooperate. It's a good thing we did or we never would have known the shipment date had been moved. Sera had originally told us May ninth."

Bowen flinched and Sera felt an answering pang in her chest. He still thought she'd set him up. She consoled herself with the reminder he wouldn't think that for much longer.

"What does he mean by cooperated?" Bowen asked Connor

dully.

"They offered me a way out of this place and I took it."
Connor looked uncomfortable, the first time Sera had ever
seen him anything but confident, apart from the night he'd been
shot. "I've got people to look after besides myself, and the way
things were headed, I wouldn't have been around much longer
to do it."

"Way out?" Bowen asked.

Troy nodded. "It took some convincing, but between Sera
and me, we managed to persuade the deputy commissioner."
He flipped the file back open. "I have a contact back in Chicago.
My old lieutenant. Derek Tyler. He's a captain now with the
Chicago PD and he needs men like you and Mr. Bannon. I've
spoken to him, informed him of your backgrounds, and he
thinks you're exactly what he's looking for. He's rarely wrong
about anything."

Bowen raised a single eyebrow. "You just arrested us for
transporting stolen goods, probably breaking at least twenty
different laws, and you're deputizing us? What am I missing?"

"Nothing. But I'd refrain from repeating that little recap
outside of this room," Troy said drily. "This is why you two were
a package deal. You're all heart, Bowen. Connor's the thinker.
If you can work together, you'll do well."

Connor threw an arm over the back of his chair. "They're
forming a new squad, from what I understand. They need *us*
because we think like criminals." A muscle jumped in his cheek,
obviously disliking that description of himself. "At first, I said
no deal. But they made me an offer I couldn't turn down. Guess
I'm a Cubs fan now."

"Chicago," Bowen mouthed. "What's my other option?"

"Prison time."

"Go Cubs."

A smile tilted one end of Troy's mouth. "Don't act so grateful. I might blush."

Bowen sat back down, looking far less satisfied than he should have been at receiving his get out of jail free card. "Thanks, man," he said quietly. "Although we both know if you put me in prison, Ruby would have had your ass."

"That played a part. It always does. But it was mostly Sera. As of now, the brass has managed to keep this quiet. They've sent Newsom out as if he's resigned for health concerns. But she raised hell, threatening to go to the media about corruption in the department, unless they gave you a chance. They can't afford the scrutiny." Troy paused, watching him closely. "She was something else."

Bowen didn't speak for a long time. Sera could see he wanted to believe it, but was still not ready. When he seemed to realize both men were waiting for a response, he tossed an absent glance at Connor. "So which one of us gets to be Batman and who's stuck playing Robin?"

"I'm Batman," Connor said.

"You wish."

"Actually," Troy started slowly. "You'll be traveling with a third. She's not exactly a criminal, but she's had some experience living among them. I guess you could call her Batgirl."

Sera watched as Bowen went so still, he didn't even appear to be breathing. That was her cue to go in, but she couldn't judge his expression and it made her nervous. What if he couldn't forgive her? What if he didn't want her in Chicago? With a deep breath for courage, she left the observation area and joined the three men in the room. Bowen locked eyes on her the second she walked through the door, intense as always, but unreadable.

Troy and Connor stood abruptly, both appearing all too eager to flee the awkward situation. On the way out, Connor laid a comforting hand on her shoulder. It caused Bowen to tense, his fingers to curl against his thighs. That telltale sign he still felt possessive toward her boosted her confidence in a much-needed way.

When the door closed behind Troy and Connor, she didn't bother sitting. This was her chance to explain everything and she wouldn't waste a moment, wouldn't risk him tuning her out again. "I asked my uncle to pick you up to keep you safe. That night in Marco's, I overheard a discussion about everything changing on the ninth. That you wouldn't be around for much longer after the score." She wet her lips. "That's why I went outside…to call him. I didn't know any other way that wouldn't blow my cover. And I'm only sorry because my uncle turned out to be someone untrustworthy. Not that I did it, though. I would have done anything to keep you from being hurt."

His face remained impassive.

"I should have told you everything. About what my brother did, how my uncle hid it. Everything that happened while I was undercover. I'm sorry I didn't. It put us both in danger and I'll never forgive myself." She swallowed hard. "I don't have an excuse, except I've never had anyone to confide in before. It felt like a failure and I didn't want to face it. Didn't want you to know I'd failed."

"It wouldn't have made a damn difference."

Bowen's rusty voice made her insides jump. *Wouldn't have.* Past tense? "You told me once that you started falling for me before we met. From just a photograph." Her voice dropped to a near-whisper. "It happened that way for me, too, in a way. Before I found out your name, you were already overwhelming me. I saw *you*. It was already too late for me when I realized who you were."

Still he said nothing, the picture of stillness in his metal chair, watching her.

"And you are *not* your name. You're more. So much more. To me, you're everything." She drew in a deep breath. "I need the mural artist, the fighter, the man who might have lost his way for a while, but still remained good where it counted. I want the man who loves one minute and rages the next. The man who suffers through church and makes me egg sandwiches. The man who touches me so perfectly." His lack of response made her want to scream and cry. "I'm coming to Chicago. If you don't want me there, too bad. I'm going to be right there, every day, standing beside you, because standing anywhere else doesn't feel right anymore. I love you. No, I've *loved* you. And I'm not saying take it or leave it. I'm saying *take* it." Tears blurred her vision. "Please, take it?" she finished shakily.

Every second that passed where he didn't move or speak felt like broken glass raking over her heart, her exposed skin. He didn't want her. Okay, okay…she would just have to work harder. She'd earn his trust back in Chicago and eventually he'd come around. What they had didn't just go away overnight. Did it?

She swiped a hand over her damp eyes and turned for the door, everything moving in slow motion around her. As soon as her hand touched the knob, she heard the metal chair scrape against the floor and go flying, colliding with the opposite wall. Bowen's body heat suddenly surrounded her, wrenching a sob from her throat. His arms banded around her from behind, molding her to his chest, warm, rapid breaths in her ear.

"Jesus Christ, Sera," he rasped. "You just handed me everything I've ever wanted in this world. I needed a minute to believe it was real." The tension in her body evaporated with his words, but Bowen simply held her tighter so she wouldn't fall into a heap. "I love you. So fucking much I'm not sure I have room for it all."

She let her head fall back against his shoulder, incredible relief making her movements languid. "Make room. I'm not going anywhere."

He pointed a shaking finger at the doorknob. "That's the last time you make me watch you walk away. Never again. I'm *keeping* you, dammit."

"I'll never walk away again. I'm keeping you, too."

"Thank God for that." Bowen turned her around. She looked up at his beautiful face, running her thumb over a cut under his right eye. He leaned into the contact with a quick release of breath and laid a fist over his heart. "Sera, I'll be dead in the ground before an ounce of this goes away. There's nothing you can do to make it lighter and if you could, I wouldn't let you. I want to be heavy with loving you, baby. Don't question it again, okay?"

"Okay." She nodded vigorously, sending tears falling down her cheeks. "Okay."

He used his lips to brush away her tears. "Are you sure you don't want to work as a nurse in Chicago? Something safer? I'm not above begging."

"And miss out on all the action?"

He pinned her against the wall with a low growl. "You'll be getting enough action at home."

"Home," she repeated breathlessly. "I like you saying that."

Their lips met for a lingering kiss. "You're my home, Sera. The only one I've ever had. I want to be yours, too. Let me."

Love expanded in her chest. "You're the only home I'll ever need, Bowen."

EPILOGUE

With a muttered curse, Bowen dragged Sera off the sidewalk and into a shadowed doorway to kiss her. At first, she laughed at his spontaneous gesture, but as soon as his tongue stroked over hers, her amusement disappeared along with his sanity. Cool fingers slid into his hair, tugging a little the way he liked. He pressed his palms high against the door, knowing if he touched her, they would need to find somewhere to finish each other off. Too bad they were already late for their first meeting with the Chicago PD. The meeting to which his wickedly hot girlfriend had decided to wear a tight skirt, probably to drive him crazy until they could get back to the brand new king-size bed he'd insisted needed to be rechristened several times a day. The bed they'd bought together, in a furniture store, holding hands and making decisions like a couple. Bowen had decided *that* day was the best one he'd ever lived through. Until the next day with Sera had started. And the next. Now every new day with her became his new favorite.

Sera looped her fingers around his belt and tugged his body closer. Her curves meshed with his harder form, her sexy little moan blanketing his brain in a sensual fog. Against his better judgment, one hand dropped from the door and smoothed over her ass. He'd seen her tug on a red thong while they were dressing to leave and now all he could think of was massaging her pussy through the material. Would be thinking about it straight through this meeting and the entire way home until he got her alone.

Since they'd moved to Chicago last week, he'd been doing this kind of thing with growing frequency. Reminding himself that the one-bedroom apartment he shared with Sera was real by painting her on every wall. Reminding himself that she was real by kissing her sweet mouth every chance he got. These reminders always ended with her legs wrapped around his head, neck, or hips, screaming for mercy. Part of him hoped the need for confirmation of his dreams coming true never went away completely. If they did, he might forget what a lucky bastard he was for a second. That wouldn't work for him. He never wanted to take a single second for granted with his girl. His Sera.

Her hips started to move, which gave him no choice but to push his hardening cock against all that hot friction. She broke the kiss with a whimper, and then the brown eyes that ruled his dreams were locked on his. Bright, excited, lusty. Trusting. Fuck, what had he started? Recognizing the point of no return, Bowen forced himself to rein in the urge to reach a hand under her skirt and give her relief. Instead, he stepped back and adjusted himself.

"Unfair," she breathed.

He brushed her hair back over her shoulder. "I'm sorry, Ladybug. I needed a reminder and got carried away."

Her eyes went soft. "You still need them?"

She really had no idea. Not even a clue how thoroughly she owned his thoughts. At first, he counted it as a blessing. If she knew the depth of his obsession with her, she might freak out a little. The more time went on, though, he felt hope bloom that she wouldn't even flinch if she knew. That she might be a little obsessed with him as well. God, he fucking well hoped so.

He twined their fingers together and reluctantly pulled her from the doorway. "What's wrong? You don't like my reminders?"

"I love them." She tucked into his side. "You take them as often as you want. No complaints from this corner."

"I've created a monster."

She growled playfully, but he could still see the need in her eyes. He'd make it up to her later. Several times. His blood went hot just thinking about it.

"Is Connor meeting us there?"

"Yeah." They stopped at the corner and waited for traffic to pass. "He's helping his mother get settled in. Said he'd head to the station afterward."

Bowen hadn't found out until the day they left New York what the NYPD had offered Connor to turn informant on his cousin. His mother's declining health had been the driving force behind his decision. The driving force behind *every* one of the guy's decisions, really. Bowen still didn't know how the man he now considered a friend got himself booted from the navy, but he wouldn't press for more information. He was glad his instincts had been on point where Connor was concerned, though. Like him, Connor had been in a bad situation with no easy way out. If it weren't for Sera, and okay, Troy, he'd still be treading water, just waiting for the day when he would finally sink.

Not anymore. He looked over to find Sera smiling up at him, the Chicago wind lifting the hair from her shoulders to brush across her still-swollen mouth. If he lived to be a hundred years old, he couldn't repay what he owed her. She'd given him a life worth living, helped him begin to bury the past. Before they left New York, she'd gone with him to see Pamela, his mother. He'd listened to her explanation for leaving, thanks to her fear of Lenny. She claimed she'd thought of him every single day. There wouldn't be any family vacations or Thanksgiving dinners in the near future, but he couldn't deny feeling a sense of peace that night.

News about Newsom's corruption had leaked and the NYPD had been given no choice but to come clean about what had taken place behind the scenes. Newsom had been indicted on several charges including conspiracy, misappropriation of funds, and bribery. It seemed as if each day brought a new confession, a new crime he'd committed within the department. The NYPD hadn't succeeded in keeping the media uninformed completely, and he suspected Sera didn't like seeing her family name dragged through the mud on the evening news. He sure as hell didn't like it either, but as long as her identity stayed protected, he could sleep at night.

She'd had a harder time coming to terms with her brother's dishonesty, but in the end, she'd seemed to realize that shades of gray existed everywhere, just as they did with him. That her happy memories of Colin didn't need to go away. They could stay along with the bad ones. Bowen had done his part to help her heal by scouring the Chicago pawnshops looking for a Nintendo console. Wouldn't you know it? The owner had unearthed an ancient Tetris cartridge from the back room. If having Sera in his life hadn't already proved his luck had changed, that would have done it. Their tournament had started the same night.

When they reached the precinct, Bowen felt a prickle of unease at the officers staring at them curiously; some even eyed him with open hostility. Wisely, none of them turned it on Sera or they would have been much later for the meeting.

Bowen held open the door for Sera, following her into the bustling front office. Phones rang loudly; men in navy blue uniforms shouted to one another across the space. He might never

get used to this, working with cops, going to work at a fucking *police station* every day. Especially knowing these people
planned on putting his girl in danger. It pissed him off royally,
even though he knew how capable she was. As if sensing his
discomfort, Sera squeezed his hand. It was the only reminder
that he needed. He'd go to work on an oil rig in the middle of
the Atlantic if it meant sleeping beside her at night.

And come hell or high water, he's protect her through it all.

A tired-looking receptionist whistled at them. "You here
for the meeting with Captain Tyler?" Bowen nodded once and
the woman pointed to a closed door. "In there. You're late."

He traded an amused glance with Sera and led her toward
the door. When he pushed it open, they both came up short.

Around a giant conference room table sat five people, all
staring back at them. Well, almost all of them. Connor was busy
glaring across the table at a gum-chewing half-blond, half-pink-
haired girl who wore a T-shirt that said *Bitch Don't Kill My
Vibe*. Beside Connor, an ancient man in a newsboy cap looked
absolutely delighted with himself. Closest to the door, a black-
haired girl twirled her hair with nervous fingers, back ramrod
straight, obviously agitated by her surroundings.

Who the hell were these misfits?

Bowen didn't have much time to think about it, because the
fifth person at the table stood and blocked his line of vision. In
a suit and tie, badge clipped to his belt, the guy had such an air
of command, Bowen immediately stepped into his space to let
him know he wouldn't be following orders from just anyone. To
his surprise, the guy nodded as if he approved. After the stories
Troy had told him, he knew this had to be Captain Derek Tyler.

"Nice of you to show up. Now sit down. We've got work to
do."

KEEP READING FOR A SNEAK PEEK OF

UP IN SMOKE

BOOK TWO IN THE CROSSING THE LINE SERIES

UP IN SMOKE

You can take the man out of the SEALs...

You can take the man out of the SEALs...
Connor Bannon stared across the empty conference room at the clock, watching the second hand tick past 3:00 p.m. Impatience prickled the back of his neck. He hated being late. Hated *other* people's being late. If the Navy had taught him one thing, it was how to show up on time. Even now, when his military career wasn't even visible in the rearview mirror and the consequences weren't nearly as severe, his ass showed up when it was supposed to. He couldn't be late if he tried.

Apparently he'd been banished into the midst of an undercover squad that didn't share the same quality.

Connor tapped his fist against his knee, breathing through the need to look at the clock again. The blank whiteboard and the room's six empty chairs mocked him. He didn't like going into meetings blind. It went against his nature to be unprepared, but he'd been given no choice. All he knew was Bowen Driscol and Seraphina Newsom were on the squad, sent from New York City to Chicago in exchange for favors, same as him. For the first time since his short-lived stint with the SEALs, he was going to be on the right side of the law.

Or the wrong side, depending on who was doing the asking.

He'd be working with cons, criminals who wanted to stay out of prison. That was where his knowledge started and ended, truly pissing him off. If they'd been given the same options as him, they'd decided helping the Chicago Police Department catch criminals such as themselves was the lesser of two evils.

Another valuable lesson he'd learned from the SEALs? If it doesn't look like a bomb, it's probably a bomb.

The door of the conference room flew open, crashing against the opposite wall. Connor's hand flew toward the small of his back, searching futilely for his gun—a gun the uniforms had taken away from him upon arrival, *dammit*. He shot to his feet instead, focusing on the...threat?

"Relax, Trigger. I like to make an entrance."

A girl sauntered into the conference room, her combat boots jingling with each step, as if there were bells attached. She wore a shirt that said *Bitch Don't Kill My Vibe* over a pair of ripped jean shorts that ended just below her ass. An ass that he'd noticed even before he registered her bright pink hair. *Who the fuck?*

She tossed a frayed canvas bag onto the table and sprawled into the seat across from his currently empty one, head tilting slightly as she regarded him. Amusement transformed her features from merely beautiful to interesting *and* beautiful. From distracting to *the* distraction he didn't need. Like she fucking needed the extra push.

Since when did he get mad at girls for being good-looking?

Very slowly, she looked him over. Connor felt her gaze slide over his crotch and bit back the urge to adjust himself, to hide the wood he'd sprung in honor of a girl who'd been in his presence for thirty seconds. He didn't like this. Didn't like feeling out of control of the situation. He let people see only what he allowed, but somehow this girl had walked into the room, said eight words, and thrown him off his game.

"Well." She sat back in her chair and winked at him. "I guess the nickname Trigger is appropriate in more ways than one."

Connor sat back down and dug his fingers into his knee, forcing himself to show no outward reaction. He hated the nickname she'd just christened him with, but he'd be damned before he let her know. "Your name, please."

Her lips twitched. "So formal, aren't you, baby?" A flicker of calculation entered her eyes before disappearing, but it told him to expect her next move. She dragged her full lower lip between her teeth and propped both feet up on the table, giving him a view of her thighs that clogged the breath in his throat. She crossed her feet at the ankles, but not before he glimpsed where those legs led. The tiny patch of denim covering her pussy. "Call me whatever you want. Just don't expect me to answer."

Jesus Christ. If she made him any harder, he'd have to excuse himself. "I wouldn't say your name unless I had a good reason."

She swayed her feet back and forth. "Give me your best one."

The urge to shift in his seat was strong. "You've already looked right at it."

Her feet stilled. He caught a flash of surprise and uncertainty, confusing the hell out of him. Had he read her signals wrong? One minute she was challenging him, and the next, she looked frozen in the headlights. Or maybe he'd just called her bluff? His ability to read people had been his saving grace more than once since being dishonorably discharged from the SEALs two years ago. Working as a street enforcer in Brooklyn for his cousin's underground crime ring, the skills he'd honed in the Navy had been utilized on a daily basis. Often in ways he didn't like to recall, but forced himself to anyway. To remember what he'd been reduced to.

But reading this girl was difficult, even for him. She'd flashed her thighs at him as if wanting a reaction, but when he'd given it to her, she'd clammed up. Whatever the reason, he refused to show another ounce of interest. He *wasn't* interested. This girl couldn't scream trouble any louder. He was through with trouble. Done.

"*So.*" She finally recovered her entertained expression. "What kind of piece were you reaching for when I walked in?"

He simply narrowed his eyes at her.

"Hey, you're preaching to the choir. They took my favorite Ruger." She pouted. "Has my initials painted in Wite-Out on the side and everything."

Oh, I get it now. She's crazy. "Why are you here?"

His abrupt question didn't faze her. "Three o'clock meeting, same as you. Some people just don't value punctuality."

The way she smirked when she said it made him think she'd read his mind upon walking into the room. But that was impossible. Who the fuck *was* this girl? A tempting weapons enthusiast who also happened to be perceptive? He needed to know more. Just enough to solve the formula she presented, so he could pack up his curiosity and store it away. "I wasn't asking why you're in this room. What landed you on this squad?"

She inspected her fingernails. "Ah. The old *what are you in for* conversation. I don't want to play." Her boots abruptly hit the ground. "Just kidding, I'm in. But you have to go first."

"Nope."

"Impasse," she whispered, walking her fingers across the table. "I could guess why you're here, but you'd dislike that more than simply telling me."

Connor said nothing. He *would* dislike that. Guesswork had always been a source of irritation for him. He dealt only in facts. Again, he got the feeling this girl saw more than most people.

The air of mayhem she wore like a second skin probably made people underestimate her. He wouldn't be one of them.

"You have a military background. But you're not there now, are you?" She leaned across the table and he caught a whiff of smoke. Not cigarette smoke. Like the strike of a match, or the lingering scent of incense. "It isn't difficult math, soldier."

"Don't call me that."

"You don't like Trigger, baby, or soldier." Her tongue lingered against her top lip. "If you don't like any of my nicknames, better tell me your real one."

Connor almost laughed. Almost. The nicknames had been her roundabout way of getting him to spill his name first. He'd nearly walked right into it. Why were they waging a battle over something so minor? When this meeting started, they would find out each other's names anyway.

It was time to let this girl know he didn't play games. At least not the kind that took place while fully clothed. As he leaned across the table, he watched her blue eyes widen and knew she had to be a blonde underneath that pink hair. Her eyelashes and eyebrows were light, her coloring fair. *She'd look goddamn perfect against my black sheets...arms stretched over her head, unable to free herself. Not really wanting to get free at all.*

"I never said I didn't like you calling me baby."

Dammit. Had he said that out loud? He'd decided not to show her any more interest. Once he made a decision, he stuck to it. Every time. He resented her for being the one to make him deviate. If she weren't leaning so close, her small tits pressing against the front of her shirt, maybe he'd have kept his resolve. He'd always liked women with bouncy little tits, and he'd lay ten to one odds she wasn't wearing a bra. "Maybe I just want to hear you call me that under different circumstances."

When her confidence visibly wavered, Connor wanted to

curse. These contradicting sides to her were only increasing his need to know more, and he did *not* want to get involved. Couldn't afford to. Her chin went up a notch, and that show of fire amid the uncertainty turned him on. "What circumstances would those be?"

Too soon. Too insane. He'd just met this girl. They'd be working together. He couldn't sit here in the light of day and detail the many activities he'd like to perform with her. Even if he wanted to, just to see her reaction. To see if she wanted him, too. But what would he do if she did? Drag her onto the conference room table, tug her shirt up to her neck, and get a look at those tits? He'd have to get her back to his apartment if he did that, damn the meeting.

Change the subject. "Why do you smell like smoke?"

Her eyelashes shielded her eyes a second before they flashed wide, hitting him square in the chest with the force of their impact. "I set things on fire."

A ny other time, the expression on the hot, bearded former-soldier's face would have made Erin O'Dea dissolve into a fit laughter. It wasn't the usual response men gave her when she played the crazy card. Not at all. Maybe that was why she wasn't laughing. This guy wasn't typical. Didn't fit her profile of what men should be like. They all wanted to get inside her until she performed her fun little reveal. *Surprise, sweetheart. I'm a convicted arsonist. You might be next.*

Cue haunted house cackle.

They never asked why she'd done it or questioned the circumstances, simply vanishing into a puff of smoke. Exactly as planned. This guy wasn't vanishing, however. He hadn't flinched, not once, and the trickle of relief in her chest pissed her off. The words "proceed with caution" flashed across her consciousness, sparking and flaming around the edges. This man *would* ask why and question the circumstances. Having only met him mere minutes ago, she shouldn't be so certain of that fact, but it would be reckless to put him in the same category as other men who scared easily. His steady green eyes were so intent on her, she worried her mask might slip underneath the weight of them. She didn't want him to be the first person to ask her why. She didn't want *anyone* to ask her why. Her secrets were all she had. After you'd lived behind bars among hundreds of women with your privacy stripped clean away, you held on to what you could. You didn't let it go for a pair of muscular biceps.

This one just needed a few more nudges and he'd lose interest. It was possible he already had and could hide his emotions better than most. She knew all about that. Although some people, her stepfather mainly, *wanted* her to be certifiably crazy, it was probably only half true. Yeah, she was a little off. For good reason. The man sitting across from her would recognize it soon enough and stop looking at her like he wanted to devour her, bite by bite.

His gaze became too much to bear, and Erin focused on the window. Only one pane of glass between her and the outside. She could survive anything, face anything, as long as that was the case. Which is why she was here. You could dodge only so many bullets before one caught you in the back. This place, this job, was her bullet between the shoulder blades. *Woman down.*

Working for cops. Hell must be having a fucking snowstorm. She hadn't spit on the sidewalk on the way in for no reason. Cops were the enemy. The men and women who took away her freedom. Laughed as they stripped away her dignity. They thought handcuffs and a gun made them smart, but it only made them complacent. At age twenty-five, she'd already proven that. Twice.

The ex-soldier's raised eyebrow told her she was smiling. After what she'd just said to him, he probably thought that smile meant she was a lunatic. Mission accomplished. For the first time since she'd sworn off men, she regretted sending one running. But it was entirely necessary. This man—this big, rough-hewn *male*—was an enforcer. More than that, he had a brain working behind all that stoicism. Even if she were inclined to call him baby in certain *circumstances*, it would be disastrous. It didn't take a rocket scientist to figure out he would be dominant in bed. The way he was clenching his fists as if fighting for control, even with her a full two feet away, told her that. He'd be the type to hold a woman down while he pounded out his lust.

That image might have turned her on at one time. Now it terrified her.

Still. She allowed her gaze to drop to his lips. Who knew she could find a beard so appealing? It wasn't rugged, but close-cut. Well-maintained. He looked like a man who could survive on his own in the wilderness with nothing but string and a Windbreaker. Capable. Made of steel. What would that beard feel like against her cheeks, her chin? If she leaned a little closer across the table, he might let her find out. If he hadn't already decided she belonged in a straitjacket. *Take a number, pal.*

"You'd better decide now if this meeting is important to you," he growled. "Because if you keep looking at me like you want to kiss me, neither one of us is going to be here for it."

Hooo boy. Something she'd thought long gone shimmied in her belly. "That's pretty confident."

"Realistic."

Erin drummed her fingers on the table before reaching one hand out, intending to tug his beard. "I'm just curious about what this feels like. In places."

He caught her wrist in midair before it made contact. "You

touch me, you'll find out."

Ice formed beneath her skin, so freezing cold that it burned like blue fire. Her muscles tightened to the point of pain. She focused on her breathing. *In and out. In and out.* Just a little tug and her hand would be free. Nothing could contain her. She'd made sure of that. He might harness a lot of power in that muscular frame, but she didn't sense that he would use it on her. Unless she asked. Which she sure as hell would *not.*

Her brain commanded her to pull out of his grip, but her body wouldn't obey. She focused back on the window, zeroed in on the patch of gray sky visible through the glass. "Please let go," she whispered, furious when her voice shook.

He dropped her hand like it was on fire. She didn't like the way he was looking at her. Eyes seeing too much. Discarding theories, thinking of new ones. Like he knew a damn thing about what was wrong with her. Half the time, *she* didn't know.

"My name is Connor."

Erin went still. Inside and out. She felt warm all of a sudden, like someone had draped a fleece blanket over her shoulders. If she thought she'd had him at least partially pegged, she'd been wrong. He didn't have to give in to their silly name war. He'd done it because she'd shown a chink in her armor and he wanted to give her a victory.

Connor.

"What about a tiny little kiss?" *Shit.* Where had that come from? "No tongue."

"This isn't summer camp." Those hands clenched. Unclenched. "If you want to kiss me, you'll get everything. I'm not going to hold back."

His gruff tone made her shiver. That voice held promises she couldn't begin to interpret. It had been so long since she'd let a man touch her, but she knew instinctively that Connor would be a whole new experience. One she definitely wasn't ready for and never would be. Still. She felt as if...gravity were pulling her toward him. She'd originally leaned across this conference table to unnerve him. It worked with most people. Invade their personal space until they back off for good. Now that she was this close to him, though, she found herself wanting to stay there. It didn't hurt that he'd released her hand without hesitation. Maybe it was premature or bad judgment on her part, but his action had made her feel safe. She didn't feel safe very often, if ever.

Deciding to trust the instinct that rarely failed her, she climbed onto the table and crawled on her hands and knees the remaining distance. Connor's facade slipped just a little, lips parting on a gravelly exhale, broad chest shuddering as he watched her. "That wasn't a challenge," he grated.

"Everything we've said so far has been a challenge." Erin knew he liked what he saw as his gaze ran the length of her back, snagging on her ass. She gave it a quick shake. He groaned low in his throat and she was shocked to find herself excited by it. "Kiss me. Just...don't touch me, okay?"

"*Jesus.*" He dragged both hands down his face. "You've got the wrong guy for that, sweetheart."

Of course, that made her want the kiss even more. She was drawn to fire. Connor had enough inside him to burn down a major city. The fact that he kept such a tight leash on it only made her want to watch it crackle and race. "I didn't say *I* couldn't touch." She gripped the collar of his shirt and dragged him forward, bringing their mouths an inch apart. "Just you."

A muscle ticked in his jaw. "I'll make you beg for my goddamn hands on you."

Ah, Connor. You have no idea what you're up against.

"You're welcome to try."

UP IN SMOKE

BOOK TWO IN THE CROSSING THE LINE SERIES
BY TESSA BAILEY

COMING JUNE 23, 2015

AVAILABLE FOR PREORDER NOW

ACKNOWLEDGMENTS

A huge, heartfelt thank-you to the following people who were instrumental in putting *Risking It All* on bookshelves and inspired or helped me along the way.

My husband, Patrick, and daughter, Mackenzie. We've become quite a team over the last two years, since I started writing full time. I can't believe how lucky I am to have you two in my life. Thank you for believing in me.

My editor, Heather Howland, for dangling the Bowen carrot stick in front of my face. It's probably why I wrote so many books so fast—I wanted to get to *him*, this man who'd been dwelling inside my head. I never would have gotten this far without your hard work and foresight. Thank you.

My publisher, Entangled Publishing, and Liz Pelletier for believing in my books.

My assistant editor, Kari Olson, who can brighten any day with one of her tweets/direct messages.

My publicist at Entangled Publishing, Katie Klapsadl, for all the work that goes into promoting my books.

My friends/fellow authors who beta-read/pleasure-read this book when it was just a first draft: Cari Quinn, Edie Harris,

Jillian Stein, and Donna Soluri. Thank you. Your feedback was invaluable.

My parents for being proud of me and encouraging me to achieve my goals. I love you both so much.

My neighborhood of Bay Ridge, Brooklyn. I know the characters in this book exist because I pass them on the sidewalk every day. This borough is a constant source of inspiration and exasperation. But I love it and hope I never stop using it as a setting.

My Facebook group, Bailey's Babes, for being so freaking awesome I can't stand it. Some mornings, you guys are the one thing that gets me writing.

My fellow authors who continue to selflessly support me with tweets and Facebook posts even though you're drowning in work. Most of my readers have been turned on to my books by *you* and I'm consistently overwhelmed by the love. Special thanks to: Cora Carmack, Laura Kaye, Sophie Jordan, Sarah MacLean, Megan Erickson, Edie Harris, Bree Bridges, Robin Covington, Cari Quinn, Shayla Black, Monica Murphy, Jennifer L. Armentrout, Katee Robert, Samanthe Beck, Phoebe Chase, Nicolette Day, Jennifer Blackwood, Christina Lee, and Jennifer McLaughlin. So many more.

The bloggers/reviewers who have supported my books since the beginning. I'm not sure I'd have a career at all if you guys weren't working your butts off and promoting authors, often for free. Special thanks to: *Scandalous Book Club, Smexy Books, The Literary Gossip, Book Whores Obsession, Dirty Girl Romance, Read-Love-Blog, S&M's Book Obsessions, Dear Author, The SubClub Book Club, Scandalicious Book Reviews, The Book Cellar, Totally Booked Blog, The Bookcrastinators, Fiction Vixen, Ana's Attic, Maryse's Book Blog, Scorching Book Reviews, Joyfully Reviewed, Fresh Fiction, Talking Books Blog, Rock Stars of Romance, Night Owl Reviews, Books Over Boys, The Book Lovers, Sizzling Pages, Confessions of a Vi3tbabe, Aestas Book Blog, Book Sniffers Anonymous, Sinfully Sexy Books, A Bookish Escape, Straight Shootin' Book Reviews, The Book Bellas, Reading Between the Wines, Lovin' Los Libros, Kimberlyfae Reads, Read Your Writes, Cocktails and Books, Romance Novel News, She Hearts Books, Gravetells, ThreeChicks, FicTalk, Under the Covers, Ramblings from this Chick*, and so many, many more. I appreciate you all so very much.

FIND OUT WHERE IT ALL BEGAN WITH TESSA BAILEY'S BESTSELLING LINE OF DUTY SERIES...

PROTECTING WHAT'S HIS

Sassy bartender Ginger Peet just committed the perfect crime. Life-sized Dolly Parton statue in tow, Ginger and her sister flee Nashville. But their new neighbor, straight-laced Chicago homicide cop Derek Tyler, knows something's up—something *big*—and he won't rest until Ginger's safe...and in his bed for good.

OFFICER OFF LIMITS
ASKING FOR TROUBLE
STAKING HIS CLAIM
PROTECTING WHAT'S THEIRS
UNFIXABLE

THE STORY CONTINUES IN THE EXCITING NEW CROSSING THE LINE SERIES...

HIS RISK TO TAKE
RISKIER BUSINESS

COMING SOON

UP IN SMOKE

FIANCÉE FOR HIRE BY TAWNA FENSKE

Former Marine MacArthur Patton is used to handling top-secret government contracts and black-ops missions, but his new assignment involves something more dangerous—*marriage*. Enter his little sister's best friend Kelli Landers. She can't wait to bring Mr. Tall-Dark-and-Detached to his knees, and her longtime crush on the commitment-phobe makes her plan to seduce him even sweeter. Love wasn't part of the plan, but soon Mac and Kelli find that more than a weapons deal is on the line...

ALIVE AT FIVE BY LINDA BOND

When Samantha's mentor dies while skydiving, she suspects he was murdered. Her investigative instincts lead her to irresistibly gorgeous Zack Hunter. An undercover police officer, Zack is investigating his uncle's diving death with the same adventure vacation company. He doesn't want Samantha's help because he's terrified of being responsible for a partner again. Still, Samantha's persistence is quite a turn-on, and he finds it harder and harder to stay away from her. But when the killer turns his attention to Zack, Samantha could be the only one who can save him.

HIGH-HEELED WONDER BY AVERY FLYNN

Sylvie Bissette is the woman behind *The High-Heeled Wonder*, a must-read blog for fashionistas everywhere. Tony Falcon wouldn't know a kitten heel from a tabby cat, but when a murder investigation leads him to Sylvie, he realizes the feisty fashionista may be his best chance at catching the criminals who killed his best friend. But solving that case means going after the people Sylvie cares about, and soon his attraction for her—and the danger she's in—has him wondering if solving the case is worth hurting the woman he can't stop fantasizing about...